DEFECTS

THE REVERIANS ◆ BOOK ONE

SARAH NOFFKE

Preston,
Thank you for
your amazing support!
I look forward to
hearing what you think
of this series.
Best!
Sarah Noffke

One-Twenty-Six Press.
Defects
Sarah Noffke

Summary: The easiest way to control people is to make them think
they're defective—but that only works until they realize they're not.

Published in the United States by One-Twenty-Six Press
ISBN: 978-1515193210

Praise for Previous Works:

"There are so many layers, so many twists and turns, betrayals and reveals. Loves and losses. And they are orchestrated beautifully, coming when you least expected and yet in just the right place. Leaving you a little breathless and a lot anxious. There were quite a few moments throughout where I found myself thinking that was not what I was expecting at all. And loving that."
-Mike, Amazon

"The writing in this story was some of the best I've read in a long time because the story was so well-crafted, all the little pieces fitting together perfectly."
-The Tale Temptress

"There are no words. Like literally. NO WORDS.
This book killed me and then revived me and then killed me some more. But in the end I was born anew, better."
-Catalina, Goodreads

"Love this series! Perfect ending to an incredible series! The author has done this series right."
-Kelly at Nerd Girl

"What has really made these books stand out is how much emotion they evoke from me as a reader, and I love how it comes from a combination of both characters and plot together. Everything is so intricately woven that I have to commend Sarah Noffke on her skills as a writer."
-Anna at Enchanted by YA

To one of my oldest and dearest friends, this one's for you, Heidi.

Prologue

My fingers tremble as I assemble the pieces.

He'll be back in a few minutes.

I blink away the sweat dripping into my eyes. I can't afford to swipe it away.

The two ceramic pieces chip at the edges as I try to match them up to how they should align. I know he keeps glue in his front desk drawer. Everyone does. *We fix things that are broken.* I slip the tube from the drawer and dab a glob of adhesive on the center of one of the broken pieces and then press it against its counterpart. I'm so used to fixing things, but now I'm not doing it because it's the law. I'm doing it because if he finds out I was here he'll punish me with night terrors again.

The pieces slip just as the glue is setting. Ragged breath hitches in my parched throat. *If he finds out I was here, that there was a trespassing...* I press the pieces together so firmly the glue seeps out and threatens to cement my fingers to the statue. Footsteps in the hallway. Soft-soled shoes. His. I know *his* gait.

I release my fingers from the statue. It teeters but stands, looking unmarked by the fall it recently experienced. But will it stay up?

The envelope still sits neatly on the mahogany desk. It was my own nervous reaction to it that shook the statue down from its high place on the shelf. I knew I should come here and look first. Knew I'd find information. My father always told me, "Instinct is the gods tapping you on the head." Still, I wish I knew what lay inside the folds of that envelope that bears my name.

The key slides into the lock, a sound like a reluctant bell. I close my eyes and dream travel back to my body, pulling my consciousness out of its current location.

1

Chapter One

My house is haunted. I've never seen a ghost in it, but Tutu, whose gift is seeing the dead, says there are many who reside in our home. I haven't received my gift yet. At age seventeen that's rare. My sister, Dee, teases me that this is a sure sign our mother had an affair with Ed, the mailman, who's a Middling—a person who can't dream travel, has no gifts. I pretend this is a joke but with each passing year I believe it could be a possibility. My family is pureblooded Dream Travelers and they're all gifted with strong talents since puberty. And although I dream travel I have no other talents, which is a first in the Fuller family. My grandmother, who I call Tutu, has three abilities. My mother, two. Even my older sister, Dee, has her gift—which she spends every single opportunity rubbing in my face. Since I have no super power I've reverted to spreading false rumors about her all over Austin Valley.

"You're going to be late again," Dee says, sounding pleased by the prospect.

"Thanks for the reminder," I say, not meaning it.

I slip my favorite organic bamboo blouse over my head and hurry out of the room I share with my sister. With one hand I smooth my hair and the other guides me down the banister as I take the stairs two at a time.

"I'm sure his mother would love the opportunity to be interviewed," my mother says to a visitor in her usual subdued tone. I don't even chance a glance at her as I scurry to the entryway, head low. Maybe this visitor will actually save me from being scolded. The brass doorknob is cold under my palm. I wrench the door open and pull it back, a rush of warm June air greeting me at once.

"Not so fast there, Em," my mother says.

I freeze. Push the door closed. Turn and face her.

My mother stands in the threshold of the sitting room, her hands firmly pinned to her hips. "You're late for your meeting with your father."

"Which is why I'm rushing to get out of here," I say, sweeping my eyes to the person my mother was talking to. Zack. He's giving me a curious expression, arms crossed in front of his suit jacket.

2

"Have I not instilled in you the proper manners to know you should greet and say farewell to everyone you come in contact with?" she says, shaking her head at me.

"Hi, Mother. Hi, Zack. I'm leaving before Father kills me for being late. Goodbye," I say, turning on my toes. I slip my hand onto the door handle again, but don't even dare to open it.

"Em?"

I turn and stare at my mother. Her red hair is pulled back into a tight low bun. Her sleeveless black turtleneck must be stifling in this heat. "Yes, Mother?" I say, working hard to keep the irritation out of my voice.

"You weren't planning on leaving the house like that, were you?" she asks with a disappointed glare as she sizes up my appearance.

"I was—"

"Looking for your blazer, right?" Zack plucks my black blazer from underneath a cushion on the settee behind him and holds it out for me.

Reluctantly I eye it and then him. He's wearing his most encouraging look. It partners well with his slick blond hair and winning smile. He's right, politics is the right career for him.

I take my blazer from him and slip it on. "Thanks," I say, pulling my tangled blonde curls out from underneath the jacket.

"Oh, you're still here?!" Dee says, tromping down the stairs behind me. "You really take advantage of our father's unending patience, don't you?" Her black heels make note of each of her steps. When she meets me at the landing she pushes my hair behind my ears. "And really, if you're not going to at least dress like an upper-class Reverian you could brush your hair once in a while."

I bat her hand away and clench my teeth together. Insulting my sister will not release me from my mother's wrath, which seeks to make me even later for my appointment. Still, someone should say something about how my sister looks more and more like an obsessed Goth whose only mission in life is to give the Catholic clergymen a heart attack. She wouldn't understand that reference though. Most people in Austin Valley wouldn't. My sister is wearing her usual get-up: short pleated skirt, starched black button-up shirt open to reveal too much, heels, and an assortment of gold jewelry.

3

Instead of commenting on how she looks like a confused Catholic schoolgirl I lick my finger and press it to a flyaway by her hair line. "You have a hair out of place. Here you go, dear."

She steps back, grotesque horror written on her face. "Eww, don't touch me." My sister turns to our mother. They don't just share the same disapproving scowl, but also the same straight red hair, which they wear similarly. "Oh, Zack, you're here," my sister says, strolling in his direction. "I had no idea."

"Are you blind?" I say dully.

She throws me a contemptuous glare over her shoulder before turning back in Zack's direction. "You could obviously teach my sister something about dress, couldn't you?"

He coughs nervously, flicking his eyes over her shoulder to me. I know Dee makes him nervous. Hell, she makes the devil nervous, probably because she's soulless. I shrug and sling my bag over my shoulder.

"Well...I..." Zack begins.

"There are not many students who choose to wear a suit before they're chosen for positions," Dee says, having cleared the space between them. Her long pointy fingernail has found his shoulder and is now tracing its way down his pinstriped sleeve until she finds his hands. She pulls his fingertips up close to her face and inspects. "And such clean nails. This says so very much about you. Obviously you take a great deal of pride in your appearance."

"I'm merely tryin—"

"Zack is actually here because he'd like to interview your tutu in order to better understand cultural changes which have transpired within our society over the generations," my mother informs Dee, pride evident in her tone.

"Impeccable dresser and ambitious," Dee says, her hand still gripping Zack's.

"Yes, I dare say that if you stay on this track then you'll make great contributions for the Reverians once released from your studies," my mother says, her stare not on Zack, but rather on my sister.

Although I realize I'll be punished later for interrupting this crafty attempt at mating I dare say something. I have other punishments way worse I'd rather avoid. "Well, I really must take my leave," I say, injecting pleasantry into my voice. "I don't want to

keep Father waiting any longer than I already have. Goodbye."
Again the brass knob greets the palm of my hand.

"Yes, you are *so* late," my sister says, eyeing the ancient grandfather clock in the entryway. "He's going to be livid."

"I'm going that way too," Zack says, taking hurried steps in my direction. "I'll walk with you."

Just over his shoulder I catch a fiery glare flash in my sister's eyes.

"Sure," I say with a shrug and turn at once and hurry out the door.

The humid breeze is a welcome relief from the frigid air in my house. Sunlight greets my eyes with a quiet satisfaction and I smile at the blue sky like it's an old friend.

"You always do that, don't you?" Zack says, hurrying to keep up with me.

"Make my mother and sister furious? Yes."

"Well, yes, that, but I was referring to your reaction to the outdoors. You always break into a relieved smile when you walk outside."

I snuggle my shoulders up high, enjoying the warm sun on my cheeks. "I do love it," I say, pausing to allow a group of elderly Reverians to pass in front of us. Zack pauses with me but gives an irritated expression while we wait. "I'm already late," I finally say to him when they've moved on and we continue down Central Boulevard.

"I don't get you, Em," he says, shaking his head. "Why do you make your life harder when you know what they want you to do?"

"I just find it difficult to conform to their standards. I mean, why in the hell should I have to wear a blazer in the middle of the summer?" I say, scratching at my forearms which are already sweating under the tight-fitting jacket.

"It's just customs. If you followed them then they'd leave you alone and let you do what you want."

"Somehow I doubt that," I say, raising an eyebrow at Zack.

"It seems you're looking to get in trouble: being late when it's easy to be early, dressing inappropriately when they supply you the right clothes, and not following etiquette."

"And may I point out that you seem to only notice my shortcomings," I say, taking an early turn. It's a shortcut down a less

5

than desirable neighborhood, but still completely safe and will save us an extra minute on the commute.

Zack's hand clamps down on my shoulder. I stop and look at him, ready to defend the route I've chosen. His denim blue eyes lock on mine. "That's not all I notice," he says, a firmness in his voice.

"Mmm..." I say, gauging his expression which is so familiar and also year by year growing indistinct, like my father's. "Yeah, what else do you notice?" I say, turning and continuing our trek. The alleyway here is a little more crowded, but only because this is a Middling street where they build the houses too close together and the insides are too small for the families who are forced to reside within them.

"It doesn't matter," Zack says, eyeing a man leaning in his doorway up ahead. "We can finish this conversation later. Let's just get you to Chief Fuller's office quickly."

"Right," I say, kicking the contents of a puddle, which is no doubt a result of poor drainage from the sprinkler system. It splatters droplets on my shoes and bare legs, but doesn't irritate me in the least.

At my father's office Zack stops, eyeing the door and then me with an uncertain expression. "You know I'm just trying to help, right?"

"Then you shouldn't have offered to escort me here," I say, pushing him playfully in the chest. "Dee will probably set fire to my bed while I'm sleeping tonight as retribution." Literally she's done that a time or two. I have no idea why the most hostile Dream Traveler born to the gods was given the gift of pyrokinesis.

Zack doesn't respond, but instead gives me his usual commiserative expression. He doesn't know what to say. I get that. "Yeah, I know you're trying to help," I finally say. "You may want to consider there's no help for me. I'm a Dream Traveler whose only talent is I disappoint my family."

"Oh, Em, I've told you that your gift is delayed. It will come on soon and when it does you'll blow all of them away."

"Thanks, Zack," I say, reaching out and straightening his tie. It isn't even that crooked, but I know he likes when I do it because it sharpens his appearance. "Are you off to go take over Austin Valley?"

6

"Not quite yet," he says with a wink. "I've got a thing or two to learn still."

"Don't we all," I say, returning the wink and then dismissing him by facing my father's ornately carved door. I've stalled long enough. Now I must face that which is certain to be extremely unpleasant.

Chapter Two

The redwood door is carved with leaves and vines and depictions of Greek gods. It's intricate, like everything in Austin Valley. We should be using our resources for offering better living quarters for Middlings or educating their children. Instead, we make sure our doors have detailed carving, our silver is polished, and our hair isn't holding chemical residues because it's washed with the finest shampoos.

The wood hardly registers under my calloused knuckles when I knock. I want to be too calloused for my father also, but I'm not. He'll respond exactly six seconds after my knock. I know this. One. Two. Three. Four. Five. Six.

"Come in, Em," he says to his empty office, loud enough so I can hear.

I lock down my thoughts before I enter, shield them the best way I know how. My father's office has always reminded me of one in a dollhouse, too small for the person who plays in it and too small for the things that happen within it. My eyes search the space. The statue I broke this morning still stands high on its shelf, solidly.

"You do know you're late?" he says, pushing back from his desk, which is half the size of a Cadillac.

"I realize that, Father, and I do apologize," I say, rushing forward. "It's Dee."

"Dee?" he says, standing up and pinning his hands on the surface of his desk. My father is blond like me, but gray hairs are starting to streak his slicked back hair. "Why has she caused you to be late?"

"Oh, I thought you knew about her current situation," I say, slipping down into the seat beside his desk. It's firm and gives me the extra support I need right now.

"Em," he says, his tone demanding. "I do not know so tell me at once why Dee caused your tardiness."

"Well, as you know, she's trying to make a pleasing union with Zack Conerly," I say and pause.

"I *am* aware of that. But what does this have to do with you?"

8

"Well, Zack was completely insulted by her lack of decorum, so I spent a few extra minutes just now encouraging him to give her one more chance. I'm sorry if my lateness has angered you, but I risked this thinking that my sister's long-term happiness was worth it," I say, pretending to fidget with my hands.

My father pauses and considers me. "Well, I'll dismiss your punishment this once, but in the future remember that others' well-being isn't your concern, even if it will benefit your family. You've been taught that, haven't you?"

"Yes, Father. And thank you," I say, forbidding a satisfied smile to grace my lips.

"Em, I've called this meeting to inform you that you'll have to schedule an extra visit to the lab each day."

"What? But I have—"

"To do what you're told," my father completes my sentence.

"Of course, but you know I have agriculture hours that would have to be cut."

"And so they will be cut," my father says, striding around his desk. "Since your gift still hasn't surfaced I want you to have two injections a day, as well as regular evaluations."

"Two?" I question, flinching with dread. "But why?"

"Why can't you move something with your mind? Read thoughts? Do anything that Middlings can't?" my father asks, standing stockily in front of me. "The President and I would love answers to these questions. Wouldn't you?"

"Well, yes, but—"

"Then you'll attend as many lab visits as we request and endure all the tests, won't you?"

"I want to know why my gift hasn't surfaced, I really do," I say, straightening my blazer, knowing that the result will probably not garner much favor from my father. "It's just that the hours I spend at the farms are so satisfying and I really need that."

He presses his eyelids tightly together, shaking his head. "Maybe the problem, the reason you have no gift, is you're more Middling than you are Dream Traveler."

"Father, just because—"

"All logic fails to explain why my daughter chooses to spend her extracurricular hours doing the work of Middlings."

"I enjoy it and that work feeds our community."

9

"That work is not your responsibility. What if eagles chose not to fly, but rather hop around from branch to branch like a toucan? That would be a waste of great talents. Species and races are divided for a divine reason. You're obviously confused on your place in this hierarchy and I'm drawing to the end of my tolerance with it."

"Father, I'm sorry to disappoint you, but—"

"This conversation is over. You *will* report to the lab every morning and afternoon from this point forward, is that clear?"

"Yes," I say.

"And starting next week you'll meet with a skills assessor the President has hired to work with all Defects."

Defects. That's what they're calling us now. The term was no doubt picked to encourage shame, which my father thinks will inspire perseverance.

"Okay," I say, threading my fingers together in front of me. The letter I saw this morning still sits where I spied it, but the label is hidden from my view. Still, I know what it says on the front: "Top Secret Case: Em Fuller."

How did I become a top secret case? That's what I need to figure out, but the only way I'll do that is through compliance.

"Thank you for helping me, Father. I really want my gift."

"And it will come, Em," my father says in a tired voice. "Just follow all my instructions."

"Yes, Father. Of course."

I swing open his door and go to exit.

"Oh, and Em?"

"Yes?" I say, stopping in the doorway.

"Thank you for helping your sister. Zack is a smart match for her. And I fear the gods above have punished us and we'll never be rid of you and your sister, Nona."

"Yes, Father, you are right, we're insufferable," I say with a small curtsy.

***

The dirt is cool and moist under my fingertips. The perfect combination for fertile soil. Morning sun is my favorite. It has a quality of pureness to it. Although I had to go to the lab and skip agricultural hours last night, I'm here now. It feels good. Firmly I pat soil around the base of each plant. I enjoy this phase in the growing process, but harvest will come in a few months and I'll find true

10

satisfaction. There's nothing like breaking a vegetable from its stem. And there's nothing like the satisfaction of knowing it has become whole enough to make something else wholesome.

I turn to Dean, who's working beside me. He smiles back. He's always smiling while he works. His family lives in one of the small dwellings on the street where Zack and I walked yesterday. Dean deserves more.

"The crops are looking good this year," he says, standing and sizing up the field with a sweeping glance.

"Maybe if we have a big harvest this year then there will be a bonus," I say with a hopeful smile as I pile my tools into the box.

"Never, ever been a bonus, miss," he says, swiping sweat from his forehead with the back of his tanned arm.

"But I've been putting in the suggestion. Bigger efforts lead to bigger gains and they should be rewarded."

He claps me on the back. Laughs. He nods at me like we both heard a joke, but he's the only one who got the punch line. "Wish the others thought like you."

"They will, some day," I say, brushing dirt off my fingers.

"Maybe my children's children will have that privilege, but I won't."

"Why don't you leave? Go and run your own farm?"

He shakes his head with a deliberate force and throws me a confused look. "I can't leave."

"But you're not a prisoner here," I say.

"No, I'm no prisoner. But I was born here, same as my father. I don't know anything else but Austin Valley."

It's interesting that the longer we confine ourselves to a place the more it imprisons us. I wonder if long-time captives refuse to leave their cell even when they're handed the key.

"Have you tried to leave before?" I ask.

"Oh, yeah, a decade ago. 'Fore the kids," Dean says, looking at his hands but not quite seeing them. "Now I choose to stay. Every day I choose to serve the Reverians. The same as the rest of the Middlings. Because when I left, I didn't sleep so well. I wasn't happy. Only gone a few weeks, but it was different on the outside. Harder. People here, the Reverians, they make it easy. Outside Austin Valley, you have to do everything on your own. Make it on your own." He shakes his head, looking overwhelmed by the idea.

11

"That's harder than you think. It's hard to survive in the world out there. Harder than I ever imagined. I realized when I came back, what I'd taken for granted. And if that ain't enough to choose to stay, well, my children are happy here, safe. You know? It's a pretty good place. They do good by us," he says, not making eye contact with me. His eyes stay trained on his dirt-stained fingertips. A sliver of a smile forms on his mouth, but it's not quite genuine. "You know they helped Patsy and me to forget about what we lost, don't you?" I nod, a knot rising in my throat.

"Think about how much harder that would have been if we'd had to endure it out there," he says, pointing just over the ridge where the world is less organized. "If we weren't in Austin Valley, under the care and protection of the Reverians, then things would have been harder. That ain't worth no farm, I tell you that much."

A few years ago Dean and his wife lost a child. I heard they rushed the baby away before Patsy could even hold her. And after thirty-six hours of labor I'm certain that's all she wanted. Apparently when the doctor returned his hands were empty and his face grave. Dean wasn't the same for a month, missing work and making mistakes on the job. President Vider authorized for the modifier to be used on him and his family. All their memories of the child they lost have mostly disappeared, all but a single strand of the moment the child was taken away. I overheard my father tell my mother they kept this memory so that Dean and his family would be grateful, knowing that the President's administration saved them from a lot more emotional anguish.

"I bet those seedlings you planted will hatch tomorrow. Be nice to see them push through the dirt," Dean says.

"Well, I'd like to see them when they're fresh and new, but I'm not sure I can spare the hours tomorrow. I'm kind of overloading my schedule by being here now," I say, grabbing my bag full of clean, presentable clothes and slinging it over my shoulder.

"Whew, I praise the gods above they didn't make me a Dream Traveler. I can't imagine having the pressing demands you all have to put up with daily."

"Oh, I don't know," I say with a wink. "I think they blessed you with more talents than a Dream Traveler could stand. No one knows the earth and phases of the moon quite like you, Dean."

"If I have a rival, then it's you, miss," he says, pulling his ball cap down low from the sun rising higher in the Oregon sky.

"I'll see you tomorrow if I can," I say, saluting him and rushing down the fields, grazing various plants with my fingertips.

Chapter Three

For four years I've been coming to this lab. One might think I'd favor it somehow, have a certain bond with the space. I don't. The people have grown on me, though, despite the painful associations I've unfortunately attached to them. It's not their fault. They're doing their job. And each year their job becomes more difficult as the list of Defects grows. I used to be one of only a few patients. Now I have to wait for my injections.

"Ms. Fuller," Tammy says, poking her head through the lab door. Her soft brown curls remind me of yarn made from alpaca's wool. "Dr. Parker is ready for you."

I smile and nod. Tammy never says much to me, although we've habitually gotten used to seeing each other. She seems to keep an extra distance from most of the patients, and maybe I would too in her position. The room she leads me to is different from the normal one I'm used to. It's not a patient room, but rather the open lab behind the exam rooms, where test tubes and other equipment I'm unfamiliar with are kept. My speculative glance at Tammy must give away my confusion.

"We're getting busier, and since you're a veteran at getting injections Dr. Parker decided to do your treatment here. All the rooms are full at the moment."

"Okay," I say, taking a seat on a swivel chair and watching Tammy's long brown hair bounce as she retreats.

"Dr. Parker will be right in," she says, dropping my chart into the holder on the wall.

Curious objects all around me suck in my attention. At my back is another door, one with a small wired window. I half want to get up and spy through it, but I don't want to be caught being inquisitive so I stay seated. Still, this is a forbidden place. The back of the labs. For as long as I've been coming here I've never been allowed to step into this room. I always imagined this was where the chemicals they formulated and tweaked to try to fix us were being mixed. I figured this was a place that should be kept without disturbances, so great is the mission of the lab in trying to fix an epidemic of Defects.

"There's my favorite patient," Parker says, not looking at me as he plucks my chart from the wall. A couple of years ago he asked me to drop the Doctor part, said it would make our relationship more relaxed. "How are you feeling after this morning's injection?"

"Sore," I admit.

"I'm afraid that you'll notice this injection hurts far worse," he says.

"So you're not sugar coating it for me anymore, are you?"

He sighs and gives a defeated nod. "Afraid not. There's not much I can do to lessen the pain and the extra injection is usually not as easily tolerated by patients," he says, flipping through my chart and then laying it down. His brown eyes pause on me, a sympathetic smile on his mouth.

"But the results? Have they been good? For the patients who are now getting two injections? Have those patients gotten their gifts?" I ask, hopeful.

He shakes his head, his dark brown hair moving with it, breaking out of the shiny gel. "Unfortunately, we've just started doing the two-injection method so it's hard to tell. No results yet," he says with perfect diction. Parker grew up outside Austin Valley, in a Korean family, but I've never spied a hint of an accent.

"Well, maybe you can tell me a funny story while you give me this, huh?" I say, allowing him to run the thermometer across my forehead. He eyes the reading and smiles.

"As healthy as ever," he says, tearing open the package containing the alcohol swab.

I sit up tall, since I know that's the best position for receiving the injection, as Parker takes the position behind me.

"Hmmm," he says, readying the syringe. "I think, at this stage in the day, I'm all out of stories, but I'll have one ready for you tomorrow, all right?"

The tip of the needle is twenty-two gauge, not big unless you consider being stuck with it daily. Parker told me that was the right thickness for a needle that has to enter the brain stem. "One. Two. Three," he says. The needle punctures into the base of my skull, a sharp paralyzing sensation. And then the pain. Three seconds of mind-numbing fire. I've learned to count backwards during this part, until the fire turns to a slow burn. That's precisely the moment that Parker injects the meds, a cold, pink fluid. It makes my head feel on

15

fire and also like I have the worst case of brain freeze in the world. This time the sensations are so overwhelming I hardly register when he slips the needle out the back of my neck, bandages the injection site, and releases my hair.

"Em, you know not to move for fifteen minutes," Parker says, already turning to the exit. "Usually I'd stay and watch your vitals, but I think you'll be fine. I've got a long list of patients to get to so I'm going to expect you as a veteran to keep yourself here until a quarter after and then show yourself out. Can I trust you to do that?" he says, his long skinny fingers on the doorknob. A nervous rush in his voice.

"Of course," I say; the smile I brandish actually hurts my head.

"Good girl," he says with a relieved smile and exits.

Parker is right—as one of the first kids to start receiving the injections, I'm familiar with the protocol. Patients are supposed to remain still, head up, no neck movement for five minutes. Parker tells everyone fifteen, but he once slipped and told me that five minutes was fine and the extra bit was just precautionary.

The pain is more manageable when I close my eyes, but it's hard not to slump like that so I search the room and take in all the strange equipment, all used to try to create a solution for Defects. Mother thinks the Defects are a part of a cursed lineage who've finally been chosen for redemption by the gods. So according to her logic we're paying the price for her ancestors' misdeeds. It doesn't make sense to me why random kids within a generation would be chosen for punishment for things that happened centuries before our birth. Still, all I want is for this to be over with. I want my gift. I'm tired of being punished.

At five after, I slip off the stool. Maybe if I rush to the farm, I'll have a chance to spy on the new plants and see if they've pushed through the soil yet. I'm almost to the door when a baby's cry arrests my attention. It's a flat, aching wail, like that of a newborn. And the cry is unmistakably coming through a crack in the other door. The one that's labeled in giant red letters: *Authorized Personnel Only.* Someone forgot to the shut the door all the way. The deadbolt is still resting on the strike plate, not yet engaged.

My mind flashes to the letter with my name on it in my father's office. To the series of events which have been building my

16

suspicion. To the fact that an infant is crying behind a door where only lab technicians should be working.

A cautionary glance through the door's small window confirms no one is in the general vicinity of the next room. I slip the door open and poke my head around the corner. It's empty of people. What it doesn't lack is objects. Beakers, test tubes, microscopes, and vials of pink liquid crowd the work surfaces in the next room. The space actually surprises me. It's way too untidy and is dangerously close to violating laws. Some cabinets are still ajar, their contents obstructing them from being closed completely, and the same can be said for a closet. The disorder feeds my curiosity so I tiptoe further into the large room, keeping my body as close to the wall as I can. Another lab door stands on the other side of the room, this one unmarked and unlocked.

Since I'm not sure what I'm looking for, the complete disorder of this room confuses me. How can I find clues when I'm not certain what the riddle is? All I know is my father is hiding something. Probably for my own good. Probably to protect the Reverians. But the President definitely has him covering something up. And I'm not even sure why I suspect the labs, but again I've got that feeling like the gods are tapping me on the head.

The baby cries again. It echoes through the other door. I half rush to the door, fearing the child needs something I can provide, but still each of my steps are tentative. Halfway to the door I check over my shoulder. The lab I came through appears still to be empty. How long until Parker returns? Maybe he won't. I'm just about to rush forward when a tired voice echoes from the door in front of me.

"Can you make that one shut up already? I can't work with all that racket," a woman says. She has her back up against the window of the lab door on the other side, only a few feet away. I'm frozen in place. Unable to retreat. Unable to find a proper hiding place. She pushes the door open with her behind, a tray of tubes in her hands as she backs into the room. "And once you're done with that kid come help me sort these tubes. I'm way behind."

I have seconds to move. To do something. Anything before the blonde lab tech turns around and sees me. I remain frozen, standing in the lab.

"Yeah, I'll be there in a sec," a guy calls from the other lab room. "And we're all behind so join the freaking club, would you?"

She nods. I watch her balance the tray on her legs and smile. "I started the club, buddy." And she turns, eyes trained on the contents in her hands, but soon they'll look up and find me.

A hand slips around my wrist and jerks me through the closet door. Instantly I'm blanketed in darkness and arms. I squeak out a breath but only after a hand clamps down on my mouth, stifling my cry. Another arm wraps around my waist and wrenches me back. I'm pressed up against someone. In a dark closet. Now no breath fills my body. Only fear. Lips touch the back of my ear. A hot breath follows.

"Shhh! I'm not going to hurt you. But be quiet or you're gonna get yourself in serious trouble," the voice says.

"Okay," I mouth against his hand which is still covering my lips. In this small space I instantly suck in everything about the person who's just captured/saved me. He smells of bark and rosemary. A lot of rosemary. The hand pressed over my mouth is calloused. And his heart is keeping pace with mine, doing double time. It thumps against my back, since he has me pressed so firmly against him.

"Shhhh," he says again in my ear. "They'll be gone soon. Just stay still."

I nod and he drops the hand from my mouth.

"Sean!" the woman who almost caught me snaps. I jump and the person behind me steadies me, tugging me tighter into him. "Get in here already!"

"How in the world am I supposed to get a child to quiet down with you yelling?" a guy says, his voice drawing nearer. Through the crack I spy a figure move past the closet where I'm hiding and hurry to an opposite workbench.

"Oh, never mind that," the lady says, sounding tired. "When are you going to do the withdrawal on that one?"

"As soon as possible. The parents are waiting to take him home, but he was so upset I couldn't do it just now. And after him there's a dozen other babies being brought in."

"Sheesh," the lady says, exasperation in her tone. "I can't keep working like this. Look at this place! If we weren't under exemption we'd all be fined for the disorder. We've got to get a chance to catch up or the work will suffer."

The stranger's hand around my waist drops, yet I don't dare look up at the guy I know stands behind me. I feel him just over my shoulder, breathing hard, but I can't force myself to turn my chin and take him in. And still my attention is owned by the conversation happening outside this closet. I'm not sure what any of it means, but bits and pieces are starting to trigger strange cues in my brain. *Gods above, tell me what all this means. Why would anyone get an exemption?*

"Look, I don't care if President Vider wants us to work without breaks. I need something to eat. I'm getting lightheaded," the whiny lady says.

"Not sure if disobeying a direct order is a good idea. He told us—"

"Oh, come on. Let's just grab a quick snack. My blood sugar is dropping faster than the DOW," she says, and I watch the two figures move across the crack in the closet door and then the door on the other side gives a gentle click as it locks back into place.

They're gone. And the most terrifying thing is not what I've just heard or that I was almost caught in a forbidden place. It's that I must now turn around and face the person who's sharing this tiny space with me. I first take a step forward. The idea to just rush out of the closet, never meeting the person who saved me, courses through my mind. But the gods stop me at the threshold of the closet. With light streaming in from the lab I turn. All belief empties out of me in one hyperventilated breath.

"Rogue!" I say entirely too loudly. "What are you doing here? I thought you were dead?!"

Chapter Four

Rogue rushes forward, claps his hand over my mouth again. A fierce look upon his face. "Shhh!" he says up close, his forehead against mine, an act meant to subdue me and then also one meaning more. One full of a fondness that instantly wraps around me. "Oh, gods. I didn't know it was you, Em." He sucks in a breath. "Hi," he says, a coyness in his voice.

I push back from him, looking him over from his head full of chaotic dark curls to his dirt-caked boots. The weirdest feelings take hold of me and that's precisely when I realize I'm in shock. That's what these feelings are. The cold numbness. The dizziness. The swimming head. I utterly can't believe Rogue stands before me. He can't. He shouldn't. Not in the world I live in. "Hi?" I finally say in disbelief, careful to keep my voice down. "That's what you have to say to me? Hi?"

"Good to see you," he says, backing up until he's flush against shelves crammed with supplies.

"Did you not hear me properly?" I say through clenched teeth. "I thought you were dead. We all did." I almost reach out to run my fingers down his flannel shirt, to ensure he's real. "Rogue...is this really you? How can this be? We thought something happened to you."

He smirks, a cute crooked smile, a mischievous spark in his almond-shaped green eyes. "Something did happen to me."

"What? Are you all right? Where have you been?"

"Hiding," he says.

"Hiding? But why?"

He shakes his head, a quiet smile on his face like he just heard a joke. "Oh, Em, you were always good at drawing me out of my hiding places. I should have known it would be you who found me."

My mind flashes on a memory so long ago it feels like a distant life, but we aren't granted reincarnation by the gods so I know this is a memory from this life. As a child, many times when we played hide-and-seek, I'd pretend to trip and sprain something. Rogue would come out to save me or make sure I was all right. Zack always stayed hidden until the bitter end.

"Rogue, where have you been? Everyone thinks you're dead," I repeat.

"Yeah, about that. I'm not dead, but you can't tell anyone."

I shake my head, ultra-confused. "Wait, what are you doing *here*?" I say, looking around the crowded closet we share.

"What are *you* doing here?" he says, his dark curly hair falling down in his eyes. He's grown since the last time I saw him, four years ago. He's taller. Stronger. His features more pronounced. And his black hair is an absolute mess. His father would kill him right now if he didn't already think he was dead.

"Rogue, you've been gone for four years. We had a memorial service for you. The gods were asked to bless an empty resting place. Do you know how many times I brought flowers to—" Tears suddenly constrict my throat. Ones I haven't felt for him in so long. Tears I thought had dried up. Gone away.

"Shhh. Shhh. Shhh," Rogue says, moving forward, wrapping arms around me I recently felt, but didn't know belonged to him. "I'm sorry, Em. So sorry," he says into my hair. "I couldn't tell anyone where I was. I had to go away."

"But your father?" I say, pushing back so I'm looking at him directly.

His eyes suddenly tighten. "Don't tell my father anything about me. You have to promise."

"But—"

"Please, Em," he pleads, his hands now pinned on my forearms. "I'll explain some stuff, but you can't tell anyone about me. Please promise."

"Okay," I say, a new thought occurring to me. "We've got to get out of here."

"Yes, *you* do," he says. "But I've got to stay a little longer. I'm not done yet."

"Wait, you're not coming?"

He shakes his head. "No."

"But you said you'd explain."

"And I will. Can you dream travel to meet me tonight?" he asks.

"I can't, it's not a sanctioned night."

"Then meet me in the park."

"I don't know if this is such a good idea." I can't believe he's here. "I have to think about it. If I'm caught... Well, I was just punished recently."

"How long?" he asks, a look of concern in his eyes.

"A week." One long week of being hooked to the night terror generator, forced to sleep through nightmare after nightmare, my subconscious exhausted in the morning by serving up every horror it knew of.

He shakes his head. "I understand. I'll be in Lidill Park if you choose to meet me."

"I still can't believe you're here. You're alive," I say, this time reaching out, clutching his hand.

He grips my hand back. Smiles. "Time for you to go, Em."

Chapter Five

Even with the blanket tightly wrapped around my shoulders I'm still shivering. In June. Furiously I rub my hands together, blow my hot breath into them.

"Child, you're sitting on a spirit," my tutu says, trudging through the living room on her way to the dining area. Her cane knocks against the wood floor with each step. "Move to the chair and you'd be warmer."

"Which ghost is it?"

"Ronald," Tutu says, leaning on her cane, her shoulders rounded.

"Well, Ronald," I say, talking to the air. "This is my house now, so why don't *you* move." I stick out my tongue at Tutu.

She sticks hers out back at me. "Ronald tells me you aren't washing behind your ears enough."

"Gross, he's watching me shower."

"Don't get all flattered. He watches Damien shower too."

"Even grosser. He watches Father shower?" I say, sliding over on the sofa to a slightly warmer spot.

Tutu shrugs. "He's more bored than he is curious," she says, craning her head over her shoulder at Zack. He's leafing through one of the stories my younger sister, Nona, wrote and pushed into his hands as soon as he entered the house. "Oh, come on, Mr. Conerly. Do you want your interview or not?"

Zack smiles at Nona, ruffles the hair on the top of her head, and hands back her handwritten pages. "I'll check them out later, how's that?" he says to her.

She blushes. Nods.

"Come over here, Nona," I say, pulling the blanket down around my legs. "Come warm up my feet and I'll read your story."

"You already read my story like twelve times," she says, but still takes the spot next to me, lying down slightly on my feet.

Zack's eyes graze mine as he passes on his way to meet Tutu in the dining area, the usual focus written on his face.

"Well, how about I play with your hair and you can tell Ronald and me about your next story," I say to Nona as she lays her head against my curled up legs.

"I like Ronald," she says, a smile in her voice. "Maybe I'll put him in a story."

"Hey, Nona," I whisper. "I might need your help again. Need you to cover for me while I dream travel one of these nights."

She flips up her head and rolls her eyes. "No, I don't wanna. Mother's already talking about having me see someone for a psych eval because I'm too much of a baby to sleep alone."

The other night Nona covered for me. Wore my sleep cuff so it appeared I wasn't dream traveling, although that's exactly what I'd been doing so I could investigate my father's office. She wore her cuff on one wrist and mine on the other. The sleep cuffs go on promptly at bedtime and if they come off during the night or indicate a wearer has dream traveled, then the punishment is a week of night terrors. I learned that the hard way. Nona has to pretend to be too scared to sleep on those nights so I have the reason to spend the night in her room. The irony is Nona, who's four years younger than me, isn't scared of anything. She's the toughest Reverian I've ever met, but no one knows that because most don't notice her.

"Nona, I think I'm on to something and need to investigate it soon," I say, stroking my fingers through her hair.

"Why don't you have Tutu do it? She probably would," she says with a sigh.

I flip my head around and spy my tutu and Zack in the dining room. He's sitting up tall, scribbling on a notepad, seeming to record her every word. Tutu's eyes are directed up high as she tries to recollect old memories. "Back in those days, people dressed how they liked, did as they pleased," she says, a hint of fondness in her voice. "Let's say you dented your bike, well, you fixed it or you didn't. There was no law saying you had to. No scripture saying that the proof of mistakes led to more mistakes." She scratches her chin, a thought obviously churning under her curly gray hair. "You know, it's funny because the gods are supposedly as old as time, but I don't remember them always being so rigid. Actually the gods I grew up with were a bit more like the President I grew up with. I guess it isn't that funny that the gods who rule our lives always seem to take on the personality of the President who rules us currently."

Zack flicks his eyes up just in time to catch Tutu's wink. He doesn't return it, but instead repositions himself nervously. "Well, yes, President Vider is a bit stricter than his predecessors," he says. She smirks, but doesn't respond. Still, I know her well enough to know she has a crafty retort at the ready in her head but won't waste it on Zack, who would probably dismiss it. His father works for my father and has been strategic in his rise up the political ladder. Zack would never spoil that for him by discussing President Vider unfavorably, even with his Chief of Staff's mother.

"One thing that hasn't changed is the devotion to the gods," my tutu says, a smile lighting up her face, bringing with it a dozen wrinkles. "Middlings and Dream Travelers have always seemed to feel the gods' weight in their lives, their purity." She toggles her head back and forth, a question in her eyes. "Still, I don't believe they created us as the golden race, like the President does, meant to protect Middlings. Never have. I just think they created us differently and their divine plan isn't for us to know or use for our own agendas." The insinuation makes Zack straighten. He flicks his eyes at me and I slide back down on the couch, pretending I wasn't eavesdropping.

"Well," I say to Nona, who looks to be almost asleep on my leg, "you don't have to do it now, but maybe you'll consider covering for me in a few days. I'd owe you big."

"I'll consider it," she says, pushing some drool away with her hand as she slides softly into dreamland.

I twirl her hair around and around my fingers, getting lost in the rhythm of the movement and her gentle breathing. Her hair is blonde like mine, all loose curls that frizz up crazy in the humid months. And now that she's just hit puberty, she's a little more self-conscious, borrowing my hair gel to try and corral it back.

My tutu's words are a low hum for the next hour. It's only when I hear Zack clear his throat that I know he's exchanging pleasantries, about to take his leave. Stealthily, I slide Nona's head to the cushion underneath me as I stand. She lies like a doll, all round and freckled, and innocently perfect. A shiver slips out of her lips, probably due to the loss of my body heat. I wrap the afghan around her.

"Ronald, go watch Dee do her voodoo upstairs, would you?" I say to the empty side of the sofa.

25

"Are you talking to yourself, Em?" Zack says as he approaches from the dining room, a subtle smile on his mouth.

"According to the ancient artifact in there," I say, motioning to the dining room where my tutu is still stationed, "I'm talking to Ronald, the Reverian who used to live in this house. He discovered gold in the mountains west of here and helped to found this society, but yes, I'm probably talking to myself."

"That artifact has some pretty amazing tidbits of knowledge," Zack says as I walk with him to the foyer.

"How old did she tell you she is? Because she always lies about her age."

"One hundred and nine years old."

I roll my eyes. "She's ninety-nine," I say with a laugh. "She's the only lady alive who lies to make herself older."

"Except those outside of Austin Valley, trying to buy alcohol or lottery tickets," Zack says, taking off his jacket and slinging it over his arm. His pressed white shirt glows in the dim light of the entryway.

I slide up close to him, nervous tension bounding out of my chest. "I have something I need to tell you."

He eyes me speculatively, caution on his face. "Go ahead."

My eyes sweep around the various rooms that surround us and then settle back on Zack. "It's Rogue," I say so low it's hardly classified as a whisper.

His eyes pinch together, confusion in them.

"He's alive. I saw him today," I say, realizing how crazy these words make me sound.

Zack is already shaking his head. Looking at me like I'm trying to play a mean joke on him. His lips tighten, along with his eyes. "Em," he says, a warning in his voice.

"I know it sounds crazy, but I swear the gods can strike me down now if I'm lying."

We pause. Wait. They've done it before so that's a bold statement not just anyone will throw out.

Nothing happens to me.

"He said he's been hiding," I say in an urgent whispered rush. "Said no one can know he's alive."

"Em," Zack says again in the same disbelieving tone, but this time he grabs my arm.

26

"He asked me to meet him tonight," I say, laying my hand over his.

Zack pauses. Searches my eyes. Winces with acute disbelief.

"Go with me," I urge him.

"But we can't. There's curfew and—"

"I know. Just go with me," I say again. "You're not going to believe me unless you see him with your own eyes and I'm telling you he's alive. Not dead. Not missing. I wouldn't lie to you. I never have. You have to—"

"I'll go," he interrupts. "If you say he's alive, I believe you, Em."

Chapter Six

Half an hour. That's as much time as Tutu said she'd cover for me. I'm supposedly in her quarters, learning to sew. If my mother paid the least bit of attention then she'd know I learned that years ago. Her job is more to keep tabs on me, rather than know the specifics of my life. She always wanted a Middling nanny for us, but Father wouldn't allow it. He said they were good enough to clean our house, manicure us, and cook our meals, but they weren't fit to raise Dream Traveler children.

"Come on," I say, tugging on Zack's shirt sleeve. "Can you go any faster?"

Everything about him is reluctant. I'm not sure how I'd have reacted if the tables were turned, if he told me something so outlandish. I want to think I'd believe him instantly, not drudge down the path like I'm on my way to meet a mythical sea creature in the forest.

Rogue and I didn't have time to discuss where to meet, but I know where he'll be. In our spot. The place past the two ponds, far out of the way of the heavy traffic of park visitors. It's where we'd spend hours lying in the grass watching clouds slide through the sky. It's where I accidentally pierced Rogue's ear with a stick when we were pretending to duel as pirates. Zack threw up in the stream afterwards.

A broad-shouldered figure stands beside that stream now, his hair catching slightly in the warm breeze. It's hard to know as we approach if it's Rogue, since the only light is cast by the moon and he stands in the shadow of an oak tree. The figure turns his head when a twig cracks under my foot. And then I see a profile so familiar and also not quite what I remember. The jaw line is more pronounced than in my memories. The angle of his nose more defined. His hair not governed by gel, instead curling at his hairline.

And then Zack finally moves with an urgency to surpass mine. He's sprinting, tearing across the grass. In one swift movement he throws his arms around Rogue's shoulders, wrenching him in tightly. Rogue stumbles back a step and then his arms stretch around, gripping Zack's back. A laugh echoes from him. A soothing sound. I arrive at their side and over Zack's shoulder Rogue smiles at me. "I told you not to tell anyone, but I knew you knew that meant 'tell only one person.' I'm glad you did," he says, opening up his arm and pulling me in so we're all locked in an embrace. I want to live in this moment for the rest of my life. Forever and ever I want to feel Zack's disbelief come in small laughs and Rogue's arms around my shoulders, his fingers pinning into my skin like he can't believe I'm the one who's real. A sound halfway between a cry and a cough rolls out of my mouth, unleashing a tender ache within.

There's a stern look on Zack's face when he pulls back. "Rogue, where have you been, man?"

He challenges the look with a light smile. Pats Zack on the shoulder. "Oh, brother, I've been all over."

They aren't brothers, but since I can remember Rogue called him that. Zack never returned the nickname, maybe because I suspect he never felt equal enough to him. Maybe that's changed.

"What does that mean, Rogue?" Zack shakes his head, his initial relief now turning to anger. "Four years ago you just disappeared. What's happened to you?"

"I had to leave. I can't tell you everything, but I can tell you I didn't have a choice. You have to believe me." Rogue turns to me. "Em, I told you I'd tell you stuff and I'm gonna make right on that promise, I promise." He smiles, a dimple surfacing. After all this time, he hasn't changed. Is never quite serious.

I nod, feeling entranced briefly. Rogue is built more like a Middling with strong, sculpted muscles. Broad shoulders. A barrel chest. Dark olive skin. He's dressed like a Middling too. Jeans and boots. He looks so strange next to Zack, who exchanged his suit for khakis and a button-down shirt. He's slim. Lean. Pale. Hair pushed back in the usual arrangement.

"Your father?" Zack reaches out and clutches Rogue's bicep. "Does he know you're alive?"

"No!" Rogue says, clapping a hand over Zack's, gripping it. "I mean, he might, but you can't tell him you've seen me. He's who I've been hiding from."

"President Vider?" I say in disbelief. "Why would you hide from him?" My father, as his Chief of Staff, was there a lot for the President after Rogue disappeared. For months we didn't see my father, his job as support to the President coming first.

"The Reverians aren't who you all think." Rogue clutches either side of his head like a sudden pain just assaulted him. He takes in a few shallow breaths before continuing. "My father, *your* President, isn't who you think he is. Right before I disappeared I learned something so unbelievable I had to leave, had to save myself from it."

"You couldn't tell us?" Zack asks, sounding hurt. "You had to allow us to think you were dead?"

Rogue nods. Shrugs. "I didn't have a chance. I had to. I didn't want to hurt you with what I knew. You were better off not knowing." He blows out an exasperated breath. "Because once the blindfold comes off there's no going back."

"But you said you'd tell me—"

He claps me on the shoulder. "And I will." He's so much taller now. Stands a foot over me, a couple inches over Zack. "Just give me a minute to enjoy looking at your faces. I've missed them every day since I left."

My reply is imprisoned under delicate tears, aching to be released. I step forward, slide my hands around his waist, bury my head in his shoulder. With an urgency to match my racing heart he wraps his arms around me and tugs me in tightly. "Em, how am I supposed to see your face like this?" Rogue says, a laugh in his voice, his grip comforting.

I laugh and it's enough to release a single tear which streams down my cheek as I step back. Rogue spies the tear and swipes it away with his thumb. "Oh, stop that, would you, Em? Reunions are supposed to be happy."

I nod, feeling small, like a child. His thumb still rests on my jaw. His eyes still rest on mine. "In the four years I've been gone, the gods made you more beautiful, didn't they?"

I don't respond. All my efforts work to force the knot out of my constricted throat.

"Why are you back after four years?" Zack asks, pulling Rogue's attention away from me. We part, opening back into the three-person circle.

"Oh, Zachariah, again with the questions," Rogue says, a laugh in his voice. "Can't you see we're having a moment?"

A trace of a smile edges Zack's lips. Rogue was the only one who could make him a little less serious. His eyes flash on me, an unreadable expression in them, then they're back on Rogue. "Why are you back?" Zack asks again. I know the wheels of his brain are working. He's doing what he's been taught: asking strategic questions, not just the curious ones.

"Fine. Fine. I'll give you some answers. Not that one. But I'll tell you a few things I know," Rogue says, rubbing his temple.

"Why won't you tell us everything?" I ask.

"Em, there are things you're better off not knowing," Rogue says, a haunting in his voice now.

"How can you dangle the presence of some troubling knowledge in front of us and then keep it a secret?" I ask.

"Because if I could unknow some things, I would. Why would I want my two favorite people to be troubled by knowledge they can't erase or forget?" he says, a strange look in his eyes.

"Well, tell us what you will," Zack encourages.

Rogue nods. "Em"—he turns to me—"you heard that baby in the lab, didn't you?"

I nod.

"I thought so. That's what had you sneaking around, wasn't it?"

Zack whips in my direction, a punishing glare pinned on me. "You were sneaking around the lab? Are you trying to get yourself in trouble again?"

"Oh, let up on her," Rogue says. "It's how she found me. Anyway, my father has the labs experimenting on Middling children. Not just experimenting, but using them. The things he's done—"

"Are to preserve our race," Zack says, nodding. "I'm aware of this. He's been using Middlings to fix the Defect crisis."

"You knew about this?" I slap Zack on the arm and return the punishing look he just gave me.

"They're helping you," he says.

"Oh no, Em," Rogue says, pushing his hair off his forehead. "They put you on the Defect list?"

I scrunch up my face in confusion. "Put? What does that mean?"

He waves me off. "Nothing, you misunderstand."

"So you left because they're using Middlings?" Zack asks.

"I left for that reason and more."

"Look, I get that your father is a demanding man," Zack says, "but did you have to leave?"

31

I remember the bruises Rogue used to hide. The way he always kept his face light when I asked him about returning home after curfew. "No biggie," he'd say, but I always spied the pain below his mask.

"I had to leave," he says and backs up. "It was the only way for me."

"Your gift? Is it still gone?" Zack asks, stepping forward.

Rogue was the first Defect. Since he's a little older than me, by several months, I hadn't been classified yet. That was the hardest year I ever remember. I lost one of my best friends and became a Defect.

He smiles, a triumphant look in his eyes. "Oh no, my gift has come."

"That's great, man," Zack says. "What is it?"

"Well, you, my brother, as a telekinetic may be able to move things with your mind, but can you do this?" Out of the humid air a single mauve dahlia pops into Rogue's hand. They only grow in one place in town, around the first duck pond at the entrance of the park. "I have the gift of apportation."

"Wait," Zack says, taking the flower from Rogue. Inspecting it. "You transported that, didn't you?"

"Yep," Rogue smiles broadly. "I pulled it through the window, so to speak. I have to be relatively close and know exactly where the object is, but I can manifest anything of moderate size into the palm of my hand. Neat, huh?"

Zack slides his hand over his smoothed back hair. "That's incredible. There's no recorded history of an apportational in the Reverian society. You're the first."

"Well, since I'm supposedly dead, don't go off bragging, would you?"

"How long are you staying?" I ask.

"Not sure yet," Rogue says, turning his too alluring eyes directly on me. "Depends on how long it takes."

"Takes to do what?"

"Nice try," he says, shaking his head.

Zack steps up close to Rogue, tilts his head back and forth, inspecting him. "You know, besides needing a clean shave, you look pretty good."

"Oh, come on," Rogue says, brandishing a giant smile, his teeth perfect on the top and perfectly crooked on the bottom. "I look great, brother," he says, slapping Zack on the shoulder.

Chapter Seven

"You called for me, Mother?" I say, standing up tall, chin held high.

She nods, stands from the Victorian couch in the sitting room, and waves her hand in a presenting manner at the man standing next to her. He's a stranger. It is rare to find one of those in Austin Valley. "Yes, I'd like you to meet who President Vider hired to do skills evaluations on all Defects." The man beside her has spiky red hair, a similar shade as my mother's. He looks to be in his mid-forties, and by the style of his dark green suit, he definitely isn't a Reverian. Another clue is that he has a pointy red goatee and all Dream Traveler Reverians are required to be clean shaven.

"Name's Ren," he says, not extending a hand to me.

"Hello," I say with a small curtsy. "Nice to meet you. I'm Em."

"Oh, so you didn't name her after Mummy," he says to my mother, his words coated in a British accent.

She rolls her eyes. A strange gesture for her to do to someone who isn't one of her children. "Shut up, Ren. You know I'd never do something so sentimental and downright repulsive."

"No, Lyza, you'd have to have a heart to do that, and we both know you don't," he says to my mother, a smug look on his face.

"A heart pumps blood. I obviously have one of those," she says, smoothing back a strand of hair into her tight bun. "What I don't have is this useless capacity for caring."

"Always the literal one, aren't you?" Ren says.

"This man, Ren, happens to also be my brother," my mother says, not hiding the disappointment in her voice.

"Happens?" he says, actually looking amused. "Like it's one big happenstance that we were born from the same parents?"

"What I mean is that the person who was hired by the President just *happens* to be related to me," my mother says, cinching her arms across her chest.

I didn't know my mother had a brother. Never met her parents. She doesn't talk to us about them. About anything really. "Why does he have an accent and you don't?" I finally say, breaking the staring contest between them.

34

Mother sighs loudly. "Because my brother doesn't subscribe to the fact that accents lead to labeling and the best way to gain advantage is to have nothing marking you with where you're from," she says with her typical perfect diction.

"So we're British?" I ask, confused.

"No, we are Reverians."

A loud, thick yawn echoes from Ren. "Although this family reunion is incredibly touching, can we get to the reason I'm here, which isn't to exchange stories of what we've been doing for the last twenty years?"

I step forward, studying the man in front of me. Disbelief and curiosity take turns overwhelming my thoughts. "Wait, you're my uncle?"

"Don't call me that," Ren says, looking disgusted. "And yes, technically I am. I don't send Christmas presents, don't care about your grades, and I don't give piggyback rides."

"We don't celebrate Christmas," is all I say. I'd heard about this weird tradition from a new Middling who had started working at the Agricultural Center.

"No, I remember now my dear sister belongs to the Reverians' religion, which is based on myths that are likened to unicorns. Do yourself a favor, luv, and pick up a world religion book. It will blow your mind. Although, come to think about it, diverse texts are probably banned here," Ren says.

My mother throws a seething glance at her brother. "I see you haven't changed a bit, have you, Ren?"

"Oh yes, I'm just as delightful as ever," he says.

"Which is why you're still alone, hopping from job to job, society to society, is that right?" my mother says.

"Being alone is a choice, dear Lyza. Some of us don't need the money and prestige of a significant other. Some of us make our own way in the world, but you wouldn't know about that, would you? How long has it been since you ventured out of this valley? Really ventured out, on your own, not some organized dream travel field trip managed and supervised by the Reverians?"

"I still fail to see why President Vider hired you for this job," she says, her anger flaring in every word. I've hardly ever seen her this flustered, my mother, the queen of pretense.

"It's simple, little Lyzie. I'm the best. And he knows it."

"Don't. Call. Me. That," she says, her voice an octave under yelling.

"Oh, you don't love my little nickname for you anymore, do you?"

"You know I never liked it," she says, her expression pinched.

"I most likely won't remember your preferences on the name calling, so don't be offended when I call you it again. Or do. Doesn't really matter to me," Ren says, a hint of pleasure in his voice.

"Oh, just do what you were brought here for," my mother says, sweeping past me, pulling the double doors closed behind her.

I turn and look at Ren directly. Menacing isn't exactly the right word for him. He's that, but he's also thoughtful in his approach. Theatrical. And he does something most of the people I know don't: he says exactly what he wants.

He eyes me like I'm a dirty puddle he's trying to figure out how to cross. "Oh, why can't I get away from teenagers? I bloody hate teenagers."

"Well, I'm mature for my age," I say.

"That makes one of us. So you're one of the Defects. Interesting thing that's happened in this valley. Note to self, don't drink the water here," he says.

"Do you think you can help us? That's why you're here, right?"

He takes a seat in the armchair and indicates I should take a seat on the couch opposite him. When I'm settled he gives me something that almost classifies as a smile. "No, I'm not here to help you get your gift. I'm here to assess you and give a report. What valuable information I provide may or may not help. Who knows, really?"

I deflate with a sigh. "Well, when you say this is happening in this valley, do you mean it isn't happening elsewhere?"

A small smile quirks up the corner of his mouth. "As sheltered as your mother, aren't you, poor dear?"

I only stare back at him, his dark green eyes like that of St. Augustine grass.

"No," he finally says. "This epidemic appears to be confined to this valley, as far as I can tell."

"Are you religious?"

"What an abrupt and personal question," he says, shaking his head at me.

36

"Well, you don't have to answer it," I say, feeling sudden embarrassment burn my insides.

"Of course I don't."

"Do you think the gods are punishing us?"

"To be quite honest, I don't think the gods or God or any other holy entity gives two cents about us," he says.

"You're the angry type, aren't you?"

"You're the honest type, aren't you?"

I shrug.

"All righty, missy, let's get down to business. Here's how this is going to work. I'm going to ask you a few questions. Got it?"

I nod.

"Oh good, it gives brief responses. That will help." Ren leans back, crosses his ankle over his knee, and stares at the ceiling casually. "Do you hear voices?" he asks.

"No."

"Do you see things which aren't real?" he asks.

"No."

"Get flashes?"

"No."

"Control people with your mind?"

"No," I say again.

"Have objects moved mysteriously around you?"

"No."

"You really aren't much fun at all, are you?" he says.

I squint at him. "I'm loads of fun."

"Yeah, yeah. I'm sure you think so."

I shake my head at him. I've never met someone with his audacity.

"All right, you failed that phase of testing and have graduated to the next loser round," he says.

"I'm not a loser."

"No, no, of course you're not," he says dismissively. He slips a device the size of the palm of his hand out of his inside jacket pocket. With a switch the device makes a low buzz.

"What's that?"

"A frequency recorder. It's science." He says it like it's a dirty thing. "And it's an upgraded model so I'm probably getting all sorts of radiation."

"Why are you using it then?"

"Well, the daft scientist who gave it to me is probably right that it will make the assessments I have to do a whole lot easier." He pauses and only stares at me for a few seconds, an intensity in his eyes. "Did you get that message I just sent you?"

"What?" I say, dumbfounded.

"The telepathic message I just sent you. Did you hear it in your head?"

"No."

Ren slips a gold ring off his finger. It's clunky. Lays it on the table next to him. "Can you move that with your mind?" he asks, his voice flat.

I stare at it for over a minute. "No."

He eyes the device and then slides it back into his pocket.

"Did you really think under these stressful circumstances I'm suddenly going to use my hidden gift for a stranger?" I ask.

"I knew for a fact you wouldn't be able to. I'm studying your approach," he says, slipping his ring back on. "And in my extremely intelligent opinion there's no chance your gift is going to surface. What I don't get is why you appear to have the instinct but there's no power behind it."

"What?"

He rolls his eyes. Takes an impatient breath. "Dream Travelers have a certain level of frequency they exude when using their powers, but yours is on par with a Middling."

"What?" I say again. "That's bizarre."

"No, let's be honest. It's sad." He sits forward and looks at me sideways. "Tell me, have you suffered any traumas?"

"No."

"Depressed?"

"No."

"Suicidal thoughts?"

"Gods no."

"Well, I'm momentarily stumped, but if it makes you feel better you're exactly like all the Defects I've assessed. At least you have people to share your woes with," he says.

"Do you think upping the injections will help?"

"Injections?" he asks, confusion suddenly covering his features.

"The meds they've been giving us," I say.

38

"Oh yes, I heard about those. Medical science isn't my forte, thank god," he says, looking repulsed. "I don't know if these meds can help, but if I become extremely bored toddling around this place I might look into it."

"What am I supposed to do until then?"

"I don't know, you can play hopscotch for all I bloody care. That's none of my concern," he says, looking tired. "I'm only supposed to assess you and a few other snots and report if any gifts surface. Right now my job is easy. You're all appropriately named. Defects."

I stay seated as he makes for the door. He turns just before he leaves. "So, what's Em short for?"

My brow knits with momentary confusion. "Nothing. I'm just Em."

"Really?" he says, an unconvinced tone in his voice. "Your mother's not the type to name someone 'just Em.'"

"What does that mean?" I say.

"Bloody hell if I know, but it sure is curious."

Chapter Eight

My favorite night of the week. Thursday. The night I don't have to wear the clunky sleep cuff on my wrist all night. I don't have to fall into dream-filled sleep. I'm allowed to do what I was born to do: dream travel.

A blanket of wind strokes my face as I slip into the silver tunnel, the transport to the other dimension. Of course, every sensation is a purely cognitive one, since my body comfortably rests in my bed while my subconscious soars through space on its way to the set meeting place. Whatever happens to me in dream travel, however, will mark my physical body.

Rapid, automatic turns in the wormhole catch my breath. It's always amazed me that the gods instilled a silent knowledge within Dream Travelers which allows us to navigate to any place and time by only thinking of it. And without fail my subconscious pops me out of the tunnel and into the location I intended.

Helen, the coordinator for dream travel events, stands at the entrance to Carnegie Hall with her usual clipboard.

"Em Fuller," she says, checking off my name as I approach her. The foyer is full of Dream Traveler Reverians, and with a quick glance at her clipboard I confirm what I feared: I'm one of the last to arrive. "You're in the Zankel Hall tonight, with most of the other adolescents," she says, words crisp and precise.

I nod, staring momentarily at her white curls which are all uniform, making a flawless beehive. I've always wondered how long it took the Middling who styles her hair to achieve such perfection.

"Thank you," I say and pull open the brass door. My eyes are swept up to the gold and white arched ceiling. It's so bright and soft, reminding me of sunlight. Under my feet green marble stretches the length of the foyer.

His impatient sigh freezes me. Tentatively I bring my eyes up to find my father, arms crossed, feet apart, standing squarely in the hallway, a look of utter annoyance on his face. "Hello, Father," I say with a slight curtsy.

"Em, what are most of the Reverians here doing right now?"

Past him I watch people file in the direction of their assigned halls. Most probably want to get a good seat.

"Attending this week's lecture," I say, unable to meet his stern blue eyes.

"Does anyone look to be studying the architecture of Carnegie Hall?" he says.

I pretend to watch the people moving with purpose behind him. "No, Father. They all appear intent on getting to their seat."

"And aren't you?"

My eyes fall to his polished black shoes. I hate how subservient he makes me. Hate it. "I am," I say with half my voice.

"You're privileged to have President Vider as your speaker tonight. It disappoints me that you're not the first one in your hall, ready to absorb all the wisdom you could learn from him."

I raise my head and find the courage to look at my father directly. "Oh, I'm certain there's a great deal I could learn from him," I say, thinking of Rogue and the secrets I know he's hiding that are connected to the President.

My father jerks his chin down, his forehead and angry eyes pinned on me. "Em, what was that thought you just had about Rogue Vider?"

Terror sends a shiver down my neck and chest, emptying me of all breath. My teeth suddenly chatter and I know by my father's expression that he's spied my nervousness. I will my eyes to blink. I will my shoulders to loosen. I will my breath to return to my body. *How could I have let my anger overwhelm me so much to drop my defense against my father's telepathy?* I know better. Tutu taught me how to direct my thoughts when in his company and still I've failed at a crucial time.

I suck in an unsteady breath. "I still miss him, that's all," I say, the quiver in my voice obvious. "The mention of his father brought back a rush of memories. It was quite unexpected for me actually. I haven't thought of Rogue in so long, but still—"

"Allowing your thoughts to be occupied by someone who's dead is beyond ridiculous," my father says with a disapproving sneer. "Again it appears that many of your shortcomings are the result of bad decisions. Focus on yourself, Em. Not others. We are the best when we serve others by serving ourselves."

"Yes, Father," I say, my nerves still vibrating up and down my chest, making my heartbeat unsteady.

"Now, get out of my sight and don't embarrass me in front of President Vider."

"Yes, Father," I say, rushing past him, catching the hint of the musty cologne he's worn for as long as I can remember.

I slide into Zankel Hall. The lights over the podium in the middle of the stage are still dim. Thank the gods I'm not late. The auditorium is full. Most of my peers are here. The other two halls probably house most of the other adult Dream Travelers. Our population has remained modest enough that we usually fit inside most venues for our lectures.

I'm halfway down the aisle when a hand reaches out and grabs my wrist. Still unnerved by my encounter with my father, I jump and almost yelp. Zack gives me a curious look from his seat, his fingers still wrapped around my wrist.

"I saved you a seat," he whispers.

I nod, one of relief. "Right. Thanks," I say, scooching around his long legs and to the seat on his other side. "Good thinking getting an aisle seat," I whisper at his shoulder.

He's staring straight ahead, but a smile graces his lips. "Knew you'd be late and I'd have to pull you in."

"I bet you get tired of rescuing me," I say, watching his face. Watching for a hint of expression.

"Are you trying to goad me into saying that I enjoy rescuing you?" he says, eyes still fixed on the stage, attention at the ready.

I slide down in my seat. "I'd never expect you to say something so absurd." *I might wish, but...* From my slouched position, I lean over closer to Zack's shoulder, my face almost touching his starched jacket sleeve. "So, pretty amazing about you-know-who…"

He closes his eyes. Shakes his head. "I don't think we should talk about that here," he says from the corner of his mouth.

"Well, I haven't seen you since then, so excuse me for taking the first opportunity I had," I say, rolling my eyes at him.

Zack finally turns and looks at me. As usual his hair is parted on the side, slicked back—the hairstyle all men wear in our culture. He wears it best. "I came by last night to see you, but you were in a meeting."

"Yeah, being a Defect keeps me awfully busy," I say. "Met with the new Skills Assessor."

He gives a defeated sigh. "Well, Dee answered the door. She ordered me to take her to the summer solstice ball."

My initial reaction, a yelp of horror, is quickly masked by a fake laugh, which is too embarrassingly loud. As a result I receive a dozen angry glances from the silent crowd in front of me.

"Em..." Zack says, a pleading in his voice.

"Sorry," I say, my face burning hot with humiliation and then something else. Jealously, I think.

"No you're not. You think this is entertaining."

"No, I think it's disgusting and also absolutely not any of my business. And besides, my father thinks you two make a smart match. Isn't that what you want? To please my father? Mr. Chief of Staff?" I say in a dull voice.

"Well, yes, but..."

"Most of the guys are drawn to her. Why not you too?"

"She's just not who I want," he says, again staring at the stage with deliberate force.

"Well, you can't marry your dream job. But you can marry to get that job," I say, punching him in the arm.

He grabs my hand as it connects with his arm and pushes it away. "That's what you think I want?"

I shrug, a little put off by his bad attitude tonight. "Of course I do."

"Shhhh," he says just as the lights dim overhead and a spotlight shines on the podium.

Chapter Nine

"Do you want to know what most Americans want?" President Vider says, launching into his speech quickly after his introduction. No one answers the question. "They want to be protected. Inside their homes they want the protection of walls, the comfort of electricity, the knowledge that a government will build their roads and educate their children. But they also want more. They want a superpower that can step in and save them. They want superheroes. People who can do for them what they can't do for themselves. The America here, where I stand," he says, pointing at the stage, his movements sharp, demanding, "it doesn't work. It doesn't give its people what they *really* want. The America inside *our* borders does. Don't you see? We aren't in America, it is in *us*. Austin Valley is the unofficial fifty-first state. The first republic under this nation to do right by the people. To give them what they want."

President Vider steps away from the podium, and the red handkerchief tucked inside the breast pocket of his black pin-striped suit catches my attention. "What is our crime rate? Zero. What is our life expectancy? Decades past the average based on the races. What are our earnings? Double that of the average American. And why?" he asks, drawing out the last word, triumph prematurely creeping into his tone.

Again no one answers. President Vider walks to the end of the stage on my side of the hall. His black slicked back hair catches the spotlight as he walks. Rogue has his nose. His dark olive skin. His green eyes. His height. His arrogance. They both share that flare of Spanish descent, making them stand out in our mostly Caucasian population.

"We have built a system that works. One that draws upon the greatness of the Dream Traveler race and uses the excellent efforts of the Middlings. We've found a way to make the races work together for the betterment of society," he says, his voice carrying with it an unmistakable draw. A persuasion hidden in each of his words, like a subliminal message. Every time I've been in his presence I've watched him hypnotize those around him with his words. Not me

44

though. I've never trusted him. Never been able to stand his gaze lingering on me.

"Do you know that other Dream Travelers hide within the population? Pretend not to exist with their superiority? They suppress it. What good does that do anyone?" He shakes his head, mouth pinched. "Within our borders we are proud and the people who serve us know our capabilities. This makes *them* proud. And, in turn, we protect the Middlings, as the gods once told us was our role as the golden race. This role is one with a burden. One that carries a great weight. And only people with our talents can handle such a task."

Around the room almost everyone is leaning forward. I jerk my eyes in Zack's direction. He shares their same posture, hanging on the President's every word. Etching it into his brain as scripture. I admit President Vider is compelling, more so than any other Reverian; even so, I'm not perched on the edge of my seat. For some reason his spell doesn't completely work on me. As I scan Zankel Hall I silently wish it did. I wish I were more like my peers.

"I've known for quite some time that if we found a balance we would achieve greatness, and that time is drawing near. We are a small state in this nation. The smallest. But soon we can slowly start to open our borders to allow more Dream Travelers and Middlings to join our ranks. Now that we've proven we know how to effectively give people what they want, we can extend our flawless government to others," the President says and on cue the entire auditorium erupts into applause. People are polite, only clapping for a few seconds, but it's enough to unleash a sneer-like smile from President Vider.

"Since our society has existed, we have controlled parts of the national government, ensuring that we had the privacy and security to grow our state to the prosperous one that it is today. Our efforts have paid off. It is my hope that our state, our society, stay secret, but we build it with great diligence and strategic minds. That is what I call upon you for. I need people who recognize the supreme balance that creates empires and wants to build them. I need Dream Travelers who know they will be a wedge or a bolt in our empire, so that the people we support can stand firmly on top of the structure we erect." Again applause, this time longer, more fervent.

When the crowd quiets down, the President raises his chin up high and points out to the crowd. "Who out there wants to implement a strategy that works? Who wants to extend our greatness to others? Who wants to achieve the mission of the gods? Those who do, please say 'aye.'"

And in unison the entire crowd chimes a low chorus of "ayes." Mine is short, almost inaudible.

Chapter Ten

I skip agriculture hours to do the only thing that's even more satisfying. Hiking. After my dream travel last night I have a dozen thoughts needling under the surface of my brain, all of them unable to emerge completely, unable to give me a definitive path to follow. Therefore I elect to trek the paths on the hills surrounding Lidill Park. If I had the time I could take them all the way to Mount Austin.

Three miles into the hike a weight falls off my shoulders and I feel a slight release from all the strangeness that's been surrounding my life lately. Being in the wilderness for an extended amount of time always frees me somehow. I giggle at a songbird who bounces from branch to branch, singing a tune to attract a mate. His incessant tweeting is strangely compelling, although bordering on annoying. That's when an acorn drops on my shoulder. I jerk my head up. The sky is clearly visible overhead. I'm on a path not covered by the usual dense canopy of trees.

Before I can move, it happens again. This time a stone drops on the path in front of me. It's round and flat, like one of the stones found in the stream down below. I stoop to pick it up. It's still wet. *What?* Swinging around, I size up the forest. I'm alone…it appears. And then from nowhere a duckling, all fluffy and yellow, drops through the air and lands on the pine-covered ground a foot in front of me. I scream and stagger backward.

It takes me approximately three seconds to realize the duckling isn't a monster. And still, ragged breaths heave through my chest from the surprise. I step forward and the creature, frightened by my reaction, scuttles further on the path. I turn to the seemingly empty forest. Plant my hands on my hips. "Rogue, you better get out here and send this duckling back to its mother."

From a cluster of trees not ten feet away, I spy his almost black curls and then one eye peeks out from behind a birch. Even from just the one eye I know he's wearing a giant grin.

"You might think it's funny, but I bet that momma duck is worried to death," I say, my heart still hammering from the scare.

He slides out completely from behind the tree, dismissing me with a shake of his head. In only a few graceful steps he walks past

47

me, picks up the duckling, and instantly it disappears. Then he turns, trains a mischievous stare on me. "They have like a dozen babies. I'm sure she didn't even notice," he says.

"Are you trying to give me a heart attack?" I say, wanting to slap him. If he was Zack I probably would have already, but Zack would never do something like that.

"I was just playing with you," he says, slipping his hands into his faded jean pockets.

"What are you doing out here?" I ask. I haven't seen him since the other night, but I had to rush home before we had a chance to discuss future meetings.

"Oh, just hanging," he says, his eyes finding a spot on the hill just above us. I follow his line of vision.

"You're camping, aren't you?"

"What are you listening to?" he says, indicating the buds in my ears. I actually hadn't had my music on for the last mile, since I was enjoying the sounds of the woods.

"You're avoiding my question."

He tilts his head forward. "Wanna keep hiking? I'll join you."

I allow myself a full five seconds to take him in, to run my eyes over the person who shouldn't be standing in front of me. He's wearing a blue T-shirt over his jeans, two things that were outlawed for Dream Traveler Reverians to wear years ago. Again I note how different he looks from how I remember him. He's rugged now. The other extreme to Dream Traveler Reverians who are all lean and polished in their overly starched suits. Rogue looks more like a Middling Reverian now. That alone would send his father into a raging fit. "Yeah, sure."

I tuck my earbuds in my pocket and take off down the path, hugging the edge to give him room to walk beside me. "Where have you been all these years?" I finally ask. My eyes flick up to catch a smirk spring to his mouth.

"All over. Tokyo, Fiji, Serbia. It's amazing to be able to dream travel freely."

"Yeah, I wouldn't know," I say. "We're still only allowed to dream travel one night a week for less than an hour, always with a set destination and a curriculum. And we're never allowed to time travel."

He cuts his eyes at me, nods. "I remember. However, dream traveling into the past is cool but you're not missing much."

"Yeah, just centuries of history," I say, sarcastically.

"Well, I was trying to make you feel better."

"Nice try. So you've just been dream traveling?" I ask. "Where do you live?"

He angles his head at the western mountain. "A day's ride that way."

"Ride?"

"By horse," he says.

"You have a horse?"

"A few, actually."

"Wait, you have horses?" I ask in complete disbelief. This information challenges everything I've ever known about Rogue. About anyone from Austin Valley. "Why do you have horses? To travel?"

"Yes, but they're also work horses. I'm strong," he says, flexing his bicep. "But I can't build a house by myself."

"Hold on a second," I say. "You built a house? You're joking."

"Nope, I'm serious." He shakes his head, pride in his eyes. "You'd love it. It's off the grid and it's simple, but has craftsmanship to inspire."

"How did you get the resources to do all that?"

"I borrow money from the bank," he says with a wink.

"Rogue!" I stop and actually slap him across the arm now. "You're stealing!"

He tilts his head at me and gives a defiant look. "I'm borrowing," he corrects.

I purse my lips and hold his stare. His eyes, along with the rest of him, have matured. There's a loneliness in them which I don't remember. Rogue was never the lonely type; he was popular, declining tons of social invites just to skip rocks with Zack and me. And I always suspected that people wanted to be around him because of his charm and not just because his father was President.

"So you built a house and have horses?" I say almost to myself. I think my head is close to exploding. Dream Traveler Reverians aren't people who own horses and build houses. That's what Middlings do.

"I've also got goats, two dogs, a mess of cats, and a cow. I need some chickens though."

"What?" I say, still disbelieving this all. "Why do you have animals?" My brain can hardly fathom an individual having animals. We have them here in the Valley, but the ranch serves the whole town. There are a few dozen Middlings who care for those animals. The idea that Rogue alone has animals, well, it's as hard of an idea for me to digest as him building a house with his two hands.

"Em, you need animals to live off the grid."

"Well, why do you live off the grid? Why don't you live in a town?"

He shrugs. "There's something satisfying to living the way I do. An independence I crave, that I didn't have before I left."

"So if you live a day's ride that way," I say, pointing to the west, "then that's like what, fifty miles?"

He shrugs. Nods. "Probably."

"You've lived that close for so long? Why?"

"I wasn't always, but after I left I soon realized I had to stay close. I need *certain* supplies I can only get here."

"So you've been back before?"

"Oh yeah, dozens of times."

"And no one's ever seen you?"

"Nope. I'm sneaky." His smile is like a beat in the song I'd been listening to earlier. Compelling. Alluring.

"And you couldn't sneak over and find me and tell me you weren't dead?" I say, less angry and more frustrated by him and his secrets.

"What are you listening to?" he asks again, pointing to my iPod, ignoring my question.

I narrow my eyes at him. He's always been a master at avoiding my questions when he wanted to. I shrug. Resign a little. "The usual."

"You forget I don't know you anymore."

I think about how since before I could walk I'd spent most of my free time with Rogue and Zack. It was a political move on my father's part. He was trying to strengthen ties with the President through family relationships. It wasn't long after my second birthday that my father was promoted to Chief of Staff and Zack's father to Treasurer. But still Rogue's more a part of my childhood than almost anyone else. "You know me well enough," I say, a strange nostalgia making the words hard to get out. "I'm listening to indie folk."

"Oh, that's your usual, is it?" he says with a clever grin.

I stop, take a single earbud and hand it to him. I take the other and slip it into my ear. Then I play the song I've had on replay lately: "3 Rounds and a Sound" by Blind Pilot. His eyes swivel on me when the guitar starts. He's watching me with a strange curiosity. It's hard to know someone so well and then meet them for the first time in their new life. That's what it feels like to be with him now. Like we've been given a new life, but it doesn't entirely belong to us. Just as the chorus starts I realize I've been staring at Rogue without interruption for too long. The smile he gives me ensures he's spied my nervousness. He untucks the bud from his ear and hands it to me. I expect him to say something about the song's haunting words. About the singer's incredible voice.

"Gods, you've changed," he says, shaking his head. There's a mesmerized expression in his green eyes and as much as I want to look away from them, I can't.

"So have you," I say, unable to keep offense out of my voice. Rogue's presence makes me simultaneously elated and angry. To look at him alive and changed challenges every part of my brain.

"I don't mean it in a bad way," Rogue says, in a soothing voice. "It's just that you're exactly as I remembered and then also better. Didn't think that was possible."

He used to tell me he favored me over Zack, but I half suspect he said the same to Zack sometimes. I wonder if this is part of that same game. I'm not in the mood for games.

Below his expression of curiosity there's a secret in his eyes, like he just figured out something about me. He smirks and then his face shifts, like a new thought just occurred to him. He's a changing storm. "Remember that time we were playing in that old tree and you fell out and broke your ankle and I had to carry you back?"

I laugh, the memory washing over me, bringing with it sounds and smells. "I thought your father was going to kill you."

"The week of night terror punishment almost did," he says too lightly.

"It wasn't your fault. You shouldn't have been punished."

"Oh well," he says, waving his hand, dismissing my sympathy. "Em, you ever play with girls or just troublemaking boys?"

51

"Zack is the furthest person from a troublemaker."

"True," he says, nodding his head. "You and Zack ever...?"

"Ever what?"

He pulls in a long breath and appears suddenly nervous. "Ever more than friends?"

"Oh no, I'm not certain he even knows I'm a girl," I say and laugh to cover up my blush.

"He'd have to be blind and stupid not to, Em."

"Zack is my best friend."

"That doesn't mean he doesn't know you're a girl."

"Well, I don't think he sees me as a romantic prospect," I say.

"Do you want him to?"

This conversation just took a turn I'm not sure how to manage. I shrug, thinking about the pathetic union Dee's been trying to make with him. "It's complicated."

"Well, I think it's fair to say that Zack and I see you differently," Rogue says, an adorably handsome coy look on his face.

I'm unable to meet his eyes, so instead I pick up my pace, intent on reaching the first ridge before daybreak. "Yeah, so to answer your question, besides from Zack, I spend most of my time with Nona. She's a girl," I point out. "And not that much of a troublemaker."

He doesn't respond. Doesn't flaunt a brilliant smile. Just keeps hiking, keeping pace with me easily.

"I've missed you, Em," he says, breaking the silence finally. He gives me a tender smile.

Missed isn't even the right word for it. I felt like someone cut off one of my appendages when Rogue disappeared. I don't respond. He's got to read the look in my eyes. Has to. He has to know from the overwhelming raw emotions in my eyes that without me saying it, I've missed him like crazy. I hope he does.

"How is Nona?" he says, kicking a patch of bark out of the path.

"Good," I say with a genuine smile. "Indescribably she's the best part of our family and also underappreciated in every way."

"I've also missed the way you talk. You take simple phrases and make them perfect."

I don't return his smile.

"Nona started treatments last week. It's hard to watch her deal with the pain but unfortunately it turns out she's a Defect."

"No, Em, no," Rogue says, stopping, grabbing my arm. He shakes his head, bitterness in his eyes.

"What, Rogue?"

"Nothing."

"Rogue, this isn't right. You disappeared and made everyone think you were dead. And now you're back, lacking any remorse and unwilling to disclose some pretty important information, like why you're here, why you left, and what you know." I'm standing, shaking.

"I shouldn't be talking to you. I just needed to slip in and out. I shouldn't have grabbed you. You're not supposed to know about me, no one is. You're better off not knowing," Rogue says.

"You think I'm going to walk away now? Let it go? Pretend like you don't exist? I already lost you once. Why are you doing this? Just stop being you for one second and be a little less stubborn."

"If you don't shut up right now I'm going to kiss you," he threatens with a sheepish smile.

The laugh that falls out of my mouth surprises me. It instantly dissipates the anger building. Rogue laughs too.

"Gods above, I haven't heard that...well, since the last time you said it to me," I say, still laughing. Rogue always won all battles because he'd threaten me with a sloppy kiss. Since boys were awesome but disgusting it was the worst punishment I could consider. I laugh again thinking of the girl who used to pretend to gag when Rogue threatened to kiss her.

"I don't think that's going to work anymore, Rogue."

"Oh, not so deterred by that threat, huh? I have my damn good looks to blame," he says, shaking his head with a smile plastered across his face. "But I'll have you know, I'm an awful kisser."

"Nice try, but all your tactics haven't distracted me from the heart of this matter. Tell me something, like why you're back."

"I won't tell you that 'cause it's not real important."

"Then tell me something else," I say.

He opens his mouth. Nothing comes out. Inside he's battling something. His lips press together, seeming to bolt away the secrets he harbors. But I'm a pirate who won't be deterred.

"I know they're hiding something," I say. "I snuck into my father's office looking for information."

He raises an eyebrow at me, looking impressed. "I would say you're ballsy but that isn't quite the appropriate label for you."

"I know they're hiding something and I think you know what it is. And I want you to tell me."

"Em, you want me to tell you something even if you can't do anything about it?"

"Who says I can't do anything about it?"

He laughs. "Oh, I forgot you have the tenacity to change the rotation of the Earth."

"Liar," I fire back. "You didn't forget that about me." I smirk. "Now tell me what you know."

"Even if it has the potential to burst the perfect bubble you live in here in Austin Valley?"

"Who said it was perfect?"

"Fine," he says, his voice resigned, but his eyes holding defiance. He rubs his fingers over the stubble on his chin and sighs. "The injections…" he says, pauses, holds my expectant gaze.

"Yes?" I encourage.

"Well, they don't help."

Chapter Eleven

"What?" I ask Rogue. Disbelief is the first emotion to seize my thoughts. "If they don't help then why do they give them to the Defects?"

He shakes his head, a brutal look in his eyes. "Don't ever call yourself that."

"Okay, fine. But Rogue, I already knew the injections weren't working. That's why they increased my dosage. And they keep tweaking the formula to get it right."

"No, they increased your dosage because I bet they fear you're developing a tolerance," he says.

"What? *Who* exactly are you talking about? Who increased my dosage?"

"My father." He pauses, gives me a guarded expression. "His cabinet."

"What? That means *my* father..."

"Yeah, he's involved." he says, remorse in his tone. "I'm sorry."

My thoughts are suddenly clouded. Shrouded in a tight-fitting net. But I asked for this information and I must stand up to it. I shake my head, dispelling the clouds within. "Rogue, what you're saying doesn't make sense," I say, rejecting his claim, ignoring the ache in my throat. "The injections—"

"Are a suppressant. They suppress the part of the brain which harnesses Dream Travelers' gifts."

"But why would they do that? Why would they want to do that?"

The cold and honest expression on Rogue's face makes the dread of what he's about to say beat like a foreboding drum. "They don't want you to have your gift."

"Wait. You're saying *my* father is responsible for the reason I don't have my gift?"

He nods, an alarming sincerity in his eyes.

"My father..." I whisper, mostly to myself. And I know I knew it all along. Sensed it. But still, to know my father is hinged in this conspiracy is a shard of glass I've been forced to swallow. It's lodged in my throat. And soon it will threaten to cut me from the inside out.

"Well, your father is no mastermind," Rogue says, "but he's an excellent puppet to my father. And they share the same vision, which is based on fear."

"Of what? Teens who can see the future or read minds?" I almost laugh at the outrageousness of this all. "That's ridiculous."

"They're afraid of losing control."

"But not everyone's on the Defect list. It doesn't make sense why only some of us would be stripped of our gifts. Zack and Dee aren't Defects."

Rogue nods his head, understanding. "That's because those on the Defect list are kids who have shown from an early age a tendency toward rebellious thinking."

"Oh," I say in a hush. I scan through the Defect list in my head. Every single person meets that criterion. And as much as my logical brain is trying to tear it to pieces, find the holes, there are none yet. What Rogue says makes perfect sense. And that means... I feel the strain on my face as the implications fill in. How long have my parents berated me for not being normal like them? And yet they did this to me. But why? Why did they make me a Defect? And now they're doing it to Nona. I swallow down the shard of glass in my throat without concern as heat flares in my head. Rogue steps closer to me. Picks up my hand and holds it between both of his. It's warm and covers my hands completely.

"I know this is a lot to process," Rogue says in a soothing voice. "I remember when I found out how difficult it was."

"That's why you left," I state, the realization dawning on me. And then another chilling thought hits me like a block of ice. "Rogue, you were the first. The first Defect—I'm mean, one on the list. Your father, he took away your gift," I say and almost can't believe the words as I say them. But they're true and so is what President Vider did to his own son.

Rogue, to my astonishment, actually smiles. "He tried." And in his hand, out of nowhere, my iPod appears. I slap my hand on my pocket where it was a second ago. It's empty. I snatch the iPod from his hand, unable to resist smiling at his mischief. He's the most rebellious person I've ever known. Of course his father would have been afraid of who he became.

"So what do I do now?" I ask.

He gives me a pained look, his smile falling away. "I already told you, there's nothing you can do. You were given fair warning."

"But I want my gift," I say.

"The only way to get it is to stop the injections, and there's no way to do that without being punished."

"Unless I leave."

"That's not an easy thing to do," he says.

"But I have to do something," I say, almost exclaiming to the forest and birds. I begin pacing almost at once, stopping at an old madrone tree and then shuffling back the way I came. My thoughts race inside me as I make the third lap.

Finally Rogue reaches out and grabs my arm with a gentle pressure. I pause and bring my eyes up to his. The sober look on his face lays a new weight on my heart. "Em, you don't have to do anything drastic. Just think on this. Because if you leave you can't ever come back."

I pin my hands on my hips and scowl at him. "Says the guy who left and is standing in front of me right now."

Chapter Twelve

Maybe Rogue was right and I was better off not knowing the secrets he knew. Already the notion that our government experiments on Middling children has spun my moral compass out of control. Zack had said that these parents offered their children willingly and were compensated for their participation. That seemed like a good thing. But to experiment on children. And what they did to them was unclear.

But even if I didn't know the truth now, I'd be in that perpetual state of sensing there was something nefarious. For months I'd been obsessed with figuring out what was "off" in our society. That torture may not be worse than knowing what my father has done to me, but at least now I know. I'm not ignorant. I'm not in a position where I'll blindly allow myself to be manipulated. I'm a robot who has awoken to the realization that I've been damaged so I can't perform, so I can't take my rightful place within this society. And I don't want to be damaged anymore.

The waiting room is full at the lab. I slide up against the wall far away from the swinging door so I don't get hit when the next Def—Rebel enters. It's going to be hard to reprogram my thoughts. To take out the messages of lack they instilled in me from an early age. But I will. I just can't let anyone know I'm breaking out of the mold, especially my father.

Rogue told me not to do anything drastic. *To think on this.* My plan doesn't involve anything radical. It's downright sneaky, and if it works then I'll be one step closer to figuring out this mess I was born into. To stopping it. But I fear the road to freedom is long. Actually, I know it is.

"Em Fuller," Tammy says, not even opening the door more than a crack.

I catch it with my fingertips before she lets it slam shut. Already she's hurrying down the stark white hallway, her sneakers squeaking on the linoleum. I jog to catch up with her. All the rooms are full again, I can tell by the folders hanging on the walls outside of them.

"Busy?" I say, arriving right behind Tammy.

"Oh gods, 'busy' doesn't even begin to cover it," she says, leading me to the back room of the labs again. I've had all my injections here since that first time. The door I snuck through has never been left open though. "Hopefully, they'll be hiring more doctors and nurses to assist us soon," Tammy says, out of breath. "We can't keep going at this crazy pace."

Busy is good. I'd planned for this. Hoped.

We're almost to the lab door when I hear the quick steps behind me. I don't allow my smile to surface. Pretend not to notice the intrusion which is about to occur.

"Em! Em!" Nona's voice echoes down the hallway. I turn just before she halts next to me, almost knocking into my shoulder. "Sorry to interrupt," my little sister says, pushing her sweaty bangs off her forehead. "It's just that Father has an urgent message he needed me to pass along."

"Nona," I say, "is everything all right?"

"Yes." She nods her head, her face beet red from running. "It's just there's something of a personal nature I need to pass along."

"Have you had your injection today?" I say, feeling Tammy's presence growing impatient behind me.

"No, but—"

I hold up my hand, silencing my sister, and turn to Tammy. "Can we have our injections in the same room, so that way my sister can relay this information from our father to me?"

Tammy doesn't even stop to consider it. "Whatever," she says, slipping my chart into the holder beside the door. "I'll be back with your chart, Nona," she says, rushing away. I knew she wouldn't argue. Our father holds the clout of the President. A message from him would have to be delivered. And since we are a higher-class family who deserves privacy, Tammy is unlikely to speak about the matter to anyone else...except maybe to Parker.

Nona and I both clamber into the lab. Last night, I'd snuck into her room. I didn't want to burden her with what I knew, but I also couldn't keep it from her. I'm not sure how to keep her from getting her injections, from stopping the evil routine of suppression which has happened to us. But I know that if anyone can help me start a rebellion by learning more of the truth, it's Nona. And she almost made me cry when she nodded, like a seasoned solider, after hearing what Rogue had told me. "What can I do to help?" she'd said at once.

"We have to start small," I had replied. I wanted her to be the one to avoid the injections, but she refused.

"No, your powers will be stronger because you're older," she had said, shaking her head, her round cheeks glowing from the moonlight streaming in from her window. "And besides, you're the one who does investigations and I'm the one who distracts. That's how we always play this game."

I couldn't help smiling at her incredibly forgiving and adventuresome mind. When I began to suspect something wasn't right in our government, Nona covered for me while I snooped. She never seemed flustered by the idea. And as soon as she learned that our own parents were behind it she just shrugged it off. "I never liked them much anyway," she said, twirling her hair around her small fingers. "I don't think Mother has looked at me directly in years. If it wasn't for Tutu and you, I'd get no attention at all."

"You know, Nona," I told her as we sat knee to knee on her bed, "no one sees the lion either, until it's about to feast on them."

A satisfied smile sprang to her lips.

Neither one of us slept well last night, too consumed with this plan. Multiple times my sleep cuff alarm sounded to warn me that I was being reported to the sleep commission.

Now we are sitting in the back room of the lab, silently waiting for our cue. After less than a minute I hear Nona's chart fall into the holder outside the door. Now I have to wait again until Tammy is down the hallway. I count to myself, a long five seconds. Then I slip the door open, reach my hand out, and pull out the thicker folder. My chart lies in my hands. With an urgency to match someone dismantling a bomb, I flip the chart to the empty page. I fill in the date and all the information, careful to match the handwriting of the prior entry. Continuously my eyes flick up to the door, hoping Parker doesn't rush through ready to inject me with poison.

When I'm done I hand Nona the folder, a bit reluctantly. She slips it behind her waistband, careful to cover the top portion with her blouse and blazer. The smile she wields gives me the confidence which had recently dissipated.

"Don't worry, Em. I got this."

"I know you do."

"Now get out of here."

I don't respond; instead, I open the door and hurry out. If they catch us now there are a dozen lies we can use, but most probably won't work. Now our biggest hope is for me to get down the long hallway and to the exit. Thankfully it isn't back through the waiting room, where Tammy is probably calling another batch of Rebels, as Nona and I've taken to calling them. We like the label much better than Defects. It fits us and gives us a purpose, not a complex like our former title.

When I push through the exit door the sunlight greets me like an old friend, glad to see me after a long ordeal. With hurried steps I clear the lot that divides the labs from a set of boutiques and artisan stores. Conscious not to appear suspicious, I walk casually, like I'm five minutes early to an appointment. I turn the first corner and halt. Not much occupies this area. A bike rack. A green patch of grass. A water fountain.

Ten minutes I stay hidden in plain sight, smiling casually at the people who hustle by on their way to the office or on their way home with fresh-baked goods from the Middling bakery. As if she is on her way to play in the fountain in the main plaza, my sister skips down the sidewalk. She pauses after passing me by a few meters and offers me a ridiculously adorable smile over her shoulder. "Well, are you coming? We've got to go do that thing, remember?"

Hesitantly I approach her, careful not to look too tense. "So?" The one word hangs in the air like it's a long gigantic question.

"So...as we intended, it went perfectly. Without a hitch," she says, threading her arm through mine. "So get that nervous look off your face and skip home with me. That's what kids do in the summer, don't you know?"

"I know," I say, allowing myself to relax slightly. I can't believe such a simple, yet chancy plan worked. Nona had been able to slip my chart, signed off by the doctor for this morning's injection, into the "refile" stack on the receptionist's desk. I'd seen Parker do it a thousand times with other patients' charts and knew this was how their process worked. Now it appeared to the lab that I'd had my injection. I *had* been there. Been admitted. And my chart showed I'd received my injection by the doctor. Now all I had to do was pray that Tammy and Parker didn't talk about it, that she didn't mention Nona and I were both there, and that in his overworked state, Parker

61

wouldn't remember not giving me an injection this morning. There was a lot of hope riding on this, but it was worth it. I was already making progress. This is the first injection I'd missed in over three years. This was the first day of change.

Chapter Thirteen

Skipping this morning's injection was only supposed to buy us some time. There's no way I'll be able to pull that off again and I'm not certain that I've been entirely successful. In order to avoid this afternoon's injection Nona and I are going to have to work fast…and experiment.

Giorgio, our family's chef, is at the market buying fresh ingredients for this evening's meal. I know he always leaves for the errand midmorning, but since I'm never around the house during this time, I'm not certain when he returns. He won't mind that Nona and I are scavenging through his kitchen. Most likely he'll offer us a puff pastry and comment on how big we're getting. But I'd prefer not to have to lie to him about what we're doing in his kitchen, so we need to hurry before he returns.

"You check the pantry and I'll look through the refrigerator," I say to Nona as soon as I ensure we're alone in the kitchen.

"Exactly what am I looking for?" Nona asks, tucking her head into the darkened pantry and squinting. She's probably never been in the pantry before. Why would she? Giorgio has made all our meals and snacks since our first baby teeth pushed through. All we ever had to do was ring the bell and he'd trot through the swinging door, his grin wide and eyes bright. Maybe Middlings are naturally happier people. Or maybe my father drugs him, like he does us, but for different purposes.

I tap the light switch next to the pantry door and bright light fills the walk-in closet. "Look for hot spices. Something that will upset my stomach."

Nona shrugs and begins pushing jars of spices around the shelves. "And what are you doing?"

"Creating something that will make me puke," I say, pulling peanut butter, anchovy paste, and a jug of buttermilk from the refrigerator.

"Wait, but what if this mixture really messes you up?" Nona asks, plucking a jar full of something vibrantly red from the middle shelf.

"Whatever works," I say, taking a dollop of peanut butter and stirring it into a glass of buttermilk.

I flushed my immune booster down the toilet this morning. Also something I've taken consistently for years and skipped today. I've always known that a patient can't have the injections if they're sick. That's why they test our temperature before each injection. Actually, it's rare for a Reverian to even *be* sick.

The aluminum tube is cold between my fingers as I squeeze a tablespoon of the anchovy paste into my concoction. The combination of smells almost has my stomach turning. Nona takes three pinches of cayenne pepper and deposits them into my glass, eyeing it like it's toilet water.

"Maybe it won't taste so bad," she says, her voice light, but her face contorted with disgust.

"Oh, it's going to taste rancid," I say, pinching my nose and pressing the glass to my lips. I pause for too long, looking down at the orangey sludge I'm about to drink.

"Just gulp it down," Nona says. "On the count of three, okay? One. Two. Th—"

"For the love of the gods, don't drink that!"

I peel open one eye and then the other. Tutu stands just inside the kitchen, leaning on her cane, a look of amusement on her face.

"Tutu!" I say, looking from her to Nona, searching for an excuse. A lie. "I was just—"

"Dear child, I know what you're doing," she says, walking over to us, barely using the cane to support her. "Ronald filled me in entirely."

"Oh," I say, eyeing the glass and then her. She's smirking at me, obviously entertained by catching me in the act.

"It's just that I learned that the injections—"

She waves her hand at me; it's withered in a glove of wrinkles. "I know about the injections. Ronald was spying on you a minute ago and also all night while you two girls plotted."

I switch my gaze from her light blue eyes to Nona's freckled face, which has gone white as a ghost.

"Then you know I have to do something," I say, facing Tutu, who is almost a head shorter than me now.

"All I know is if you drink that"—Tutu indicates the glass still pinned between my fingers—"you're going to have a fierce stomachache."

"That will work," I say, bringing the crystal glass to my lips again.

"And then Damien might suspect you've been drinking or doing drugs with Middlings," she says, as though offering a hypothetical course of events.

I pause. Think it over and then bring the glass back close to my lips. If that's all my father suspects and I still get dismissed from injections then it's not so bad. "Yeah, but that would still work for my purposes."

"Or…" Tutu draws out the word, hinging my attention on it, "he might think it was Giorgio's cooking and terminate him." She shrugs, her face giving a comical "who knows what will happen" expression.

A frustrated sigh falls out of me as I slam the glass on the marble countertop. "Well, I don't want to risk that."

"No, I suspected you wouldn't," she says, taking in a long breath like she's enjoying this revolting moment.

I turn and stare at my tutu. "You know why I was going to the trouble?"

"I do." She's rubbing the raccoon head that is the handle on her cane.

"And I was able to avoid my first injection in years this morning," I say.

"Congratulations."

"I was hoping to keep it going."

"I see that."

My tutu and I have always spoken in abbreviated sentences, never needing to say more than the bare minimum. We're quite efficient.

Tutu and I both watch wordlessly as Nona licks the spoon from the peanut butter jar and takes careful bites of it, chewing and swallowing, her mouth slowly getting stuck together in places. Finally Tutu says, "May I suggest a strategy that is mysterious and also not easily traceable?"

I angle my head sideways, staring at her with interest. "Go on."

65

She scuttles forward. Extends her hand and gives me an encouraging look. Funny how this ninety-nine-year-old woman sometimes reminds me of the fairies in classical lore. She's small and unsuspecting. And most people walk away from an encounter with her not realizing they've been "handled" until she disappears into the mist…or the eastern wing of our house, as it were for her.

I extend my hand under hers. She opens her fingers and something light touches my palm. When she pulls her hand away I spy a medium-sized capsule, gray and oblong, resting on the creases of my palm.

"Now, go ahead and take that if you dare," she says. "You'll have only one symptom, and alone it will be a conundrum, but enough to keep you home for the day."

I eye the pill in my hand. It's about the size of the immune booster I'm used to swallowing. If I thought I had a chance to consider whether to take it or not it's defeated by the urgent manner in which Nona presses a freshly made glass of water into my hand.

"Go on, Em," she urges, giving Tutu an excited smile.

I return it with my own nervous one and pop the pill into my mouth, swallowing it down with three large gulps of water.

"Good choice," Tutu says, turning on her heels and shuffling back to the kitchen door. "I'll call the labs and tell them you've got a fever." She pauses at the door. Hardly turns to swivel her head over her shoulder. "Oh, and you may want to strip off that blazer and most of your other attire. You're about to be roasting."

Chapter Fourteen

"Well, well, well," I say, looking Zack up and down. "I bet now that you've gotten a look at yourself in a tuxedo, you're not going back to suits. And I also bet that getup is really uncomfortable and you love every minute of it."

He scowls at me. "I don't like being uncomfortable. I only like looking my best."

"Is that why you hang out with me? Because I make you look better with my slouchy dress?" Zack actually looks quite handsome in the black tuxedo, but I wouldn't dare tell him that.

He ignores me and takes a seat on the edge of the bed, careful not to wrinkle his jacket. It isn't my bed. The sheets on this guest bed are musty, most likely because we never have guests. Dee kicked me out of our room as soon as word spread that I was sick. Fevers are my new favorite thing. They get me out of gift-numbing injections and away from my demon sister. If I didn't feel like my brain was currently frying from the heat then I'd want to keep the fever going.

"How did you get yourself sick?" Zack asks, looking sincerely concerned.

I give Zack a sly smile. "An 'ancient artifact' knew an old trick too strong to best the defenses of immune boosters."

"Wait," he says, looking startled. "You made yourself this way? Oh, Em." He shakes his head, eyes closed.

"I had a good reason," I say, pushing my covers down low, although Dr. Jahn told me people with fevers were apparently supposed to sweat them out. It's my first. Tutu called the doctor at once and she rushed over. Dr. Jahn confirmed I had a 103 fever, no other symptoms, and it was probably just my body fighting off a virus which would pass in a day. From over the doctor's shoulder I watched Tutu's face grow with a mischievous pride at the news.

I'd been laid up in the unused bed most of the day with nothing to entertain me except a pile of books. Having Zack here is a real treat, especially because I can tell he's dreading the summer solstice ball with my sister. I love to tease him when he's already feeling defeated. It's our thing. And the fact that I know he doesn't want to be her escort to the ball makes the whole thing much easier to digest.

He leans forward, voice low, a worried look on his face. "Do tell me, why would you want to be sick?"

"It's the injections," I say in a whisper. "But if I tell you what Rogue told me you have to be careful, especially around my father, who's a vulture at stealing thoughts."

"Wait, you saw Rogue? When?" As I suspected, he looks upset. Left out.

"I ran into him, so to speak," I say, pushing the covers off entirely and curling my legs up underneath me.

He nods, this explanation seeming to make him feel slightly better. He flicks his eyes to the open door and then back to me. "Gods, I want to see him again," he whispers.

"I know, it felt good, didn't it?"

"No, it felt weird, like a ghost came back to life. I still don't believe he's alive, that's why I want to see him again," he says, sitting farther on my bed, taking up the place where my feet were a minute ago.

"Oh, that's why," I say dully.

"Em, of course I've missed him. I just think we need to be careful. He's obviously in trouble."

"I agree, which is why we're going to figure out why and help him."

"Em, I'm not—"

"And I'm in trouble too, Zack."

He stops, examines me. Nods his head reluctantly. Rogue and my problems have always seemed to weigh heavier on Zack than us. "Yes, I'll help."

"Of course you will," I say, pushing him with my toe. "You're Zack Conerly, and saving misfits is what you do when you're not training to run this 'empire,'" I say, impersonating the President's commanding tone.

He rolls his striking blue eyes, but still lets loose the tiniest of smiles.

"Meet me tomorrow afternoon in our old camp area before I have to go to the labs," I say.

"No, but you're sick. How can you go to the labs?"

"It will only last twenty-four hours," I say, pouting my lip.

"You're the only person in Austin Valley who wants to be sick," he says.

"If you knew why then you'd understand. You'll find out tomorrow, I promise."

"Okay," he says, resignation in his eyes.

"All right, you better get out of here before Dee lights your coattails on fire."

"Do I look all right?" he says, sitting up tall in his tuxedo, smoothing down his jacket.

"Just about." I push forward on the bed and lean over to straighten his bowtie a little. "Now you're perfect."

A smile reaches all the way to his eyes. "Thanks, Em."

A cough echoes from the doorway. My father's way of commanding attention. Zack stands at once but doesn't give the same flustered response that I do. He holds my father's piercing stare. Smiles at him. "Good evening, Chief Fuller," Zack says, bowing his head slightly.

"Hello, Father," I say, fury flaring across my chest at the sight of one of the thieves who has stolen my gift. I'm careful to corral my thoughts back to the mundane so I don't give my father any information.

"Mr. Conerly, do you think it is a good idea to expose yourself to Em when she's in such a mysteriously sickly state?" My father wears a tuxedo too, a burgundy rose pinned to his left lapel. It gives him some much needed color, makes him almost seem soft.

"Chief Fuller, I understand your concern but my immune booster has never failed," Zack says.

"Yes, mine either. Strange this has happened to you, Em," he says, now studying me. "It's probably those Middling farmers you choose to congregate with."

"Yes, I'm sure you're right, Father."

"Well, Mr. Conerly, you shouldn't keep my daughter Dee waiting," my father says, angling sideways, showing Zack the path he intends him to take now.

"I hope I have not made her wait at all. I was merely checking on this misfit," he says, ruffling my hair in that way like I'm his little sister.

My father shakes his head at me, disapproval evident in his look. "Get better, Em," he says like it's an order. "I want you back to normal routine immediately."

69

"Farewell. I hope you have a nice night," I say to the pair as they leave.

"I'm sure we will," my father says without another look.

Chapter Fifteen

I tuck my head into the sitting room, thinking the guest I was told to meet with is a mistake. Browsing a map of Austin Valley on the wall, Ren stands with his hands behind his back. He's wearing another odd suit, this one grayish silver, not tightly tailored like the ones men wear in Austin Valley. "Hello, Ren," I say to get his attention.

He turns, looking irritated. Nods. "Hi," he says without inflection.

"I don't understand," I say, taking a few steps into the room. "I have to meet with you today? But I have a fever." I slept fitfully the whole night, but that was fine because when I awoke I still had a fever, although it had come down.

"I have a fever," Ren says in a high-pitched squeal, mocking me. "And I have an ingrown toenail, but you don't see me being a loaf."

"It's just that we weren't scheduled to meet until next week."

"That's right. Very good with keeping up with your own schedule, but it's changed. Damien, your father, has requested you have a midweek evaluation."

"Because I'm sick…" I say mostly to myself.

"I don't believe being sick will make a lick of difference. You'll probably still flunk my assessment," Ren says, removing that small box device from his inside pocket.

"Right," I say, aware Ren is doing something at the drawing desk in the corner but unfocused on it. I ruminate and fume on how my father is continuously trying to oppress me to ensure that I don't become a problem for him. How can such a powerful man be so scared of those much younger than him? And why? What do he and the President fear we're going to do if we rebel?

Ren steps back from the desk and turns to me. "All right, I want you to focus on the contents of the drawer inside this desk. I've inserted objects you're unfamiliar with. Can you sense what they are?"

I lower my chin until it's close to an inch off my chest, stare at the drawer like it's possible to see through the wood. Again and again I wait for something to spontaneously spring to my mind, an epiphany of sorts. Nothing happens. Luckily Ren isn't watching my face grow redder from intense concentration; he's eyeing the device in his hand.

"I don't know," I finally say.

Ren doesn't give a response. He takes a step and removes an object from the drawer. I've never seen it before. It's a gold coin and on it is a woman's profile, a crown atop her head.

"Take this," he says, depositing the coin into my hand. "Now tell me if you sense emotions, ideas, or anything of relevance from it. Anything at all?"

I clench the coin between my fingers and palm; it grows warm and sweaty in my feverish hands. I feel the contours of the figure on the coin, but that's the only sense I get from it.

"Well?" he finally says, breaking into my meandering thoughts.

"Nothing," I say, opening my hands and looking more closely at the coin. "What is this?"

He rolls his eyes and grabs it from my hand. "Crikey! It's a pound. You're more sheltered than I thought."

"You have no idea," I say.

Ren looks at the device briefly before slipping it back in his pocket. "I'm sure you're baiting me, hoping I'll ask in a sympathetic voice how you are sheltered. I won't. I don't care. I'm not your shrink, I'm the guy who was hired to report on how defunct you are within our race."

"I didn't want you to ask," I say, responding in a common voice, one I don't usually use with people of higher status. "I'm more or less letting internal banter slip out of my head. Let's say it's due to the fever."

"Or maybe you're going crazy," Ren says with a grin, looking entertained. "It does run in the family, you know."

"I didn't."

"Tell me, does your mother still only have that lame gift where she reads fortunes in tea leaves or whatever it is?"

"She's clairvoyant too," I say.

Ren doesn't respond, instead eyeing the carpet, something working in his brain.

"What's *your* gift?" I ask, not caring if I'm interrupting his thoughts.

He lifts his gaze to me, a clever look in his green eyes. "I have many."

"What are they? Can you show me?" I ask, strangely excited by the prospect.

"I'm not a circus act," he says, sounding offended. "And I could show you but one of them might kill you, and you probably don't want that, do you?"

I shake my head. "Are you clairvoyant, like my mother?"

"No," he says, leaning against the desk. "What I can do makes her gifts look as lame as balancing a spoon on your nose."

"Oh, gifts that are fantastic and lethal, huh? Now I definitely don't want to know. Don't tell me. Seriously," I say.

Ren pushes off the desk and yawns. "So you may be interested to know your frequency actually measures up perfectly with a Dream Traveler's now, one who's performing using a cognitive skill."

"What?" I say, struck by the abrupt delivery. "Like a gift? I'm showing signs of a gift?"

"No, gosh, why doesn't anyone ever listen? Your frequency is matching up with that of someone *demonstrating* a gift. Maybe you're going to get yours, or maybe it's just a fluke. And maybe the fever has helped you."

"Oh, it has..." I say, threading my fingertips together, satisfaction rising in my chest.

"Whatever," Ren says, turning to leave.

"Wait!" I say when he's at the door.

He turns and gives me an impatient stare. "Make it good."

"You can't report this finding," I say.

He scrunches up his eyebrows and then turns and faces me directly. "I do believe you've gone completely batty from this so-called fever. Did you not hear me the first ten times I told you this was my job?"

"But they can't know that I'm getting close to my gift." My eyes dart to the clock on the wall. I have roughly two hours until I'll be called in for injections since my fever is below midgrade. If I'm close enough to normal then they'll dose me and this will all be over. All I have is this time to try and figure out who I am.

Ren studies me with a strange determination. "You know you and I aren't pals or buddies, right? I'm not here to help you. I was

73

hired to report if anything surfaced, not to lose brain cells listening to you spew banter from your sheltered brain."

"Right," I say, nodding. "We aren't pals. And you should do your job. Just don't report this for a couple of hours. It won't make any difference to you and it will make all the difference to me." Because as soon as they know I'm close to getting my gift they'll intervene and I can't have that when I've come this close.

"I don't do favors," he says.

"Right, only those who need things do favors," I say, spewing one of my father's famous lines. "And you obviously don't need anything from me."

"Right you are, missy," Ren says, and then he flicks his eyes up over my shoulder. "What do you want?"

I turn to find my mother with her hands pinned on her hips, her lips pressed into a thin line. "I want a report. Has my daughter made any progress? Shown any signs of not being a complete shame to her family?"

I seethe, my head suddenly burning hotter. She dares to call me a shame when she's made me this? Maybe she isn't privy to what the injections do to me. Maybe... It's a hope, but one I have little faith in. My mother has always looked at me like I'm an old piece of furniture in need of replacing.

"I don't believe I report to you, Lyza," Ren says, crossing his arms.

"Don't play games with me," my mother says, her voice climbing. "She's my daughter. Tell me what I want to know."

A slow smile stretches across Ren's face. "I'm not playing games, but I think we both know if I wanted to I could play some nice ones on you. Just like old times, remember, Lyzie?"

"Don't threaten me with your mind control and hypnotism. I'm not a child you can bully," my mother says.

"Your gift is hypnotism?" I ask Ren, astonishment making my features go wide.

"Shut up, Em. This conversation doesn't involve you," my mother says, narrowing her eyes at me.

My eyes jerk to the floor. My hands squeeze together. "Yes, Mother," I say, hating being scolded in front of Ren.

Ren clicks his tongue three times in disapproval. "Telling your daughter to shut up. That's not very nice."

"Stay out of my family affairs, Ren," my mother snaps.

"Oh, that's not going to happen since I do believe I'm a part of the family," he says.

"Ren, you are not—"

"Our dear mummy would never have spoken to you that way," Ren says, with a gloating look on his face.

My mother's face is almost the same shade as her hair. It's rare to see her so worked up and it's taking everything I have to suppress the delight it gives me. "Don't you talk to me about her!"

Ren smiles coolly. Looks extra pleased with himself. "You really still hate her, don't you? And all because—"

"Shut up, Ren!" my mother yells again. I've never heard her so out of control, her voice not poised.

Ren pauses. Smiles again. This one is subtle. "All because—"

"Get out of here, Em."

I nod and turn for the door.

"All because she's a Middling," Ren says in a rush.

I whip around and stare at my mother, who's wearing a look of horror. Ren's eyes are on me, a mischievous grin on his face. He rocks forward on his toes and then back on his heels a few times. "That's right, luv, your grandmother was a Middling. Surprise."

"REN!" my mother nearly screams through clenched teeth. "You have no right to—"

"The look on Em's face confirms my suspicions," he interrupts. "She doesn't know. I bet no one knows you're a half-blood, do they, Lyzie?"

I'm not sure where I get the gall, maybe from Ren's display, but the words rush out of my mouth. "So I'm not a pure-blooded Dream Traveler?"

My mother turns on me. She whips her hand high in the air, a mean icy threat in her face like she's seconds away from slapping me. It pauses in the air. She's shaking. "You do not breathe a word of this to your father, is that understood?" she says, a threat in her voice.

I stare at her hand raised in front of me and then to her cold, burning eyes.

"Do you understand?" she screams.

"Why would I tell him anything?" I say, unable to keep the disgust out of my voice.

"Don't you disrespect your father, Em."

"Oh, Lyza," Ren says, daring to push my mother's hand back down. And he steps in front of me. "That's quite a statement for *you* to make."

"Damien is worth respecting, unlike our father who married a Middling," she's says like it's a repulsive thought.

"Our father married for love, which I think is rather respectable. It's much more honorable than seeking status in a bogus society," Ren says.

"No one asked you what you think."

"Actually, President Vider did." Ren turns and looks at me, then walks to the exit. "And to answer your original question, Lyza, Em has displayed zero signs of receiving her gift. Such a shame, this one."

Chapter Sixteen

The old camping area, where we spent many a summer night, is now overgrown, with no direct paths leading to it. This is probably because the Parks department decided a couple of years ago to close off access to this part of the hills, encouraging citizens to hike down lower, closer to the stream. This means Rogue's camping grounds are perfect for keeping him tucked away from the general public. Bad for me, as I'm constantly having to finagle my way through dense brush and tangled vines. I'm not used to hiking off the path. It's actually illegal.

If it wasn't for Rogue's blue denim shirt, then I wouldn't have spotted the campsite. His tent is built into an arch of trees and camouflages perfectly into the woods. A small area to the side has been cleared away of brush and leaves. That's where he has the campfire set up. That's also where Rogue sits. Hunched over, face bent to his knees, hands covering his head. He's rocking slightly. *Wait, not rocking...he's convulsing.* I push through the overgrowth faster now, ten yards still dividing me from Rogue. The way he sits, the way he moves, is all wrong. And then a muffled yelp of pain falls out of his mouth, like someone stuck a sock in his mouth and then cut off his pinky.

Thorns tear my clothes, scratch my calves and ankles, but I keep moving until I reach him. I expected to arrive and find him bleeding or see an object to blame for his obvious pain, but the area around him is empty. I expect him to notice me, even just a little bit, but he stays crouched over. Shuddering.

"Rogue!" I say, reaching for his head cradled in his hands. "Are you all right?"

He jerks away. Not looking at me. Keeping his eyes covered by his arms.

"Rogue," I say again, afraid to touch him, but not satisfied by only sitting next to him, not doing anything. I place my hand on his back and rub, watching him burying his head deeper into his arms and knees. Biting down on the pain. The areas of his face I can see are splotched with red. Obviously he's battling a pain so great in his head that he can't speak, can't even look at me. Otherwise he'd probably tell me properly to leave him alone. I can tell by the way he's moved away from my hand that he would prefer for me not to be here. Rogue never liked anyone to see him in pain. He'd gone to great lengths to hide injuries and now I realize again he's hiding.

For ten minutes I sit beside him, only touching him that once. The pain in him goes from the searing, screaming pain I walked up on to a slower, more stubborn one. Toward the end he's only groaning, a soft sound that still accurately communicates the discomfort. And still his hands never move away from his face. His arms cradle his head, sometimes his fingers going white by the pressure. Shallow breaths finally replace his painful moans. Shaking replaces the convulsions. And I'm surprised when he pulls his head out of hands and lays it on my shoulder. He takes exasperated breaths, seeming to breathe through smaller bouts of pain. With the weight of his head on my shoulder and a confounding turn of events, I have a hard time determining what to do. How to help him. I finally reach out and grab his hand. Instantly he holds on to it like a person clasping onto the rope thrown over the cliff to rescue them. I return his pressure with my own firm grip. "It's okay, Rogue," I whisper against his head. "You're all right. I'm here."

I don't know what I'm here for, but I guess it shouldn't really matter. Something's hurting Rogue, something he's struggling to battle. Then like a clear, winter's wind it hits me, blowing me over more with its cold than its momentum. "Rogue, *they* did this to you, didn't they?" He doesn't stir from my shoulder, but I feel his breath pause. "Your father…"

Rogue pulls his head away from my shoulder, leaving a patch of sweat where it had been. His hair is stuck to his brow in places, curling wildly in other places from the moisture. Red eyes etched with exhaustion catch mine. His elbows rest now on his knees. And I have a feeling he'd prefer to be lying down now.

"Or emptying the contents of my stomach," Rogue says, his voice mostly a growl.

"What?" *Why did he just say that?*

"You thought I'd prefer to be laying down right now. You're right, but I'm also hella nauseous," he says.

"Wait? What? You're telepathic now?"

He shakes his head. "No," he says, taking a steadying breath. "It's just after an episode everything heightens. I'm telepathic, telekinetic, clairvoyant, and a whole bunch of other things, but only the first few minutes afterwards."

"You can lie down," I say, indicating his tent. "I'll stay close by and watch over you."

Rogue takes a swig from the water canteen by his feet. Shakes his head. "I'm not laying down and you should just leave. You shouldn't have seen that."

"But I did see it and I want to know what's wrong with you," I say.

He gives me a tired look. Pushes his dark hair out of his eyes. "Em, don't be offended when I tell you to mind your own business."

"Don't be offended when I tell you to stuff it."

"Oh, you're such a beautiful pain the in ass," he says, pushing to a standing position. "Now, what brings you to my neck of the woods?" he says, trying to inject lightness into his strained voice.

"Zack will be here soon. We wanted to see you."

Rogue walks off a few paces and turns to me, staring at the dirt-covered ground. Nods.

"Tell me what they did to you. Tell me how I can help," I say, taking a few steps closer to him.

He shakes his head. Gives me an annoyed look. "It was a headache, Em. People in the real world, who don't have mega vitamins and unnatural chemicals, get 'em. That's all."

"Bullshit. I may not know much about the world, but I know what just happened to you isn't normal." I pause and stare at him; he's actually stunning when he's being stubborn, like a cat.

"You know nothing, Em. Just forget about it."

"Look, you can pretend I'm naïve, but I think they did this to you. Actually, I know it, so let me help."

"You can't," he says, not rejecting my claim. "If you do then you're gonna put yourself in danger."

"I'm already putting myself in danger. I can make my own decisions. Today was the first day in over three years I didn't have an injection. I beat the system," I say proudly.

"Damn it, Em!" he yells so loud a flock of nearby birds takes flight. His face burns red. "That's what causes the headaches. You can't just stop getting the injections."

"But you told me—"

"And I told you not to do anything drastic!"

79

"So that's why you get the headaches?" I say, piecing it all together. "How do we stop them?"

"Keep taking the injections for one," he says with a growl, looking like he's about to pounce on me for my stupidity. He shakes his head. "But since that's not an option for me, there's a med they make."

"That's why you're back, isn't it? To get the drug?" I say.

"Yes, but I can't find it. They've moved or hidden it," he says. "Maybe they figured out someone was stealing it every several months. Maybe my father knows it's me. I've been through the lab a dozen times and can't find it. But I know how my father thinks and the people he employs think the way he tells them, so I'll find it. Then no more headaches."

"Well, I'll help you find it," I say.

"No you won't. I don't want you involved," he counters.

"I'm going to do it anyway. If you don't allow my help then I'll probably get careless. Then I'll get caught. And it will be because you didn't involve me and allow me to help properly."

"That's the stupidest thing you've ever said," he says, no lightness in his voice. All irritation.

"I'm going to help you, Rogue. Involve me. I've already gone off the injections. I'll need to find this medicine anyway."

"Em, you need to go to the labs now and get your injection. Don't go down this path. It's not one I want for you."

"You, my father, and your father don't get to choose my path. It's mine to decide. My gift is surfacing, my Skills Assessor confirmed it. I'd rather die than give up what rightfully belongs to me."

"You don't get that you might die," he says in a hush, his words haunted. "That's how serious this is. They've been giving you those injections a lot longer than they gave them to me. You don't just quit them cold turkey, not without sending your body into seizures. You really want that more than some stupid gift?"

I watch him move, pace. Watch his anxious hands push through his hair. I watch him look me over, like at any moment I might convulse with a seizure. I shake my head, resign a little. "No. To hell with my gift. What I want is to help you. To get whatever this medicine is that will fix you. That's what I want more than anything else."

80

"No, Em," he says through clenched teeth.

"Yes, Rogue," I say, matching him.

"I think you should leave. Stay away from me."

"Because I'm trying to help you? That's ridiculous!" I yell.

"Yes, because you're trying to help me! And you're gonna get yourself in trouble."

"Well, I'm not going anywhere, so just deal with it."

"Leave," he says, a quiet warning in his voice, his hands balled by his side.

"No!" I fire back.

"Em, if you don't get out of this—"

"You'll what? What are you going to do? Kiss me?" I actually laugh, knowing I have Rogue where I want him. He's powerless.

A dark shadow falls on his face. He brings his green eyes up to meet mine, and they pair with a threatening grin. "Maybe."

My heart shudders, but I force myself to stand tall. Take another step forward. "Well, as awful as that sounds, I'm not leaving. I'm not forgetting you need help."

"I'd reconsider your judgment on this. I'm a sloppy kisser."

"Do your worst," I say, trying to sound bold, brave. Relentless. I take another challenging step in his direction, daring to separate us by inches. "I'm not leaving."

Rogue's eyes swivel down on me, a strange expression in them. Disbelief maybe. He sucks in a breath. Pauses a few inches away, seeming to measure my resolve.

His fingers find my chin, angle it up. And he leans down, his warmth blanketing me. My eyes close just as Rogue's lips close on mine. All my dreams and realities and strange alter realities rush until they meet this one. The one where I'm kissing a guy who should be dead. The boy I've loved all my life, but never thought of in this way. In a way in which I'd press my lips again and again to his. Take breaths that smell of him. Encircle him in my arms. This moment is beyond surreal and also feels good enough to be a dream. My fingers reach up and slide through his loose hair. He slips back only an inch and squints down at me, since the afternoon sun is at my back. "Awful, huh?" He's close, but I still spy the grin on his mouth.

"The worst," I say, tracing my fingers down his neck, my hand stopping on his chest.

81

"I warned you," Rogue says and leans down and kisses me again, each one so tender and slow, I lose my place in it. I lose myself in him. He kisses me exactly how I feared, in a way that makes me want more.

I step back, despite my desire, and give him a punishing stare. "Don't think I forgot why you just kissed me."

"Because I wanted to," he says, stepping closer.

"And also you wanted to distract me from the argument we're having."

"Or I just wanted to." There's a tempting heat in his eyes. I almost let him pull me to him, but I pivot away.

"I'm still helping you," I say, a defiance I learned from him in my tone.

"Helping with what?" a voice calls from a few yards away.

"Zack!" Rogue says without the same hint of nervousness I feel. He takes a few long strides and throws his arm around Zack's shoulder. "How's my favorite friend doing?" They walk until they're back to my side and then Zack breaks off to inspect the camping area. Rogue turns and whispers in my ear. "That's not true, you're really my favorite."

"Of course I am," I say under my breath, smiling at him. "How many times you kissed Zack?"

Zack turns, giving me a strange look over his shoulder like he heard but also misheard what I whispered to Rogue.

"How many times have you and I kissed, brother?" Rogue says, throwing his arm around Zack's shoulder again. "I've lost track, myself." Then Rogue plants a kiss on Zack's cheek, which Zack wipes away looking only half disgusted.

"Oh, you scorn me." Rogue grabs his chest like he's suddenly pained. "You shouldn't wipe away my love. Em knows better." Rogue turns to me and plants a gentle kiss on my cheek, lingering a few seconds too long. My eyes flick up to Zack's just as Rogue pulls away and drapes his arm over my shoulder. "Now don't wipe that off or I'll put you in a headlock, Em," he warns.

My face is hot, my eyes unable to hold the evolution of confusion growing in Zack's expression. I twist out of Rogue's arm and stand in a spot a safe distance between him and Zack.

"I think Rogue has something he should tell you." I turn to Rogue. "Tell him about the injections. Zack will have a better time with it. He's not on this list. And maybe he can help you."

Through clenched teeth Rogue says, "I don't want help. You two shouldn't get mixed up in this."

"What would you do in our position?" I say, hands firmly planted on my hips.

"Would the two of you stop and just tell me what's going on?" Zack says, looking impatient.

***

"Em, why in the world would you think once I knew this all it would affect me less?" Zack says, his eyes having grown heartbroken as he learned the news. "They're not doing it to me, they're doing it to you. That's worse. Rogue's right though, you shouldn't have gone off the injections."

I roll my eyes at the two of them. They love to gang up on me.

"And also, Em, Rogue is right about another thing. We just need to think on this. Nothing drastic." Zack holds my eyes, a stubborn weight in his expression. "And you're not leaving."

"I wasn't—"

"I know that's what you're planning," Zack says, a firmness in his tone. "I know how your brain works. You're staying and we're facing this *together*. Quietly though."

He's right. I'd been thinking about it. I shrug, not meeting his eyes.

"First things first, we need to find the med—"

"No," Rogue protests.

"Yes, Rogue," Zack argues. "If you're suffering we have to help. But we'll be careful. We won't get caught. I can check inventory for the labs. Em, keep your eyes open while you're there. And you, Rogue, lay low. No more strolls through the park." Zack is good at this. A born leader, for sure.

Rogue looks at me, a not-so-serious expression on his face. Then he turns, stands tall, and salutes Zack. "Yes, President Conerly."

Zack shakes his head, but smiles still.

"I love you, brother," Rogue says, relaxing, clapping a hand on Zack's shoulder.

Everything feels better now that Zack is involved, like we have a chance. I'm not sure what we have a chance at, but it will be better than where we are, because I can't watch Rogue have another of those attacks.

"Now"—Zack turns and gives me a demanding look—"go to the labs, Em. Your father will be on your case otherwise, and we don't need you getting these attacks before we have a plan of how to fix them."

Chapter Seventeen

I feel Rogue's kiss on my lips as I stroll to the labs. I never in my life thought there was a reality where I would press my mouth to Rogue's, but a week ago I didn't even know he still breathed in this world. And his breath haunts me now. Makes me want to breathe it again. Having him so close felt too complete, like I was close to a reality where I could live my own life. Where I could know what his life felt like, experience it with him. But I remind myself I only shared a kiss with him. I'm not Rogue's. I'm just the girl he kissed...today. I'm sure I'm a part of a club. Should have a punch card or something. I'm sure Rogue kisses lots of girls. Guys like him don't have to try to get attention.

I know without them testing that I'm not running a fever. I can feel it, the absence of heat in my body. I'd felt it so acutely that I'm more aware of the normalcy. I've been too aware of my every action and instinct, waiting to breathe fire or spy a flash of the future. There's been nothing. Aside from Ren's reading of me, I've had no other indication that I have a gift trying to surface. Even so, I've been trying to push every leaf on the sidewalk with my mind or push my way into every person's thoughts as I walk down the busy Central Boulevard. I'm waiting. Waiting like a chrysalis before it becomes a butterfly. A seed before it becomes a sapling. But like all those things I have no idea what I'll become, what gift lives inside me.

I round the corner and walk into a starched black suit. The aroma envelops me immediately. I know without opening my startled eyes the man who douses himself in this scent. It's like my father's, but with more of a floral tone. I back up several paces and lower my head without making eye contact, taking an extremely low curtsy. "Hello, President Vider," I say, my eyes fixed on the pavement under my feet. *Why is the President walking down a main road? Out around the general public?*

I bring my gaze up to catch the tight look on the President's face. "Hello, Ms. Fuller. Are you on the way to the lab?" he asks, pressing down his suit and pushing back his perfectly short hair. It's too cropped to curl at the ends like Rogue's does.

"Yes, sir," I say, standing tall, trying to eject a confidence I don't feel into my posture.

He sniffs the air, like he smells something. Not something delicious, but rather interesting or different. His eyes swerve to me. "So, you've been sick, I hear, dear Ms. Fuller. My sincere apologies."

"I'm better now."

"Which is why you're on your way back to the labs?" he says, his long nose leading the direction of his face as he turns in the directions of the lab. "I'm sure you're relieved to be back to your treatments."

"Oh, yes," I say.

President Vider takes a couple of steps until he's too close, looking down on me. His nostrils pull back with one deliberate inhalation. This is not the first time he's reminded me of a werewolf. The black slicked back hair. Manicured eyebrows. Long canines. And a pronounced nose. Right now though, as the hairs on my body stand on end, I wish I envisioned him as something less menacing. Anything else.

To my horror he brings his nose down and smells my shoulder. Actually runs his nose across it. His almond-shaped eyes spring up, giving me a satisfied expression. "Excuse me for that," he says, his breath hitting me. "It's just I'm on the hunt for something and you smell awfully close to what I'm looking for."

I shiver out a disingenuous smile and step back. "It must be croissants. That's what Giorgio fixed me for lunch."

He shakes his head, his eyes trained on me with a brutal determination. Around the streets people don't even notice us. They know better than to even chance a glance at the President. They might have noticed him on the streets, but a second glance wouldn't be paid. "It's not pastries I smell on you. It's something woodsy."

My head snaps up. Too fast. "Well, I've been sick. Home all day." I stumble back.

He makes up the distance quickly, grabbing my shirt sleeve, pulling me in his direction. The President is strong. Stronger than I realized as he holds me in place, not giving me any room to negotiate. "And who in your home is responsible for ripping your clothes like this?"

I chance a glimpse down and spy the holes and tears along my sleeves and socks from my run in the woods. My shorts are unmarked, but there are several fresh cuts along my calves. I shake my head, at a loss for a response. If I set off at a run, where can I get to? How far will I be before President Vider has someone after me?

Ever so gently, he angles my wrist up, turns it over, and his eyes run over a long scratch on the underside of my arm. Blood has bubbled up on the cut and dried. He sniffs the air. His eyes dart to mine, a strange sensitivity in them. "Do have Dr. Parker treat your wounds while at the lab, Ms. Fuller, would you?"

I pull my arm back to my body, the sting of the cut registering for the first time in my brain. "I got that—"

"While farming, I'm sure," he says, narrowing his eyes with a conceited knowing.

"Yes," I say too fast.

Bikes ride past us on the street. A shopkeeper across the way refills his case. Middlings hustle down the alley way behind me, which is their thoroughfare through town. Their voices low as they walk. I'm aware of all of this, like my ability to observe has suddenly been thrown into hyperdrive. But my main focus is on the figure hovering over me, too close.

"Your father told me you were still grieving for my son," the President says, his voice matter-of-fact.

"I will always grieve for Rogue," I say, my reaction immediate, as though built into my instinct.

His eyes narrow, scanning behind me, and then studying me with a unique interest. "You know, you and Rogue were always close, and also so much alike. I could see why you miss him still."

"Thank you, sir," I say, at a loss for words. Again and again I take in everything around me, the details as exact as if I'd studied them under a microscope. I spy the tiniest of differences in Ms. Willow's socks as her slacks hike up as she walks. Know they don't match. I smell a group of Middlings who work in the sanitation department a minute before they pass the alleyway. I hear Mr. Carmichael's stomach growl a half a block away. And in front of me I spy the tiniest hint of nervousness spring to the President's eyes. It isn't something I've ever noticed before. His eyes dilate a tiny degree. His eyelid twitches.

"Maybe I should escort you to the lab myself," he says, grabbing my arm, nails pressing into it as we move up the street. I work at not tensing, at pretending this is normal. Because something is completely wrong. With him. With me. And I can't afford to do anything until I figure out why. Why can I see, smell, and hear everything around me all at once and individually? Why is the President out? He seems to be looking for something, but the President is always chauffeured in a rickshaw. Everywhere he goes. Our President doesn't walk the streets. Never has.

"The thing is," he says, now almost pulling me through the crowd to the lab, "there's something different about the Valley now. Something isn't right. I can sense it, like something dead has been unburied. And it might be nice for you to bring your head up to the land of the living. I'd hate for you to get caught up in something tragic. Like whatever happened to my dear, poor son."

I startle. Stare at him. I say the only thing that comes to mind. "I'm still so sorry for your loss, sir."

He doesn't respond. Doesn't reciprocate. Doesn't accept. Instead he smiles, one that flashes both of his long canines. "We all know that Rogue wasn't a benefit to this society. If he stayed here, he could have been," the President says, swiveling me around at the stoop to the lab.

Stayed? He knows Rogue left here. That he's alive.

"I hate what happened to my boy, but he chose his fate. You can choose differently. You can choose to serve your people. To serve me," the President says.

"Well, sir, you know I have nothing to give. I'm a Defect."

He smiles, like I just told him a not-so-funny joke. "Oh, but you do have so much you can give me. Compliance is the purest form of flattery. It means I've established what you need for yourself and others."

"But why are you discussing this with me?" I ask.

"Because I don't want dividers," President Vider says. "I don't need them here. And I want them to know where their place is on the outside. Em, the world outside our borders is cold." He stops and looks at me. "Rogue will tell you this is true. You'll suffer outside our walls and we'll allow it. And if you're ever found inside our borders then the worst will happen to you. Is that clear?"

"Yes, sir," I say, listening to his steady heartbeat, a sound that shouldn't be audible from two feet away. The look in his eyes chills me. Paralyzes me. Crucifies me. And I'm only whole when I'm away from him, where his judgmental eye can't see me as I stumble off to the lab.

"I'll wait for you to get your injection, Em," the President says, like a threat. "I want to make sure that it makes you better."

I turn and stare at him. Take in everything about the President. Behind him my senses sweep in a thousand details.

"Because right now, you really don't seem well, Em," the President says, his eyes narrowed. He stands at the bottom of the stairs like a gate.

I nod and turn away from him. I open the door to the lab, breathless to find a site that empties me of all my resolve to back down from this fight. Every single chair and every single space is crowded, filled with a person. It's never been so full in the lab.

Chapter Eighteen

There's nowhere for me to stand while I wait for my name to be called. I literally slide in front of two boys who are lined up against the wall. They're Nona's age. One of them, Scott, tried to kiss her last year. The other one, who I don't know by name, was caught a month ago skipping classes. Rebels for sure. Real hard-core criminals. Hell, why be so kind as to numb our gifts, why not just give us a full lobotomy now?

As I scan the anxious and irritated faces of the kids in the waiting room, I expect to be attuned to every detail like I'd been out on the street. It's gone though. Unmistakably and inexplicably gone. I'd felt like a lion when I was on Central Boulevard, able to hear, smell, and see the tiniest of details from yards away. Actually, to be quite honest, it was fantastic and made me feel like the strongest predator.

I expect, since I was the most recent to arrive, that I'll have a long wait. I don't. Tammy calls my name next, an annoyed look on her face.

"What?" I mouth to her when I meet her by the door. She isn't hurrying off down the hallway, making me run to catch up with her like usual. A crease marks the space between her eyebrows and she looks half past the verge of verbally tearing me in two. Then I remember the last time I was in the lab, the deception Nona and I pulled. *Has she figured us out? Is she going to turn me in?*

She indicates the direction she wants me to take with her pointy fingernail. "March. You know which room to go to."

What am I going to say? How am I going to get out of this? My adrenal gland, which is already exhausted from my run-in with the President, is pumping again, overflowing my bloodstream with adrenaline. Pulse racing, I whip around and face Tammy.

"Look, I can totally explain," I say, staring at her scrutinizing glare. And out around her the strangest thing appears. A red cloud forms, outlining her. It hovers beside her skin, bathing her in a strange glow. It's transparent like a bubble. I stumble back, simultaneously wanting to get away from whatever is enveloping

Tammy and also sensing that it's harmless. "Wh-wh-what is that?" I say, unable to refrain from pointing directly at her.

She turns and gauges the empty hallway. Swings back around looking even more irritated than before. "Em, I don't have time for your games. You've already derailed our schedule and now I have a waiting room of patients to explain this to. They're all going to want to know why you got bumped up in line and they're all going to be mad at me about it. Gods know I can't tell them the truth." She shakes her head, lips pursed as she marches past me, carrying that red glow with her.

"But I didn't have to be bumped up, I didn't ask for you to—"

"No, of course you didn't," Tammy says, chunking my file on the lab counter as soon as she opens the door. "Wouldn't make any difference if you did and you know that. President Vider just phoned the lab himself. Said to make your injection a priority because you are past due. You'll have this first one now and come back in three hours for your second one. He insist that you get caught up on your injections quickly." She shakes her head, that strange red glow still hovering around her. Then quite unexpectedly she pins her hand on the doorway, closes her eyes, and sucks in a strained breath.

"Tammy?" I say, still standing in the hallway, watching the glow around her pulse with intensity, but always red. "Are you all right?"

"Fine," she says, batting her eyelids a few times, like trying to clear her focus. "Just hit by a strange bout of exhaustion. It's these hours. All the demands of the job. And now your arrival throws a wrench in our schedule."

"Sorry," I say, meaning it.

She straightens suddenly, moves to the side so I can enter. "Oh, good, you're ready for her," she says to someone behind me. I turn to see Parker rounding the corner. Encasing him, similar to Tammy, is a greenish cloud. I rub my eyes. Open them. It's the color of an evergreen tree, but again transparent, surrounding him. Tammy has already hurried away down the opposite hallway, carrying her red glow with her.

"Hello, Em," Parker says, giving me a genuine, although tired smile. "Please," he says, extending his hand, indicating I should enter the lab room. I scamper into the room and take my usual seat. Parker enters behind me, closes the door, and the greenish glow around him instantly falls away. Disappears. I bat my eyes to try and clear my vision. When I open them, Parker's giving me a concerned look. "You all right, Em?" he says, hurrying to pull the thermometer from the drawer, along with the needle and tube of pink liquid. I shudder at the sight of the poison.

"I'm...well..." I can't figure out what to say. I want to protest the injection. To tell Parker there's something going on with my senses. Something I can't really explain, but then he'd be obligated to report it and the President is obviously suspicious of me. I shake my head, not having constructed a real sentence. "Nothing."

"I heard you were sick," he says, swiping the sensor across my head. "Missed seeing you and your bouncy curls." He eyes the reading on the thermometer then smiles. "Seems that you're all better now. I bet you're glad."

I shrug, unable to feign a look of relief.

"Well, maybe you'll feel better after your injection," he says, hurrying to take the position behind me. "You've never gone so long without your injection, I hope it didn't slow your opportunity to recover your gift."

I don't nod. Instead, I clench my teeth together as he rubs the cold alcohol swab across the top of my neck. "One. Two. Three," he says, and then the sharp intrusion I haven't missed blankets my head in pain. It's worse than any other time before. A scream actually rips out of my mouth. I can't stop it, since I'm using every ounce of consciousness to keep myself upright and not buckle over. Parker's arm actually whips around and holds me up, balancing me, keeping me still. Noises of pain continue to issue from my mouth as fire scorches through my brain and the base of my skull explodes over and over again with a cutting sensation. A single tear slips out of my eye and rolls over my cheek, finally falling on Parker's arm with a splat. The pain turns into an ebbing throb, a more manageable sensation. Parker removes his steadying arm and walks around to face me.

"I figured the drug might have a stronger effect on you now, Em," he says, squatting down and looking up at me. "I'm so sorry. And that's why we don't like you to skip injections."

I usually nod in understanding, but I know I'm not allowed to move my head and couldn't even if I wanted to.

"It's hard to watch the injections do that to you kids but if it works then it will be worth it, I'm sure," he says, standing and picking up my chart, filling out the information for this injection.

Parker doesn't know, does he? He doesn't know he's severing our gifts. If he did, I'm certain he wouldn't be doing this.

He claps my folder shut, gives me a sympathetic smile. "I see now why the President was so adamant about you getting your injection as quickly as possible. He really does care about every citizen, doesn't he?" he says, like the idea just reaffirmed in his mind.

"He must," I say, the effort to speak actually bringing more tears to the back of my eyes. The strangeness of everything I've experienced recently motivates me to talk. "Parker, can I ask you a question?"

He eyes the clock on the wall, seems to calculate something in his head. "Sure." He finally nods. "I should be spending more time evaluating you after your injections anyway."

"I wanted to get something for Tammy to thank her for being so nice all these years. I can't decide on what to get her though. Can you tell me what her gift is? I was thinking that might inspire me."

Parker's brown eyes shine behind his glasses. "That's thoughtful of you, Em. Great idea too. Tammy's gift is she can read auras." He pauses to tuck his pen behind his ear; it immediately gets lost in his thick slicked back hair. "You know, she says I have a green aura. Dark green."

Chapter Nineteen

The President isn't waiting for me as I expected when I exit the lab. My guess is that he got confirmation another way that I'd successfully gotten my injection. The evening sun is setting as I hurry to the apartment building by the old theater. I've never had a reason to go there until now. I'm not sure if anyone can help me at this point, but what I need more than anything is information.

After consulting the directory I hurry off to the fifth floor, taking the stairs so I avoid anyone seeing me.

I knock as soon as I arrive at his door, afraid I'll lose my nerve otherwise.

First I hear cursing, followed by a great deal of shuffling. Finally the door opens to a not-so-welcoming face.

"Oh, dear God, it knows where I live," Ren says, looking down at me from the entryway.

Of course I knew where to find Ren. All single Dream Travelers are given housing in this apartment building. "I need your help," I say, eyeing the hallway, cautious of anyone seeing me here. It would get back to my father. It would provoke questions I can't answer.

He rolls his eyes. A bit of an immature response for a grown man, but he doesn't seem to care about that kind of thing. "I oughtn't have given you the impression we're fast friends by covering for you to Lyza. Your mother just encourages me to act my worst, always has," he says, threading his arms across his chest. "But here's the thing, you and I aren't pals. I don't want to buy your Girl Scout cookies or help you with your arithmetic. So I say you pop off before I slam the door in your face. How's that for nice?"

I take a step forward, my foot blocking the threshold.

Ren raises a red eyebrow at me, looking slightly entertained.

"Something just happened to me," I say in a rush. "Since everybody in this society is completely brainwashed by the President, I was hoping you could help since you're relatively new and maybe not under his spell yet."

"Oh, the old 'you're the only one who's not brainwashed' approach," Ren says, leaning on his open door and giving an extremely long yawn. "Really? That's what you led with?" He shakes his head and clicks his tongue. "You really lack imagination. Since my books haven't been delivered yet and I'm quite bored I'll give you the chance to bait me one final time and then I'm sending this old door shut in your face," he says, knocking on the surface of the door with his knuckles, his gold ring catching the hallway light.

I shake my head, take a couple of steps back. "That's all right. What's going on with me is really bizarre. You've probably never encountered it and won't know what it is. I'll see if Tutu knows, she's really smart. Sorry for wasting your time," I say and turn and leave at once, making haste to the stairwell. My hand is almost to the push bar when behind me I hear clapping. I stop. Turn. Ren still stands in his doorway. He stops clapping as soon as my eyes meet his.

"Yes, a much craftier approach. I've always been a fan of the old 'you probably don't know, so I'm not going to ask you' method. It's clever. Now get in here before someone sees you," he says and disappears into his apartment.

***

Ren sits in a plaid armchair, stroking his red goatee, a look of mischief in his eyes. He hasn't said a word for more than a minute after I've divulged everything: the injections, my fake fever, my encounter with the President and Tammy. The only thing I didn't tell him about was Rogue. Even then I'm not sure why I gave him so much information. I guess it's because I don't have much left to lose. And Reverians aren't allowed to contest what our government does, but an outsider might not be so inhibited.

His living room is barebones. There's only one chair, which he's sitting in, and a coffee table with a stack of notebooks.

"You're a leech," Ren finally says, breaking the silence.

"I'm what?" I say, pushing off the empty wall I'd been leaning against.

He rolls his eyes. "A leech," he says again, slower, louder. "That's your gift. You suck out other people's gifts and use them as your own. Well, you borrow them, since they can still use their gift at the same time, but the effect can be draining." Ren flicks a few specks of white lint off his black trousers and then levels his gaze with mine. "Bet your Tutu doesn't know about that kind of gift."

"I've never heard of a leech before," I say, shaking my head at this preposterous idea.

95

"You're daft if you think the Reverians would write about those with gifts like that in their dreadfully flawed textbooks."

"Why?" I say in a hush. "Why would they hide so much from us?"

"Well, as your account with the injections has already explained, these are people who disempower and the best way to do that is to withhold knowledge."

"Are you going to stay here now that you know all this? Now that you know what they're doing to kids, all to keep us from overthrowing them?" I ask.

"Absol-freaking-lutely! I love a good conspiracy. And I've been surrounded by goody goods for too long. Nice to be the only one in government without a blackened soul."

"But why did the President bring in an outsider?" I ask, the question popping up, demanding immediate attention.

"It sounds like he's scared gifts are surfacing and wants confirmation as soon as they do. And as we've already discussed, I'm the best," Ren says.

"But doesn't all this information compromise the integrity of your position?" I ask.

"No, because I fulfill my position the way I see fit," Ren says, a sneaky grin on his face.

"But what if the President catches on to you? Realizes you know about all this," I say.

"No one ever catches on to me. I'm a master of illusion."

"Seriously, though, how are you going to fool him?" I say.

"Seriously, though, I'm a master of illusion." He sighs. "Blimey, why do I even waste time talking to people who don't listen?"

"Fine. I'm listening. Tell me more about leeches. Everything I need to know," I say, starting to pace his apartment.

"I give the orders, Emmy. So don't be a git and tell me what to do."

I stop. Nod. Wait.

"Now let me go ahead and bestow upon you the wisdom I know about leeches." He stands and takes up my former position pacing, his eyes pinned on the ground as he speaks. "Leeches are rare. My granddad, your great-grandfather, was the only one I know of. Most leeches do it as a defense mechanism, although you can train yourself to do it at will. You see, leeches aren't usually spiteful people. They do it as a defense, like a porcupine with its needles. You were feeling threatened by the President so without meaning to, you stole his gift. And then—"

"Which is?" I ask, interrupting him. He stops and glares at me, which I do my best to ignore. "Do you know what the President's gift is?"

"He sounds like he has hyper-senses. Also rare, but not someone I'd worry about bumping into in a dark alleyway. The thing that makes the President dangerous is he has the senses of a vampire and the agenda to match."

"Oh," I say, thinking of the chilling moment when President Vider slid his nose against my shoulder where Rogue's sweat had stained my clothes.

"Back to leeches," Ren says, snapping twice in my face. "Unless you'd like to stay in your daydream or wherever your tiny brain is at the moment."

I nod. "Yes, please continue."

"Another thing you should know about leeches is you can suck up a little or a lot of someone's powers. You can literally leech someone to death. However, no matter the amount, the power you take can't be stored easily, especially not much of it, not safely. Other people's power corrupts us if we hold it inside. It can literally burn you from the inside out."

"What does that mean for me?" I say.

"It means if you suck something out of someone then there's an avenue you have to use to unleash it. My grandfather expelled his through combustion. On a good day, he could level a house. Probably a good thing I never saw what he could do on a bad day."

"What?" I ask, sure that he's joking.

"Oh God, does no one speak English around here?" Ren says.

I shake my head and try to piece together my thoughts. "You're saying that whatever I take from someone has to come out of me somehow?"

"Ding. Ding. Ding," he says with zero enthusiasm. "Give her a gold star…no, make it bronze on second thought."

"But earlier, with the President and Tammy, I didn't expel anything. Where did it go?"

97

"You do realize if you keep asking me these irksome questions then I'm going to lose my pleasant manner, right?" Ren says dryly.

"You don't know the answer, do you?" I say.

He studies his fingernails, picks at one. "I haven't got the slightest," he says coolly. "You were given the injection, so my guess is it has to lie dormant in you until you aren't being medicated." Ren shrugs, still staring at his nails, his eyes growing tired. "It might kill you. Or it might give you a headache. Or it might not do anything at all. Each leech is different."

"But it's healthier for me if I unleash the powers I absorb, right?" I say.

"Yes, so the question is, how will yours come out?"

"That's a crazy question," I say, realizing it's getting late. "Thanks for helping me."

Ren huffs and sits down in his chair with a thud.

"I mean," I say, walking to the exit, "thanks for barely shining any light on this matter. Your help was hardly adequate."

At my back I actually hear a small laugh. It's covered up by a fake cough.

"Oh, and Em," Ren says when I'm almost to the door.

"Yes," I say, turning to him.

"No wonder they drugged *you*. Not sure if they know what you're capable of, but you're someone I wouldn't want to meet in a dark alley. If you're anything like granddad then they're all screwed." He smiles. "Yeah, I'm definitely sticking around to see this magic show."

Chapter Twenty

"What are you covered in?" my mother nearly yells when I enter the house. Tutu pops her head out of her book and catches a glimpse of me from the living room. A smile unfolds, lighting up her blue eyes.

"Dear, sweet Lyza," she says, snapping the book shut. "That's dirt. It's this strange substance under all our concrete. It's as old as me."

"I know what dirt is, Marylou," my mother retorts. "I'm concerned why Em is covered in it."

"Covered is a bit of an exaggeration," Tutu says, tucking her nose back in her book. "It looks like you've been gardening, dear Em. Good for you."

My mother shakes her head and rounds on me again, her face turning a slight shade of pink. "Get upstairs and bathe. I want Rachel to wash and style your hair right away."

"I can wash my hair just fine." *I can style it too*, but it's probably better if I don't argue with her about everything. Dee and my mother have Rachel wash, dress, and get them ready every day. They've deluded themselves into believing that because Rachel's Middling family has been serving us in one capacity or another for decades she enjoys the honor. I suspect Rachel would rather be doing a lot of other things. Middlings are rarely given much choice about what job they do for the Reverians. Once they commit to serve they are elected into positions that meet their skill sets, not their interests.

I tiptoe up the stairs, careful to minimize the amount of soil that flakes off me. When I'm almost to the landing I stop and turn back to my mother. Her fuming eyes are on my back, watching me leave. "Why is it that you want Rachel to style my hair? Do we have an important event?"

"If you spent more time with Reverians and less time playing in the dirt with Middlings then you'd already know. The President has called a mandatory meeting. It's in one hour."

"Right," I say, turning back around. Good thing I returned when I did. I could have spent the rest of the evening working in the fields. After another two rounds of injections today and the news yesterday, what I really wanted was to go back and see Rogue again. However, I can't chance him getting caught, not with the President watching and threateningly suspicious of me.

I hadn't had agriculture hours all week and Dean was glad to see me when I arrived this afternoon.

"It's always good to have your help, and I know you enjoy the work," he said, handing me a bucket of tools. "Thing is I don't really need your labor as much as I have in the past. We're fully staffed now." He pointed with his thumb to the field behind him, which was indeed filled with more workers than I'd ever seen at the farm.

I didn't answer, but I think the confused look on my face said it all.

"They were brought in a couple of days ago. A whole bus full of Middlings," Dean said, angling his head low so only I could hear him. "They're mostly transients and young adults, looking to make a fresh start. One of 'em told me they were recruited by a slick-looking fella."

"What do they promise them?" I said.

Dean gave me a strange look. "Same thing they promised my father and all the other Middlings: a home, food, protection, and fair wages."

"And bonuses for medical testing on their offspring," I said, a morbid laugh escaping my lips.

"What that's now?" Dean asked, like he misheard me.

I waved my hand to dismiss my tasteless remark. "Nothing. I was just referring to the program where Middlings can get extra compensation for doing medical testing."

Dean scratched his head. "I don't know nothing about that program, miss."

"Oh, well, maybe it's new," I said.

"I do know that they encouraged this lot to start families whenever they want. The officials in charge of housing said they'd build more family dwellings and reconfigure as needed. That made a bunch of these fellas mighty happy," he said, waving his hand out at the field.

"Hmmm…" I said, studying the many figures digging and plowing, working extra hard to ensure all our foods are organic and grown to exemplary standards.

"You know, it's been good for me to be around this bunch," Dean said, again indicating the field. "They've reenergized me. Made me realize how lucky I am to be in Austin Valley. How good I got it. These folks all say they're happier, healthier, and sleep better since they arrived. You can't beat that."

"It must be the immune booster," I said, assessing the rows to determine where my help could be most valuable.

"Probably the food and medicines, but definitely not the immune booster. They don't work on Middlings. Sad, but that's what was responsible for a string of infant deaths," he said, his face went from confusion to remorse, like he could just barely remember his own tragedy of losing his child. The pain and memory was whisked away with a smile though, like being washed absent by a spring rain. The gap between his two front teeth was prominent when he smiled. "Good news is they've fixed all that. And they take a sample of blood from each new baby when they're six weeks old to ensure they won't have any problems. The Reverians really do think of everything and have a solution to our every problem." He clapped a hardened hand on my back. "You should be proud of the work your father does."

"Proud doesn't even begin to explain the way I feel about him," I said through a fake smile.

I recount my conversation with Dean as I shower off the dirt. Once my skin is puffy from the hot steam, I slip on my robe and head to my room, my mind continuing to comb through the details of my hours spent in the field. The Middlings, the old residents and new arrivals, all seemed genuinely happy. Dean said they were given a chance they didn't have outside our borders. Maybe in this instance our government is doing right by them. And the testing on children? It sounds like they are trying to prevent a disease or ailment. Still, my rational brain implores me to continue doing some detective work, maybe just so I learn this is all not nefarious.

"Not so short!" Dee screams as I enter our room. Rachel sits on her knees, filing my sister's nails. "How ridiculous! You'd think this is the first time you've ever done this. Has your memory lapsed since yesterday when you did my nails?!" Dee pulls her freshly manicured hand to her face and eyes it with disgust, then her eyes swivel down on Rachel, who's almost cowering. "Well, has it?!"

"No, miss," Rachel says, pushing to her feet. She's my mother's age, but looks ten, maybe fifteen years older. Her gray hair overwhelms the rest and she moves slower than I remember in years past. She turns her eyes on me when I enter, my head in a towel and my face red from the hot shower.

"Ms. Em, may I help you get ready?" she asks, giving me an eager look.

I chance a glance at my sister. Her hair is pinned in a tight side braid, and she's inspecting it in the mirror, complaints forming in her head. "This is all wrong. And on a night like tonight!" she fusses, throwing a hairbrush across the room. "I demand that you—"

"Why yes, Rachel, I think I could use all the help I can get," I interrupt, grabbing the lady by the hand and pulling her over to my side of the room where my vanity sits in slight chaos. I turn over my shoulder to spy Dee piercing me with a hostile stare. "Oh, Dee," I say, waving at her. "Would you stop worrying? You look so good I positively want to be you."

She dabs too much powder onto the end of her pointy nose and smirks. "You wish you had a gift as amazing as mine. Well, you just wish you had a gift," she says with an evil cackle.

"How right you are. I only wish I had my gift." *Then I'd singe off your eyebrows.* I'm just about to run the brush through my hair, when Rachel's hand stops me. I look up to catch her thoughtful eyes.

"Please, allow me, miss," she says, taking the brush from me. "And you really don't want to overbrush hair like yours, you'll frizz your curls."

"What's this 'allow me' business, Rachel?" Dee says, acid in her tone. "You're never so polite to me."

"She pities me and my bad hygiene," I say, winking at Rachel in the mirror. She winks back.

"How would you like your hair tonight, miss?"

"Whatever you think is best. You're the expert," I say, cleaning the dirt out from underneath my fingernails.

"Your mother laid out your clothes for you," Rachel says, indicating the hangers draped in cream fabrics beside the closet.

"How nice of her," I say dryly. "This must be a big meeting, indeed."

"It is and you'd know that—"

"If I wasn't such a loser," I say, cutting off Dee. "Mother already beat you to that one."

"The President is going to make some big announcements tonight," Dee says, slipping a black shawl around her shoulders. "And afterwards there's going to be a big party, with music and cake. This is a big deal, Em." She walks over to my vanity and snatches a diamond-encrusted comb off the surface. "Keep your hands off my stuff."

I'm not going to anger myself and argue with Dee. It's pointless to tell her that Tutu gave me those combs for my twelfth birthday. I'm absolutely positive my sister has already concocted a story in her head, which she firmly believes, where the antique hair pieces belong to her. I'll just wait until she's sleeping and steal them back, as I have a dozen times already.

"You're good as gold," Rachel says, taking the last of several hairpins and tucking it into my curls. The hair on the sides of my head is drawn up, twisted slightly and pinned at the back of my head with hairpins with pearls on their ends. And for a rare opportunity, all my blonde curls are arranged neatly down my back. Rachel also added color to my cheeks, some lipstick, and a bit of mascara.

"It's perfect, Rachel," I say, clasping my hand on the one she has resting on my shoulder.

"You look like an angel," she says, her face making me feel too sentimental.

"Well, I feel nothing like one," I say and wink at her again.

I dress in the white silk blouse and cream pencil skirt my mother laid out for me. The nude heels I've never worn pair perfectly with the ensemble, as well as the pearl necklace I never give myself an opportunity to wear. This whole tight-fitting, pressed look is polished, but it also makes me feel too restrained, like any action will wrinkle or stain me. I guess I've always preferred to move in a way that would wrinkle clothes, would stain them. Then I know I'm actually living.

"Oh, and Em," my sister says just as she's about to head downstairs. She has that too-nice tone in her voice. It instantly brings my suspicious eyes up to meet hers. "Father left you a present on your bed. He is so thoughtful."

I wait for her to leave and then slowly make my way to my bed. My father doesn't leave me presents. Hasn't given me anything since

I can remember. Hesitant eyes fall on the two pieces lying flatly on my bed. I suck in a sudden breath and stumble back, like I've just seen one of Tutu's ghosts. The top and bottom half of a statue of Lady Justice lies on my comforter. It's the statue from my father's office. The one I broke.

Chapter Twenty-One

I take each step down the staircase, thinking that my nervousness will make my feet slip out from underneath me and I'll tumble to the bottom, broken and hopefully in a lot less trouble. From the corner of my vision I spy my mother fussing over Nona's hair. I round the end of the banister and stand staring at my family. They're all dressed in black. My mother and Dee both wear tight-fighting dresses. My father in his usual suit. Nona, a pleated skirt and blazer, but around her neck is tied a silk white scarf. I can't help it. I thread my eyes down my crisp, light appearance and then over the dark bodies in front of me. They look like they're going to a funeral. And I, well I look appropriate enough to be buried.

"Is everything all right, Em?" my mother says, a snarky tone in her repressed smile.

"I'm fine," I say, brushing off nonexistent lint from my blouse and standing tall.

"Do you think it's acceptable to keep your family waiting while you get ready?" my father asks from behind my mother and sister. The look on his stone face doesn't give anything away. It's the same mask he always wears, but I spy an extra degree of heat behind it. He narrows his eyes at me and I feel the all too familiar invasion into my thoughts. I throw up a shield to block him, to stop the trespassing.

"I apologize for my tardiness," I say with a practiced curtsy.

"She's going to have back troubles if you keep insisting she does that," Tutu says from behind my father. She takes a few hobbled steps and then comes around to my side.

Tutu isn't dressed for the affair. She has the clout to finally "stick a decline" to the President. I eye her dressing gown with envy.

"We must be off," my father says, hastening the group to the exit.

"Of course you must. That's what you people do. Hurry off to your engagements where not much engaging happens from what I can see," Tutu says, eyeing my father with a scrupulous look. She's the only one who can get away with it. "Oh, and Damien, if the cake is chocolate, bring me home a piece."

105

I smile at her brazen nature and hurry out the door. Her withered hand catches me as I try to go. A scent as inborn as my own wafts from her as she pulls me close enough to whisper in my ear. It's a mixture of salt and lavender. "Those who see the fire run. The rest die from smoke," she says, not a hint of lightness in her usual jovial voice.

She doesn't say another word, just stares at me with an intensity I think will saw me in two. I nod. The words "Yes, Tutu" fall out of my mouth.

"Good girl," she says, and then turns me around and slaps me on the bottom. "Get out of here before your father convicts you of stalling this gods-forsaken meeting."

***

My heels almost kill my pinky toes by the time we walk the three blocks to the old theater. Cars are rarely used, even on special occasions. Since there's no way I'm riding my bike in a pencil skirt, walking was the only option. I dutifully took up the rear for my family as they marched down Central Boulevard. Multiple times we've stopped so my father could shake hands with various people and exchange pleasantries. It really is a boring business. Politics. I break away from the pack when we arrive at the theater, intent on spilling some news to an important someone.

Zack spots me at once from his place stationed at the corner. His eyes actually do a double take and he freezes in place looking at me, like my head is twice its normal size. "Em?" he says, giving me a look of awe.

"Later," I say, waving my hand haphazardly at my head and dress. "I've got someth—"

"Hi, Zachary," Dee says, sliding right in front of me. She actually thrusts her hip out enough that it bounces into me. My sister is all legs and curves, which I realize is a hard combination for most guys to ignore. "Our time at the ball was so lovely, didn't you think?"

"It was grand," Zack says, taking a quick bow. His eyes dart to my anxious look and then my sister's.

After everything I've been through in the last twenty-four hours the only thing I've wanted was to divulge a tiny bit of it to him. Now I realize that's impossible. Beside me Nona strides up, pulling on the white scarf around her neck like it's choking her. "I've got something to share," I say from the corner of my mouth to her.

"Like how you're dead meat," Nona says, also from the corner of her mouth. "I can read Father well enough to know when he's about to roast someone."

Dee has moved in closer to Zack. She has her hands tracing up and down the lapels of his jacket, her shawl having dropped down low revealing her bare shoulders and backless dress. He's a goner at this point. "Sit beside me, Zack," Dee says, her voice demanding. She threads her arm through his and looks up at him like he's the President himself. "And after the meeting you can accompany me to the celebration."

I half want to laugh at how miserable Zack looks, but my own disappointment of not getting to share my news with him overwhelms the urge. Instead I give him a sympathetic shrug and turn to leave. I will my feet to stop screaming, taking each step like I'm walking on coals. I've only made it a few excruciating steps when I hear Nona's whiny voice behind me; it has a nasal quality about it that's half cute, half annoying.

"Oh no you don't, Zack!" she says. "You're coming with me. We both know you're the only one who can keep Em's trap shut during these meetings. I'm not getting in trouble on account of her…again."

I turn to see two distinct images. One is of my little sister, tugging on Zack fiercely, like a goat trying to pull a bull through a yard. They both wear slightly comical expressions, like they're playing a part in a play. And the other is Dee, standing cross-armed at Zack's back, watching him be pulled away by who she thinks is the least menacing force on this planet. Nona.

I walk off a few paces and let them catch up. "You know, he's almost grown and can make his own decisions about who he hangs out with," I say to Nona, who quickly takes the position beside me.

"Everyone needs saving from Dee," she says, flipping her long straw-colored hair behind her back.

"Thanks. I did need saving," Zack says, taking up the spot on my other side. "She intimidates me. I'm afraid to go against her."

"Afraid she'll burn you," Nona confirms.

"Right," Zack says as we walk, his eyes flicking to me every so often. He has that look of awe on his face again. "So," he finally says, drawing out the word and strangely sounding nervous. "You look really—"

"Oh, save it," I say, rounding on him. "Yeah, I almost look like one of you. Happy now? Happy that I sucked it in long enough to fit into this skirt?"

"Em, you always look—"

"Like a bum, yeah, yeah. I'm not in the mood tonight, Zack," I say.

"I wasn't going to say that. It's just tonight you look different, like a girl who can change her colors at will. It's stunning, actually."

I shake my head at him. Kind of want to punch him in the shoulder right now, but resist. "Whatever," I say. "I wanted to tell you that I figured out my gift." I revolve my gaze all around, realizing the President could be listening, from so far away.

"You have what?" Nona says too loud.

I give her a punishing look and then continue to our seats, dragging the two of them behind me. "I can't tell you about it right now, but soon I will," I say as we slide into our seats.

"Em!" Nona protests.

I flick my eyes to the stage, where the President will soon stand. "Trust me."

"You were right about the...?" She lets the question hang out there.

She's referring to the injections. "I was," I say, nodding and meeting Zack's nervous stare.

"Em, that means—"

"Exactly," I cut him off, knowing the President could be spying on us using his super hearing. "We have our work cut out for us."

"What are we going to do first?" Nona asks, her tone now discreet, bordering on casual. "What can I do?"

"Our first priority is to help a certain someone." I point with my eyes to the stage. "Because that someone's father knows about him."

Zack shakes his head slightly. "Oh no. That's disastrous."

I slip down in the seat, my eyes planted on the stage, my lips hardly moving as I speak. "And I think I'm in a great deal of trouble."

For the second time tonight, Zack does a double take at me; this time I sense fear in his eyes. "What?" he whispers.

I chance a sideways glance at him. "I think my punishment will be worse than the night terror generator."

"What's worse than that?"

"I don't know, but I think I'm going to find out," I say, staring at the back of my father's head. He sits in the front row between my mother and Dee and he's the first one to start clapping when the President takes the stage.

Chapter Twenty-Two

When the applause dies down, the President is still resting his eyes on the podium in front of him. "Tonight we will celebrate a great many things. Tomorrow we awake to a community that is even better than the one we currently have. And each day afterwards will be marked by improvements. But first we have to make some changes." His green eyes finally pull up from the podium and stare out at the middle of the crowd. A shiver actually trembles from my body. Nona slips her hand in mine and squeezes.

"Tonight we will discuss how to expand and reorganize our society so as to benefit everyone," President Vider begins in his salient tone. "It's an incredibly exciting time to be a Reverian. This society started small, just over a hundred years ago. Our forefathers knew the story of the gods, knew Dream Travelers were the golden race, and set up the place we now call home. We have been strategic in growing our population and maintaining our protection over the Middlings. It is time that we expand and spread the greatness we have to others." He smiles, one that's practiced, that looks almost genuine. "Our borders will be expanded to the east by one hundred miles, and this is only the beginning. Homes and more establishments will be built to serve our growing community. Already we have opened our arms to Middlings and they've found a great peace under our care. Very soon we will begin the process of selecting Dream Travelers from across the globe to join us, to be a part of our community. It is only through this growth that we continue our mission. And just think, you all who reside in front of me now are the founding members of this society, which will one day be so great it will have no borders."

Applause rings out. I allow my head to swivel around. The auditorium is full. Almost every Dream Traveler Reverian is here tonight.

The President holds up a hand and the crowd falls silent at once. "I've chosen to lead with this good news, because unfortunately I must also address something which has affected us all in a negative way," he says and then pauses, looking pained. "As you all know, an awful epidemic has befallen our society. One that I've sunk every

110

resource into remedying. I'm of course referring to the generation of Defects, those who are not being gifted with a skill by the gods. It appears that our race is undergoing a slight evolution. And, as is my duty to the Reverians, I have traveled and researched this extensively and found this to be the problem within many Dream Traveler societies."

"Liar," I say under my breath.

The President's firm gaze darts to me. I freeze, feeling his intensity like a laser beam. My anger got the best of me and I let the word slip. For too long he stares through the crowd at where I sit. Finally he clears his throat.

"My investigations have also determined we are evolved in our methods of dealing with this problem," the President says, pride heavy in his tone. "It is this innovation within our society that contributes to the superior quality of life we share. However, this epidemic has caused a great deal of stress and discord within our society. I realize that's unavoidable, given the seriousness of it. Therefore, I have established a plan which will end this imbalance and deliver us to a more euphoric state of being."

The breath I suck in is cold and unfulfilling. My chest is too tense to breathe properly. Nona's hand grips mine firmer. She pulls my hand into her lap and that's when I realize she's trembling.

"It's okay," I mouth to her, although I'm lying.

"I can't even begin to understand how confusing it must be for the Defects who are born Dream Travelers, but not gifted with a skill at puberty. Your pain and anguish weighs on my heart every day."

It's hard for me to keep my eyes on the President as he recites his speech of lies. I want to declare the truth to the Reverians. I want to protest, but I'd only appear like a raving teenager. Then I'd really be in trouble. I bite down on my bottom lip, urging all accusations to stay buried inside me.

"Defects have created a divide within our population," President Vider says, shaking his head at the news. "They're neither true Dream Traveler nor Middling. This divide makes it difficult for us to maintain the critical balance we need to ensure the happiness of everyone, mostly the Middlings. Now that the first of the Defects is about to come to the age where they will be granted their role within the Reverians' occupation system, it is impossible to place them. How can we place a Dream Traveler with no gift in a position of power? How will this appear to the Middlings, who are asked to work the more labor-intensive positions because they're not gifted, not Dream Travelers? You all see the dilemma we face, don't you?"

To my horror the crowd nods in unison and gives a collective, "Yes."

"It has been exceptionally difficult to find a remedy that is fair to all, but I think we have found one," President Vider says, his tone shifting to one of triumph. "And I'm confident that in time everyone will be happier. We have done everything to try and help the Defects achieve their gifts. You all know that. And we're still hopeful that in many cases the gifts will surface for these kids. However, those coming to occupational age will need to go through our process."

That's me.

"Since Defects are neither fully Dream Traveler nor Middling, we think it best to convert them to a single race, one where they will have a sense of belonging," the President booms, his tone carrying its usual enticing quality. "We recognize that it's difficult for Defects to assimilate into the Dream Traveler culture and our studies have confirmed that they feel most comfortable with Middlings."

My father turns his head sideways so I can see his face. Then something that he never does happens. He smiles. It's small, but it instantly makes my stomach turn over twice.

"We now have the technology to convert Defects to Middlings, thereby relieving them of their dream traveling abilities," President Vider says.

What!

"This is great news for this segment of the population because after conversion they no longer have to withstand the painful injections. They no longer have to fret over whether their gift is going to surface. They can relax and enjoy their lives among the Middlings. And really,"—the President stands up tall, flashes a proud smile— "I wish at times I could be a Middling. No one can argue that they're happy here in Austin Valley. We protect and care for them. We ensure they have all their needs met. And now the Defects who have suffered for too long will become valuable members within this race. And I think we can all agree that belonging is more important than any gift. That's what my council and I want for you, the Defects, we want you to belong. We want you to have a place within our society. A chance at having a family, since you can't do that with a Dream Traveler. That could risk passing along your defect. We want you to have a life. And our research has told us that the only way for Defects to truly belong is to fully become a part of the Middling race through conversion; otherwise you'll always be an anomaly and we don't want that."

The crowd actually stands, clapping and cheering. President Vider encourages it by striding out from behind the podium and clapping too. I turn to Zack, who is making the motion of clapping, but no sound emanates from his hands. He says something, but I can't hear him over the deafening applause.

When it quiets down, the auditorium of Reverians dutifully takes their seats.

"Now some Defects may still be worried about the conversion and I understand this. Please know that it doesn't need to happen until age seventeen, right before the occupational stage starts. And since this permanent conversion is a big change to consider we've already had a prominent Reverian family volunteer their Defect." The President's piercing gaze zooms until it's pinned on me. "I'm certain that when the community witnesses this seamless transition then some will elect to do their conversion early. This decision is yours to make, though, since I want you all to feel at ease and happy with this process."

Again applause. I don't clap. Neither does Zack or Nona. I don't chance a single word to them although my head is spinning with strings of worries.

"Like I said at the beginning, we are about to embark on a new age. One I'm excited to share with all of you, as well as newcomers. Our community will grow and those within it will have our support to flourish. If that's not a reason to celebrate tonight, then I'm not sure what is!" The President waves out to the crowd as they give him a standing ovation. This time it's short because he strides to the exit almost immediately.

The overhead lights fade on and the auditorium is a shuffling of excited Reverians, all cheerily making their way to the party.

Zack turns to me, his face starched and white, like the shirt under his jacket. "Em, you have to get out of here now. You have to run. You have to hide."

113

Chapter Twenty-Three

People scurry to the exit, creating a dense bottleneck. The aisle is already clogged with happy Reverians, chatting about the delicacies sure to be served at the celebration. How brainwashed are these people that they are about to toast to a segment of their race being stripped of their ability, all because we have no gift. Because we've been drugged. The President and his conspirators must have figured out that he couldn't keep up the injections and needed a long-term remedy. Convert us to Middlings. Give us happy pills and the chance at a family. It's genius actually. He's fooled an entire population into thinking he's doing right by his people. I keep scanning the crowd looking for a skeptical face, a disapproving one, but everyone wears a smile. Even the kids I see all the time at the lab are laughing, chatting with their friends about the life they'll have now.

That kid named Scott, the one who tried to kiss Nona last year, actually waves at her on his way by. "I'm going to get converted early. You should too," he says to her with a chuckle.

"Oh, gods, I think I'm going to be sick," Nona says, crouched over slightly, holding her stomach.

I rub her back. "It's okay, Nona. You don't have to worry about being converted for a while and I'll never let them do that to you."

She scowls at me. "I'm not worried about me. Zack's right. You have to get—"

"Shhh. And I know. I'm just not sure how yet," I say, staring at the crowd which seems to grow denser somehow.

"Zack?" I say his name like it's a full question, with all the concerns I have right now.

He turns to me. Nods. A look of understanding on his face. "I won't let them do it to you. Don't worry." His eyes scan the crowd. I can see his brain working, trying to piece together a solution to this all. I'm not sure if there's one.

"My stomach *really* hurts," Nona groans.

"I know," I say, rubbing her back again. "I'm sorry."

"No, Em." She snaps her head up from its crouched position and winks at me. "My stomach hurts. I think I'm going to be sick."

Zack and I stand simultaneously, bumping heads as we do. "Sorry," I say, pulling Nona out to the aisle, cutting off a group as we do.

Behind me I hear Zack. "Coming through, sick kid here. Need to get her to the facilities."

The crowd parts like they're water and we're oil, repelling away from us, afraid Nona might vomit all over their shiny clothes. Behind me I feel Zack's hand on my back steering me through the crowd. "At the exit break left," he whispers at my shoulder. "I know a shortcut."

I nod and pretend to have all my attention centered on the sick Nona in front of me. This kid can act. I'm almost convinced she's about to be sick by the pale shade of green her face is turning. We round the corner out of the auditorium into a sea of people, all congregating in small groups. Around the area various buffet stations have been set up. Middling waiters hold trays high in the air, moving through the crowd, ready to serve guests stuffed mushrooms and puffed pastries filled with plum jelly.

We dart around groups, Nona still in the lead. The crowd is growing less dense as we make our way to the back side of the Performance Hall. Zack's smart. He has us taking the exit closest to the trails, so I can get straight into the woods. We weave through a few more groups and a few pillars and come to a shuddering halt. There amongst a crowd of stiff politicians is my father. He looks up at us, no surprise on his face at all. He politely holds up a finger to dismiss himself from the group and takes three long strides in our direction.

"Where are you going in such a hurry?" His eyes are only on me.

"Nona," I say in a rush. "She's—"

"Trying to get Em to the facilities. She's about to be sick, Father," Nona says at my side, grabbing her stomach again. I give her a confused look, but then catch the hidden expression on her face. I know it well. "We're actually both feeling ill. We need to get to the facilities."

I realize now Nona knows if I'm not the one who's sick then there will be no reason for me run off to the facilities, which is my only opportunity to escape.

"And Mr. Conerly, are you unwell also?" my father asks.

115

"No, sir," he says behind me. "I was only helping them to find their way."

"Noble of you." My father turns his eyes on me. "I'm glad I ran into you, Em. Did you get my gift?"

"Yes." Bile rises in my throat. The image of the broken statue swims into my head.

"I have more where that came from."

"Oh," I say, covering my mouth like I might be sick at any second. "Father—"

"You and I have an appointment at the lab. Tonight," he says, a sinister expression in his clear blue eyes. "I see no reason to put off what is the inevitable for you. And you'll set such a superb example for other Defects."

"But the party, Father?" Nona says, tugging on my hand and still clutching her stomach.

"Neither of you look in much condition to attend this party. By the looks of it, you're about to ruin it, Nona."

"Father..." I argue, careful to keep the desperation I feel out of my voice.

"Do you really think you're going to persuade me not to have you converted tonight?" he says, careful to keep his voice low.

I shake my head roughly. "Of course not. It's just that I really think I'm about to be sick," I say, taking a page out of Nona's book, holding my stomach like I'm trying to keep its contents in.

He shakes his head back at me, no remorse on his face. "This is absolutely ridicu—"

"Chief Fuller," a woman says, striding right into our group. She looks as old as Tutu and is wearing a dress that makes Dee's look conservative. Her blue hair hangs in ringlets around her over-ripened face. "I was so hoping you'd tell me more about this expansion. I think it sounds good enough to invest my dead husband's weekend treasury fund into," she says in a gruff voice.

My father eyes me over the old lady's shoulder, then directs his attention back on her. "Of course, Mrs. Carrie. I'd love to." Again he holds up a finger to pause her. Directs his attention to the person my attention failed to notice in a nearby group. "Dee, dear?" he says and my sister's red head perks up.

"Yes, Father?" she says, breaking out of her group and scurrying over.

116

"Do escort your sisters to the facilities and then bring them back to me at once," he says, threading his arm through Mrs. Carrie's withered one, draped in loose skin.

"Of course, Father," Dee says, giving the two of us a menacing stare.

"And if they give you any trouble, be sure to *fire* them in the right direction," my father says, striding away with the old lady in tow.

"You heard Father," Dee says, trying to scoot us with her arm movements.

We break away from Zack and run for the bathrooms like our lives reside somewhere in the toilet bowls. I've never faked being sick, but with the prospects of being converted staring me in the face, it's all feeling less and less like an act as the inevitable draws near.

At the bathroom door, Dee stops. "Do your business," she says, crossing her arms in front of her chest. "I'll be waiting."

I nod and pull Nona into the first open stall. From the sounds of it no one else is in here. I kneel down low so that I'm looking up at her. "We've got to distract her."

"She's Dee. She's as easily distracted as a newborn puppy. Just leave that up to me."

I nod, glad my partner in crime is Nona. "Okay, well, I've got to run after that."

"I know," she says, sounding too grown up all of a sudden.

"I'm not sure how long I'll be gone."

"It's all right."

"Nona," I say, gripping her hand, which is almost as big as mine now. "I'm coming back for you. There's no way in hell they're doing anything to you or me. You understand?"

She only nods. A look of pure determination in her eyes.

"Okay, are you ready to go out and face the 'evil one'?" It's what we used to call Dee, but it made her so mad she started burning all our clothes so we stopped.

"I'm ready."

We exit the bathroom door and there standing, like a troll guarding a bridge, is Dee. She looks unhappy about her role to say the least. "Come on," she says, pointing at the spot in front of her. "I want to see you march to Father. Really march, like your existence as a Dream Traveler is staked on it." She giggles. "Oh, well, I guess that's a bad example since it's already gone."

Nona and I take the position in front of her and start walking, slowly weaving our way through the crowd.

"Oh, I do hope you visit after you're converted, Em," Dee says behind us. "Maybe you'll do a better job with my nails than Rachel." She gives a high-pitched squeal. "Oh, or maybe you can clean my toilet. I really would love it if you were the one instead of Heather. She's awful. Never does a good enough job. I'm sure you'll make a fine Middling."

I want to run, but I know if I do Dee will set me on fire. I keep marching, giving sideways glances at Nona, waiting for her diversion. Then out of nowhere I hear Dee squeal delightedly.

"Where have you been all night?" Zack says behind me. I wheel around to spot him with an arm wrapped around Dee's waist, pulling her into him, a hungry look on his face.

"Family duties," she says, waving at us, not taking her eyes off his penetrating stare. She arches her back, making me think she's going to fall back in a swoon.

"Oh, that's too bad," he says, bringing his chin down low on her neck. "I was hoping we could pick up where we left off at the ball."

She giggles, backs away from him, but only slightly. Her eyes flick to us with a scowl before eagerly returning to his. "I'll be back in just a few," Dee says, running her black-painted fingernail down his jacket and then bites down on her red bottom lip. "I'm obligated to escort my dear sisters back to our father."

"I do understand that," Zack says, grabbing the hand she has on him and pulling her back in close. "It's just that I can't stay long. I have early meetings tomorrow."

Dee doesn't take her eyes off Zack. "Nona," she says in a commanding voice. "Take Em to Father now. Don't dawdle or otherwise I'll burn everything you own."

Nona stands at attention and nods. "Yes," she says and grabs my hand, pulling me forward through the crowd.

I have only a second to turn back and watch Dee wrap her arms around Zack's neck and pull him down for an unexpected kiss, one he flinches against. I owe him big for making that awful sacrifice to protect me.

Nona yanks me forward, but then backtracks through the crowd until we're at a side door. "Okay," she says almost out of breath. "Get out of here."

"Nona, I meant what I said, I'll—"

"Yeah, yeah, get out of here."

"But Father, he'll be looking for me," I say.

"That's why I'm going to go distract him."

"How are you going to do that?"

"I'm going to go barf on his shoes."

I smile at her, my heart overflowing with love. "You'd do that for me?"

"That and more, now get out of here."

I push open the door and give her one last look. "I love you more than anything Nona."

"I know," she says and I swear I spy the smallest of tears in the bravest of eyes.

Chapter Twenty-Four

The summer night air greets me like a warm blanket after the frigid air conditioning in the performance hall. I tear off my heels at the door and throw them into the ground cover surrounding the courtyard. They instantly sink below the dense ivy. Sucking in a rugged breath, I take a final look over my shoulder and then set off in a jog. I want to move faster, need to, but my tight pencil skirt prevents it. Maybe my mother knew I was going to try and run away tonight and that's why she put me in something that constricts my legs from moving properly.

Since I'm not sure how long Nona's diversion will buy me I have to do the one thing they'll never expect. I forgo the paths that snake in and out of the gardens and various courtyards. The ones that meander through the park. Instead, I climb up the hill in front of me that divides the buildings of Central Boulevard from the park and then the surrounding hiking trails.

The hill I'm trespassing raises up at a forty-five-degree angle and is dense at the bottom with the ivy ground cover. It's actually easier to cross this section. Once I arrive to the forested part, it's much harder to find something to grab onto. I'm climbing, digging my nails into the dirt and pulling, pushing, doing whatever it takes to secure every hold. Several times I miss and slide back down a few inches. My calves burn from the intensity of the climb and my shirt is already covered in dirt, but somehow I manage to get up the hill.

The good news is that I'm off the main path and also have a good view of it from up here, so I won't get lost. The bad news is that I'll have to hike through uncleared territory the whole way. The hiking trail would have given me three miles of easy path. Then regardless I'd have to detour and fight the overgrowth to get to Rogue's camp. Now I'll have almost the full four miles of untamed forest to wrestle with. Barefoot. I nod at the woods. "Bring it on," I say, as I dart forward, knowing the forest can't do worse to me than my father. Than my own people.

I'm bleeding and winded by the time I make it to his camp. I've moved so fast at times that I felt my heart was going to beat out of my chest. And my neck is sore from constantly whipping my head over my shoulder to see if I'm being followed. Every noise made me pause and then charge ahead faster.

As soon as I saw a small jagged rock, about a half a mile into the run, I grabbed it and cut a hole into my tight pencil skirt and ripped the fabric, freeing my legs. When I set off again I was able to really run, sprint, tear through the brush, letting it scratch and poke and stab me. And I didn't stop once because my only advantage is that I have a head start.

Will my father have people look for me in the forest?

My father is all logic. I believe he would think that a person dressed in formal attire would never venture into the woods. They'd stay on the roads, scamper through the alleyways, and maybe find a Middling to hide them. Once they had real shoes they'd run north, where the closest border is and the terrain is easiest to pass. They'd escape Austin Valley the logical way. There's no way someone in their right mind would run straight into the woods unprepared, climb up the tallest hills in the Valley. I hope that's how my father thinks.

I'm not as quiet as Nona. She probably could have snuck up on Rogue without him noticing. When I arrive he's pulling back the flap to the tent, holding a dim lantern in his hand. I stop for the first time in four miles and my legs instantly turn to jelly. Sweat trickles down my back. The light burns my eyes which have adjusted to the darkened forest. Still it allows me to see his face, which first takes on a look of disbelief, followed by absolute concern. His eyes dart to my skirt ripped up to mid-thigh, then to my dirt-stained silk blouse, ripped in multiple places, and finally to my face, which is scratched and hot from the long trek.

"Em?" Rogue says, taking hurried steps to me. "Are you all right?"

I nod. It's so good to see him. Instantly makes me lighten. I sway as I try to will my bleeding feet forward. "Is there room enough in that tent for two people?" I say, and the smile I give makes the scratches on my face sting.

Swiftly he sets the lantern on the ground, not taking his eyes off me. Then he engulfs me in his arms and I allow some of my bodyweight to sink against him. He pulls back, but still holds me up. "If that other person is you, then absolutely."

***

121

"I knew that was my father's eventual plan, but I never thought he'd figure out how to do it," Rogue says. I told him all about tonight's announcement and my escape from conversion as I washed my face, hair, and feet using a bucket of water he had.

"You can come in," I say, unzipping the tent and tossing my dirty shirt out. Rogue had given me one of his shirts. I had to roll up the red and blue flannel sleeves several times to make it work, but it's warm and clean and that's what counts. Rogue ducks into the tent and I slide back to make room for him. He's carrying a first-aid kit. I eye it and then him. The light from the lantern isn't bright enough for me to see his eyes well, but I see the sly smile he's wearing, seems to always be wearing.

"I'm fine, Rogue," I say, scooching back to the far corner of the tent, which still doesn't put much space between us.

"Oh, no you're not." His eyes are pinned on my feet and legs, which I'm having a hard time hiding while still being modest in my torn skirt. "I'm playing doctor, so get over here."

I roll my eyes, shake my head, but don't move when he approaches. Without asking permission he goes to work cleaning the cuts on my feet and legs with an alcohol swab. Just the smell of the astringent makes me cringe, reminding me of the injections.

"How did you know what your father was planning?" I ask, watching him work.

"It's how I found out about the injections. I knew something was wrong, so just like you, I snuck into my father's office. He showed up with a few of his council members and I had to hide," he says, wrapping a bandage on my foot and then slipping one of his clean socks over it. He's so much stronger than he was a few years ago, but also more gentle. Tamed somehow. "The Council were discussing their master plan. The injections. The Middlings and testing on their children. And the conversion. This was before I left, several years ago, so the conversion wasn't something they thought was gonna work."

"Your father didn't sense you in his office?" I ask, thinking of how heightened my senses had been when I was leeching him.

Rogue flips his head up, a look of surprise on his face. "You know about his gift? How? No one does."

A smile spreads across my face. "I experienced his gift firsthand."

I explain what Ren told me about leeches and how I am one.

"You *have* to show me this. I want you to leech me," Rogue says, moving onto my other foot.

I laugh and shake my head. "I had two injections today. My gift won't come back until tomorrow probably."

"Well, as soon as it does," Rogue says, his eyes bright with enthusiasm.

"Your father knows you're alive. Knows you're hiding in the Valley."

Rogue nods, his eyes trained on the scratches on my legs. "Yeah, I know. You asked if my father sensed me in his office? Well, he did, but not at first, only after the Council members left. I thought he was gonna murder me right there. Somehow I slipped past him and ran. I didn't stop running, not until I was outside the Northern border," he says as he dabs ointment on a scratch along my leg.

I open my mouth, a volley of sympathies wanting to come out, but I remain silent. Finally I just shake my head. I've been as betrayed by my father as Rogue was by his, and still I don't know how to respond. I guess I'm unsure how I feel about it. Soon it will hit me.

"So I kissed you," Rogue says, flicking his eyes up to mine.

I immediately look away. "I remember," I say without inflection.

"Are you mad about it?" he says, a hint of amusement in his tone.

"Why would I be?"

"Because we're friends and—"

"No, we *were* friends and then you died," I say, giving him a mock scowl.

He smirks and shuffles forward until he's beside me. "I assure you, I'm very much alive."

"Maybe you are. Maybe you aren't. Maybe another of my gifts is I can see ghosts," I joke.

He brushes my hair out of my face, tips my chin sideways, and inspects the many scratches on my cheek. "Do I feel like a ghost?" he finally says.

No, he feels the opposite of a ghost. He's warm, full of life.

I can't help but to suck in a sharp breath when the alcohol pad slides across my cheekbone. "You really seem to know what you're doing," I say, keeping still so Rogue can finish with my face and finally release me from this torture.

"Well, I've become pretty self-sufficient over the years."

"Yeah, I guess you had to," I say, thinking about all that I still don't know about him.

"So you and I are fugitives. Us against the Reverians," he says a lightness in his voice.

"Yeah," I say, feeling heavy. Then it really hits me like a storm cloud. I've left everything I've ever known or had behind. I can never go back. Not really. I'll get Nona out, but there will be no more late-night chats with Tutu or pastries from Giorgio or afternoons working beside Dean. I've emancipated myself but I don't feel free. I feel scared. Nervous. Intimidated.

"Em?" Rogue says, pulling my attention out of my thoughts.

"Yes."

He looks suddenly serious. "The headaches are gonna come on after the injections wear off. Remember to focus on your breath. Don't hold it. And know the pain will be gone soon."

The headaches. I'd forgotten. The thought of having an attack like I witnessed Rogue have is terrifying, but not more so than the idea of being converted. "Okay."

"Oh, and I'll be right here when they do," he says.

I smile at him. "Well, we just have to get the meds. Zack's trying to find an inventory list for the labs. That should tell us where they're kept. But we shouldn't break into the lab until my gift comes back."

"Yes, I agree," Rogue says, stretching out beside me. He's easily the length of the tent, but there's still plenty of room for the both of us since I'm small. "And how do you suppose we occupy our time until then?" He folds his arms and tucks them behind his head, giving me a sideways smile.

I lay back, slipping one of the pillows he gave me under my head. My muscles are already starting to fatigue from the run. "Rogue, have you ever been to Amsterdam?"

He squints at me, like he wasn't expecting that question. "Of course."

"Well, I haven't. I've never dream traveled without supervision. Never had the free rein to explore like I want to."

A smile lights up his eyes as he stares at the ceiling of the tent. "Oh, yes, the first time is indeed the best."

"Would you take me around Amsterdam tonight?" I ask, feeling a little shy with the question.

He slides his gaze toward me and then back. "It would be my pleasure."

"Is it safe to dream travel tonight? Do you think our bodies will be safe here?"

"It will be fine," Rogue says, all confidence.

"What about your father? Do you think he could track me?"

"He could, but a) I don't think he'll have the inclination, and b) there's no way he's finding you here," he says, pushing his messy hair back.

"What makes you so sure?" I ask.

"My father will think this is a bear's den."

"Why would he think that?"

"Because I doused the perimeter with bear urine," he says.

"Won't that attract bears?"

"I'm less afraid of bears than my father."

"True," I say, impressed at how crafty Rogue has gotten.

He closes his eyes and a mischievous smile graces his lips. "Find me in De Wallen in Amsterdam. I'll see you in a few."

Chapter Twenty-Five

"You took me to the Red Light District?" I say in shock as soon as I find Rogue. He's leaning both his elbows on a bridge and staring out over the canal, a beautiful nonchalance in his stance.

"Well, you're the rebel who picked this liberal city. And this is actually the most beautiful part of Amsterdam in my opinion," he says, staring at the arched rooftops. "Most people judge it only on its promiscuous aspects, but if you look closer you'll find some real beauty."

I eye a tall brunette who's standing in a display window. She's wearing a thong and a bra and changing her provocative pose as each new prospective customer strolls by. "Yeah, *real* beauty." I stare at her, something I'd never do in person, but those who aren't dream traveling can't see those who are. We exist in the same world, different dimension.

Rogue offers me his arm. "How about a tour of this fine district?"

I eye his arm and then the multiple shops behind him, all lit with dim red lights and their merchandise prancing around in the doorways or windows. "When I said 'Amsterdam' I was more thinking a museum or a historical center."

"You don't get any more historical than this," Rogue says, taking it upon himself to thread his arm through mine and tug me to the end of the bridge and along the canal. "Some of the architecture here is from the fourteenth century."

He directs me down a cobbled side street. The buildings lean at strange angles, giving them a unique charm. It's undeniably an atmosphere of openness, which entices my caged curiosity. Before too long, I've forgotten my initial anger and find we're easily strolling the streets. I mostly take in the sights and Rogue seems to be amused by my interest in the happenings around me.

"Do you have any questions about the city?" he finally asks.

"Not about the city," I say, sweeping my eyes over the strange street we just walked past.

"Oh, so you have questions about other things. I should have guessed. Fire away, babe," he says coolly.

"What are your dogs named?" I ask. The idea of having pets intrigues me. We're not allowed to have them in Austin Valley. Animals are kept at the ranch, but that's run by Middlings.

"The Lab is Poseidon, because I can't keep him out of the creek, and the shepherd is Athena."

"Oh, is the cow named after a Greek god too?"

"I call her 'A-lot-a-work,'" he says.

I laugh. "Are they all right while you're gone?"

"I've checked on them a few times while dream traveling. They're fine."

I slip out of his arm and approach the canal. *I've always wondered...* I tip over the surface of the water and watch for my reflection. It doesn't shimmer there like it would if I was in physical form. I turn around and smile at Rogue, happy to have another question in my mind answered.

The look on his face is pure amusement, like he's watching an alien explore Earth for the first time. "So, what's your plan, Em? Now that you're a deserter?"

"First, I'm going to break into the lab and get us meds," I say. "Then I'm going to get Nona out. We'll figure out what to do next after that."

He nods, a quiet smile in his eyes. "It would be pretty easy to build an extra room or two onto my house. Might give you a place to start or stay depending on what you decide."

I can't hide the look that makes my face lengthen with surprise and astonishment. "Really?"

"Really."

"Thank you," I say, totally sheepishly. "That's so kind of—"

"I'd be doing it for purely selfish reasons, of course," he says, his dimple surfacing with his smile.

"Oh...really?" I say, not able to bring my eyes to his all of a sudden.

"Well, yeah. I need farmhands."

I laugh, grateful for his joke, which instantly breaks up the budding tension. "Do you have a garden at this house of yours?"

Another nod. "Caterpillars are a problem this year."

"Yeah, we had a problem with them too at the farm. Dean and I concocted a pepper spray solution that really works," I say.

"You still spend your free hours at the farm, huh?"

"Where else would I?"

"It's summertime, Em. Last one before you're assigned an occupation. Most take advantage of that last bit of freedom," Rogue says.

"Well, I think there's no better way to spend my freedom. And I won't ever be assigned an occupation...well, unless they catch me."

Rogue shakes his head sharply. "They won't find you. Convert you. Don't worry."

His short sentences are incredibly effective at erasing my worry. "Zack does the same as me. He spends all his free time at the Government Center. He's interning under my father."

Rogue whistles, his eyes lighting up. "Now there's a guy, under the right circumstances, who could make some real changes. Something great lives in Zack, something that could start a revolution."

"That's what I tell him."

Rogue shakes his head, his unkempt hair falling on his forehead. "It used to burn me up inside that you two were there living your lives together and I was on the outside."

I halt. Wait for him to turn around. His face unreadable. "Then I really don't understand why you didn't contact me. At least tell me that you were alive? Tell me the truth before now?"

He nods, seeming to understand my plight. "I didn't want to risk getting you in trouble. And I pictured you were happy in Austin Valley and I didn't want to ruin that. But like I said, I also assumed you and Zack were getting closer and that made me jealous for some reason. Now that I see that you did, it actually makes me happy."

"Why?"

He shrugs. "'Cause you needed each other."

"Well, I need Zack, but he's probably fine without me."

"I doubt that," Rogue says.

I look up as we walk, enjoying the way flowers overflow from planters on various second-story windows. And under my feet the streets are as clean as we keep ours in Austin Valley, but the vibe is the opposite. We've walked to a part of the district that appears a little more innocent than where we started. And I realize I didn't mind it so much back there. It was fascinating for my eyes to take in such a bizarre scene, one I'd only overheard a Middling transplant speak about once. Unfortunately, my education in cultures and geography is limited, but that's all about to change.

My inquisitive eyes continue roaming over all the details around me when I realize Rogue is staring at me. "What?" I ask, suddenly a little self-conscious.

He stops and I turn around and watch him study me, a curious look in his eyes. "Nothing. Just marveling at how you're still so inquisitive."

"Oh, did you expect that to change?" I ask.

"Not sure what I expected."

I continue to walk and then I stop, a weird uninvited worry creeping into my head. "When you said Nona and I could stay with you…"

He stops, regards me a bit cautiously. "Yes?"

"Well, do you have other people living with you?"

He laughs. "Do you think I'm shacking up with someone? That I have a family or something?"

"I don't know," I say, embarrassment tightening around my insides.

"Well, I don't. I live alone," Rogue says.

"And you always have?"

He gives me a sideways look. Squints at me. "Yes. Why?"

"Just figured…"

"What? That I go around kissing girls and offering to have them live with me?"

"Well, maybe."

He laughs, one so loud and genuine, it actually breaks up the tension building in my chest. "Well, I don't. I spent the last four years alone. Hard to explain to people where I'm from and about my condition."

"Oh," I say, not having moved.

He slips his hands into his faded blue jean pockets, almost looking a little nervous, although that would be a first for him. "*And* I spent a lot of those years thinking about you."

"Me?" I squeak out.

"Yes, you," he says, chuckling. "You know, right before I ran away, I was gonna ask you on a date. A real one. Not a playdate and not with Zack tagging along."

I would have been twelve. He would have been thirteen. I clench my eyes together and bury my face in my hands, giggling.

"Are you laughing at me?" Rogue asks with a smile in his voice.

"Yes," I say, pulling my hands away to catch the amused look on his face. "I mean no. I'm mostly laughing because the idea would have been preposterous to me. I would have said no."

"Because you had a crush on Zack?"

"No!" I say in embarrassment.

He threads his strong arms across his chest and gives me a challenging look. "Oh, come on, you've always favored him in that way. It was kind of obvious. And that's another reason I never came back and all. I figured you two matched up. Kind of surprised that you didn't."

I shake my head at how adorably interesting all these insights are. "Well, maybe I did long ago—favor him—but after you 'died,'" I say, using air quotes with my fingers, "we bonded more, but only as friends. And that's what we needed."

He nods. "Sorry my bogus death hurt you two so much. If things could have been diff—"

"Your father tried to kill you." I step forward and grab his hand. Squeeze it. It's so much bigger than mine. "Don't apologize for doing what you had to to survive. I get it now."

He eyes my hand in his. "Why would you have turned me down all those years ago?"

"Because my father wouldn't have allowed it. You're the President's son. He encouraged our friendship, instigated it originally, but always warned me to be nice to you. Not to create any friction that might harm his position with the President."

"I see you disobeyed your father even then. You were never nice to me," Rogue says with a grin.

I smile. Nod. "Well, so I'd have turned you down because if things went poorly between us then it could have negatively affected my father."

Rogue nods, seeming to remember how stupid it is that family relationships are arranged for political reasons in Austin Valley. "Well, if the idea of that date came as a shock, then you probably don't realize I've liked you since I could walk."

"What?"

He smiles, looking almost proud at causing that reaction in me. "If my nanny is to be believed then you're who encouraged me to take my first step." He pulls my hand up and directs it around his back so we're closer. "She says I walked so I could get to you on the other side of the room. I don't remember it, but it sounds like something I'd do."

Being given this moment, hearing Rogue's words, is a stolen dream. A forbidden one. One I never dared to have. And never before have I so badly wanted to be a criminal. "Are you kidding me?" I say, sliding my other hand around to his shoulder.

"I kid about a lot of things, but how I feel about Em Fuller isn't one of them."

"I don't know, Rogue," I say, shaking my head at him. "It's a little hard to believe that I never knew all this. That I missed so much for so long."

He gives me a sideways glance. A clever gleam in his eyes. "Oh, I don't know. I'd venture to say you miss more than you realize."

"What does that mean?"

He waves his hand at me, dismissing my demanding look. "I just meant the whole being hoodwinked by our government."

"No, you didn't," I say, spying the guilty look on his face. "What else do I miss?"

He shakes his head. "That's all. Hey, enough of this. I vote we play hide-and-seek. You pick the next location."

As kids we talked about playing this game while dream traveling in fantastic places, fantasized about it. And now it was actually coming to fruition. "The Louvre," I say.

"You're it," Rogue says, and disappears.

Chapter Twenty-Six

After eight hours of exploring and running around museums, monasteries, and the Great Wall of China, I awake in the tent to find my body cuddled against Rogue's. My head lies on his chest and my arm drapes across his abdomen. Somehow as my subconscious dream traveled the globe, my body found its way over to Rogue's side of the tent. Besides from our brief embrace in Amsterdam, he kept his distance the rest of the night, probably because he was trying to hide from me. Even so, I'm embarrassed by how intertwined I've made my body with his while we slept.

Gingerly I pick up my arm and bring it back to my body. He hasn't stirred yet and was still searching the Great Pyramid of Giza when I left him. If I'm swift then I can roll back to my side of the tent before he awakes. However, my first attempt is met with a small snag. Literally. My hair is locked under his arm. Angling my head up and away I manage to free my long strands with a gentle pull. I'm just about to scoot back when Rogue's arm circles my waist and pins me to him. "Where you going?" he says against the top of my head.

"I was just—"

"Stay here." He brings his other arm around, locking me in place.

I can't help but smile into his chest. "Okay," I say. My dream travels with Rogue last night had been absolutely perfect. Deliriously so. I hadn't laughed that much since…well, since before he disappeared. And every single moment had the backdrop of an incredible location I was free to explore at will. We talked between games and in one night I found the bond we always shared grew exponentially. And also I kept realizing he was someone new to me, not the same boy I grew up with anymore. His mannerisms were as familiar as Nona's, and then there was a host of mysteries behind his green eyes that intrigued me.

"I'd ask you how you slept, but I'm fairly certain I already know," Rogue says, his voice sounding thick with sleep. He pulls a fleece blanket from the side and across us, making sure it covers my back. "In my haste to get to Amsterdam I forgot to cover us up."

I let go of the reservations I awoke with and snuggle into him. He smells of pine and campfire. "I think I figured out how to stay warm during the night."

"Yes, I see you did," Rogue says.

Outside the tent the forest is stirring to life as the sun streams over the hills opposite of us. Waking up to the songs of birds reminds me of my childhood.

"Hey," he says.

I flip my head up and stare into his green eyes; his eyelashes are impossibly long. The stubble on his face is a little longer, although I love it. No Dream Traveler is allowed to leave their house in Austin Valley unshaven. It's such a handsome look and makes Rogue appear more perfect in his unkemptness.

"Yes?"

He cranes his neck until his lips are close to mine. His breath is warm in the crisp morning air. I scoot up, making it so he doesn't have to bend so much. He pauses an inch away.

"Em?" Rogue whispers.

"What?"

"I want you to leech me."

I deflate slightly. Sigh and roll off him to the side. "I don't think it's a good idea."

He rolls over on his side, propping his head up on his bent elbow. "And I think it's a fantastic one. You said yourself you have to figure out how to unleash the power you leech."

"But Rogue, I could hurt you. Tammy looked exhausted at the lab, like she was going to pass out."

"You might hurt me, but just a little and I don't mind. I wanna see it."

"Rogue."

"Em," he says, mocking my tone. "I won't kiss you if you don't. Not anymore."

I purse my lips at him. "You're so immature."

"I know you are but what am I?" He leans in close, tempting me, his breath on my lips. "Leech me, Em."

"Oh, fine," I acquiesce.

He flashes a brilliant smile before pressing his lips into mine.

"I'm not even sure how to do it," I say once we're outside, stationed in front of the tent. "When I did it to Tammy I was scared, and with your father I was terrified."

"Yes, fear is a great motivator. You just have to find a similar one. Think of preserving yourself maybe, like you were when my father tried his intimidation tactic," Rogue says, his face haunted by something.

I close my eyes and picture I'm running through the woods again. I think of the need to get away from my father, from the President. I think about surviving as the gods intended me and not being altered by the injections. I feel that motivation inside me stir. "Now what?" I say, snapping my eyes open.

Rogue unfolds his fingers and sitting in the palm of his hand is a silver compass. "Take this using my apportation ability."

I don't have the slightest idea how that ability works, but I didn't know how President Vider's did either. It was all instinct inside me, the way I'm sure Rogue's is for him. With intense focus I picture the compass popping out of his hand and into mine. I desire it to be in my possession. And as second after second ticks by it stays sitting firmly in his palm. "Maybe it hasn't been long enough since the injection."

"Maybe, but my guess is that it has," Rogue says. "We dream traveled the whole night and you'll find it's incredibly regenerative. That's why my father only allows Reverians to do it one hour, one night a week. Otherwise everyone's skills would be more powerful."

"But I've dream traveled illegally before and it didn't combat the injections."

"How long did you dream travel on these occasions?"

"An hour or two," I say.

"Yeah, well, we dream traveled for twelve hours," Rogue says confidently. "Your gift might be weak, but it will be there. Now try thinking of a different motivator, really feeling it."

I think of Nona. Of protecting her. Of taking something in order to protect her. Of stealing whatever it takes to keep her safe. I look at Rogue and for a second I picture he has what I need for this. That all I need is to borrow it from him and that it really belongs to me anyway.

Rogue slumps slightly, lets his head fall and then looks at me under hooded eyes. "It worked."

"What? How do you know?"

"Besides that I'm suddenly in desperate need of a nap?"

"Oh."

He opens his fingers again and the compass twinkles back at me. "Take it."

Not even a full second passes before the compass disappears from his hand. I open mine thinking it must already be there, but it's not.

"There's always a slight delay," Rogue says, staring at my hand.

And just as he finishes his sentence I feel the slight weight of the compass in my palm. It's warm from Rogue's skin. I squeeze my fingers around it and allow a smile to unfurl.

"Now that's cool!" Rogue says, giving me an exhausted smile. "If it's even possible I'm even more attracted to you now. You can do anything you want! Have any power you decide. You're like the queen of super powers."

I smile back at him shyly, opening my fingers again to spy the compass in my hand. It's beautiful, engraved with the initials "RV" on the back.

"My mother gave it to me," Rogue says when my questioning eyes flick up to his.

I remember now the part of Rogue's past that I'd forgotten. His mother, Violet, died when he was five. Since a Reverian rarely dies before old age, it was considered strange, but no explanation was given about her death. Rogue spoke about it rarely, but I know it weighed on him all the time. I open my mouth to ask the question I've always wondered, but he cuts me off.

"Now we need to find how you unleash the energy."

"How do I do that?"

"Hmmmm... Do you feel the energy?"

"I don't know. Maybe," I say, closing my eyes, concentrating on the depths of my insides. Not the internal ones, but the energetic part of me. "There does seem to be something new, like a buzzing light. That's the best way I can describe it."

"Focus on expelling that."

"Okay," I say tentatively.

"First though." Rogue stands, grabs both my shoulders, and angles them so I'm facing him on profile. He nods at me. "I don't want to get blown up or whatever it is you can do."

I give him a devilish smile. "Don't cross me, Rogue."

"Noted. And I never would anyway," he says, winking at me. "Okay, here goes nothing."

"Says the girl who just sucked my gorgeous energy out of me leaving me exhausted," Rogue says with a chuckle, taking a seat again on a large rock.

I smile at him. "Remember, I've had this hidden from me for almost four years."

He nods and pushes his hand at me, imploring me to focus on the task. I think of pushing the buzzing light out of me. For some reason I see it with a tinge of blue. My instinct tells me to raise my hand. I point it out in front of me, aware I look like a loon. I reverse the feeling from before when I leeched the power from Rogue. I focus on letting it go, pushing it out of me. And then, although I'd been looking for the release, something quite unexpected happens.

"Whoa!" Rogue says and then laughs in astonishment. "Was that what I think it was?"

Chapter Twenty-Seven

Four more times Rogue makes me leech him, explaining that I need to have the process built into my motor memory like walking. He's stretched out in the tent when Zack approaches. I'd been paranoid all day that someone might be searching for us, so I'd been watching for the slightest sign of movement in the distant woods when I spotted Zack's blond hair. I toss a packet of granola at Rogue and rush off to meet Zack.

He darts forward when he catches sight of me. His arms wrap around me in a way I've never known from him and he twirls me around with an overexuberant excitement, lifting me off the ground. "You're all right?" he asks, holding me out at arm's length.

"I'm fine," I say.

"I've been so worried about you," he says, and from the lines under his eyes I know he's telling the truth.

"Thanks for taking care of Dee. Not a bad job, I guess, considering," I say, giving him a sly smile. He shakes his head at me, his eyes not finding mine.

"You're welcome, but it was actually an awful job," Zack says. "Still worth it to protect you."

"Come on," I say, tugging him toward the camp excitedly. "I have something to tell you."

Zack stops, skepticism and caution swathing his features as soon as he arrives in front of the tent. First his eyes stare at Rogue, who's half asleep, and then to me. His gaze follows down to my still ripped skirt and then to my face. He slides the mailbag he has slung across his shoulder off and hands it to me. "I brought you some clothes. Thought you'd need them. They're my mother's and a few things Nona was able to round up as well."

"Thanks," I say, rummaging through it to find a pair of shoes. I'm overly excited by the idea of having something besides Rogue's oversized socks to wear.

"Em, are you really okay? You got here all right?" Zack asks again, taking in my ridiculous getup.

"Beside from breaking every fashion law in the city, I'm fine. A little bruised, but Rogue fixed me up."

137

Rogue smiles from his place lying flat on his back in the tent, his eyes closed, but his ears apparently listening. "I did, indeed."

Zack's eyebrows knit together, a question on his face, but I cut him off before he can ask it.

"What's going on in the Valley?"

"Your father's madder than I've ever seen him. He gave Dee two days of being hooked to the night terror generator. Nona would be in extreme trouble, but she's mysteriously come down with whatever you had and is under quarantine. It was your tutu who actually handed your belongings off to me."

I smile, realizing that Nona and my tutu are going to be all right as long as they have each other.

"Your father is having the Middling neighborhoods searched for you," Zack continues. "He's already had the farm shut down for the day for a full sweep. And border patrols have been stationed at the north and east end."

"They don't suspect this end?" I ask.

"No, they don't think you'd be able to get over this or the southern pass."

"Fools," Rogue sings from the tent, his eyes still closed.

"Rogue, are you okay?" Zack says, ducking down and checking on Rogue laid out under the green mesh of the tent. "What has you looking so exhausted?"

Without opening an eye, Rogue points straight at me. "It would be that girl, brother. She damn near killed me. Exhausted me to hell, but I begged her to do it, so who am I to blame."

I laugh and want to simultaneously slap and kiss him.

Zack twists around, a confounded look on his face.

"You were warned," I say to Rogue.

"And I don't regret a minute of it," Rogue says, stretching up to a sitting position. Looking somehow adorably half drunk, he says to Zack, "It's her gift. You have to see it." He slides his eyes to me, the effort looking excruciatingly difficult. "Show him, Em."

Zack looks at me with disbelief. "You did that to him? Using your gift?"

I nod.

"Show me," he says eagerly.

"No," I argue. "Are you paying attention? Look at what I did to Rogue," I say, pointing to him half slouched in the tent.

"Worth it," he sings again, a chuckle in his voice.

"Oh, shush it, Rogue." I turn to Zack. "I think it's best that I explain my gift to you. That's the safe option."

"That's the boring one," Rogue says. "Show him. It's more fun."

"For who?" I say, turning to Rogue and planting my hands on my hips.

"For me," he says, shaking his head like he's trying to shake off the tiredness, his hair whipping around wildly. He pushes it back with both hands, but it's still a complete mess. "I wanna see his face."

"Em," Zack says, taking a seat on the rock beside the campfire, "I've been dying for you to get your gift. Show me."

"You don't understand though. I'll drain your energy."

"That's your gift?" Zack says, looking at me, confused.

"Oh no, brother. That's only part of it," Rogue says, looking proud.

"Do it, Em," Zack says, nodding, looking to prepare himself internally. "I'll be fine."

"Are you sure?" I ask.

"Yes."

"Okay," I say.

First, I evoke the motivation that I built into my leeching protocol the last two times I did this to Rogue. He's right that practicing makes the process easier. Now it feels simple, like I've done it a hundred times. Zack doesn't slump or change in appearance at all, but still I feel the space in my body change, like something new has entered me.

I know with certainty that in Zack's breast pocket his lucky charm resides. He's religious about keeping it there. Always has been. With a skill I don't own I slip it out of his pocket and allow it to hover just in his line of vision. It takes a second or two for his eyes to register the coin hanging in the air a foot and a half in front of his face.

He recognizes it and snatches it from the air. Stares at it in his hands and then me.

"Did you just do that?"

I nod, feeling a little guilty for taking his prized charm from him.

"You're telekinetic?" he says with elated astonishment.

"No," I say, muffling my laugh. "You are."

"Wait," he says, holding up his hand. "Did you just steal my gift?"

"Borrow," I say.

"That's amazing. And you can do that to anyone?"

I nod, smiling at the dirt, unable to look at Zack directly to catch the smile he has to be wearing right now.

"That's not even the best part," Rogue says, his words a little slurred but still sounding giddy. "Show him," he encourages.

I turn, line my shoulders up in front of the dry kindling in the campfire. My nervous eyes hover over it and then flick to Rogue's. He's sitting all the way up, a smile tucked at the corner of his mouth. He encourages with a nod.

And as though controlled by instinct, I will the energy I leeched out of Zack out of my body. My hand raises up. From it a bolt of electricity shoots out and lands in the pit, igniting it into a spark and then lighting the dry wood, turning it to a small fire.

Zack jumps up, startled.

"Now *that's* the best part!" Rogue says.

"You did that? How?" Zack asks, staring at me and then the fire I created.

"I'm a leech," I say, like that should mean anything to him.

"And she's electrokinetic," Rogue says, lying back down.

Zack steps forward and grabs my hand, eyeing it like he's looking for holes or damage. He shakes his head. "I've never heard of anything like that."

"I told you, you had to see it," Rogue says with a smile, his eyes closed again. "You can lay down next to me if you want to, brother."

Zack's eyelids slip closed for a second longer than I expected. He takes in a breath and opens them. "I'm a little tired, but fine mostly."

"Yeah, she steals your gift, turns it into electricity, and sucks the life right out of you," Rogue says with a whistle, like he's enjoying the drained state I put him in. "Pretty cool, huh?"

"Yes," Zack says, looking at me in disbelief. "Em, that's—"

I smile at him, wave him off, and turn away before he can finish his thought. I walk over to the tent, carrying the bag of clothes Zack brought, and toe Rogue's mostly lifeless body. "Hey, can I have the tent for a second. I want to change."

He opens one eye and smiles at me. "Of course, babe." He sits up, a groan making mention of the effort it takes him. Then he half crawls, half walks out of the tent. "You sure you don't need help?" Rogue asks, his voice low in his throat like he's been asleep for days. "I can help you zip or button or whatever it is you need."

I zip the flap up, creating some privacy as I say, "I think I've got it covered, but thanks."

From inside the tent, I hear the guys roll into an easy conversation. I slip on a pair of khakis I often wear to the farm, a sleeveless knit blouse, and a pair of sandals. I fold up Rogue's shirt, but wad up the ripped skirt.

Both guys are staring at me when I exit the tent, like I've interrupted their conversation. Rogue's eyes roam over me, a satisfied grin on his face. I toss the ripped skirt on the still burning fire and he gives me an alarmed look.

"What?" I ask, afraid I did something wrong.

He dismisses me with a shake of his head. "Just gonna miss that skirt. Fond memories."

I roll my eyes at him and take a seat on the ground, as far away from the hot fire as I can manage, while still being close to Rogue and Zack.

Zack returns his attention to Rogue, who's gone to lie back in the tent. "So they have a guard on the lab. You can't dream travel in there."

"Tell me something I don't already know," Rogue says, using my duffel bag as a pillow.

"Yes, thought you would have come up against that security," Zack says, nodding. "So I'm going to try and find you the codes to get in there. Before you've been sneaking in during open hours, right?"

"Can't sneak a thing past you," Rogue says with a nod. "Not easy to sneak around there during the day."

"Right, but if we get you in there during the night then you'll have more freedom."

"Sounds like a plan," Rogue says.

"We need to know where the meds are though," I say. "Otherwise we could be there all night searching. That place is huge."

Zack agrees with a nod. "Rogue, can't you use your apportation ability to retrieve the meds you both need?"

Rogue shakes his head, one arm over his forehead. "Don't you think I already would have the meds and be out of here if that was the case? I have to know where an object is to displace it. Just the same way Em needs to be close to leech someone or you have to see an object to move it. There are rules. Always stupid rules. Screw the gods," he says bitterly.

"Okay," Zack says, not deterred. "Then you need to dream travel into Government Center and find the inventory list. I've been keeping an eye out for them and my best guess is that they're kept in Em's father's office."

"Let's go tonight," I say to Rogue.

"No," Zack says as once, a punishing look on his face.

"Zack, I know that office. I've already searched it once," I say. "The inventory list will tell us where the meds are kept, right?"

He nods.

"Fine, it's settled. You find the codes for the labs and we'll find the location for the meds," I say with conviction.

"Em, I just don't think it's a good idea for you to be out right now," Zack says.

"Brother, do I need to remind you *why* you shouldn't argue with her?" Rogue says and then rolls over like he plans to fall off to sleep.

Chapter Twenty-Eight

That night Rogue awakes with a howling scream. He'd been asleep since before Zack left. During the afternoon hours Rogue slept, I sometimes dared to tickle his brow and watch him clamber about trying to swat what he thought was a pesky bug. Now, though, I know an unbearable headache is ripping him in two. He's not even all the way awake. I don't know what to do. I stand watching as he scrunches up, burying his head underneath him, like he's trying to entomb the pain. He moans, sucks in breaths, barks out indecipherable complaints. I watch, again and again paralyzed by the sight.

Rogue wouldn't want me to watch him in pain, but I can't turn away. Can't leave him. And approaching him feels wrong too. My own undecided emotions of what I'd want in his situation plagues me. Pain isolates us. The last thing I can accept when in pain is comfort, although it's exactly what I need. And all day long I've been waiting for my own headache, the first one, but so far nothing. It's like waiting for a forecasted storm; each breeze is a potential threat and when it passes without incident there's relief and also a foreboding.

Because I don't know what to do for Rogue I prepare him water and a cold compress and station myself as close to him as I can without touching him. He said he'd be there for me when my headaches start. Why do I feel wrong being here for him? But Rogue is a lone wolf. Has been one for so long. He was never good at being vulnerable; he's probably downright awful at it now.

After twelve excruciating minutes, Rogue rolls over on his back, knocking into me. It's then that I realize he was so incapacitated he didn't even realize I was that close. His eyes bolt open and stare up at me from his lying position, frustration lying dormant under the exhausting pain.

"Hi," he says with a growl.

The bleary look in his face. The red edges to his beautiful eyes. The pain he's trying to hide. It shatters my insides, tears me bit by bit, until I'm nothing which could ever be made whole again. Our fathers did this. Our government scarred Rogue. The look in his eyes makes me crave something I never thought I'd ever want. Retribution.

"What do I do for you the next time that happens?" I ask.

"Do?" he says and somehow an amused smile forms on his mouth. "Nothing. Sometimes you have to just allow yourself to be helpless."

I offer him the water, but he declines it with a shake of his head. "Rogue, I understand that you're used to not having help. I realize you've been alone for a long time."

"All this time," he corrects. Even after recovering from pain he's still playing with me, giving me a teasing look from his laid out position.

"Well, you don't have to be all alone anymore."

"Are you saying you want to be with me, Em?"

I scoot over closer to beside where his head rests, encouraging him to slide it into my lap. When he does I stroke his hair off his sweat-covered forehead and wipe his brow and temples with the cold compress I made. He closes his eyes and sighs, one of relief. "I'm already with you, Rogue. What I want is for you to want me to be here. To allow me to be here during the hard times."

His green eyes flash open, their beautiful slant a little more pronounced from my viewing angle. He reaches out and strokes the side of my face. "I'm just not sure it's necessary."

"Is that because you don't think I know how to take care of you? Do you think I'm that sheltered?"

I expect him to withdraw, to deny me, but instead he smiles back. "There's no one else who knows how but you."

***

I arrive a full minute before Rogue does. Every second waiting for him to appear in my father's office is enough to make the panic overwhelm me. I don't want to be here alone in this place. There's an energy to my father and his belongings now that crystallizes my blood. I always knew he was cold, unaffected by his children, but now I know he's soulless. How else could he do what he's done to me? How else could he try and take away my ability to dream travel?

Rogue's form solidifies in front of the cold fireplace. He looks out of place in my father's neat office, arranged with perfect precision, without an ounce of dust. Rogue stands unshaven on the Oriental rug, his boots slightly covered in dirt that thankfully can't flake off in dream travel form. Actually everything about Rogue here right now is perfect. He's alive when he's supposed to be dead. His appearance in my father's office is a mockery to everything my father holds true. And Rogue represents that we are truly Rebels, not Defects.

I wave him over to the file cabinet. "There's files in there that I know will give us the information we need."

"Well, open it up," Rogue says, his perfect smile crushing my focus.

I tug on the cabinet to prove that it's locked. "I can't. But you could get them for me."

"Why don't you do it," he says, stepping up close enough that he's pressing into me.

I smile at him and push him back. "Stop that," I laugh. "I don't want to leech you. I can't have you passing out here."

He bites down on his bottom lip and looks down at me. "Okay. But I don't know what I'm looking for. I'm gonna be pulling random files out of there. Seems a little inefficient. We should just pick the lock."

"You know how to do that?"

He gives me a look of mock offense. "No, I'm not a common criminal."

"You rob banks," I remind him.

"That's not common at all."

"Okay," I say, failing to keep the smile off my face. "If you take the files out using your gift, then can you put them back?"

"Sure, sure," he says, nodding.

"Okay, we've got all night. Give me a file."

He nods. Smiles. And three seconds later a file appears in his hand, which he dutifully hands over to me.

***

Good thing we have the entire night to find the inventory list for the lab. I'm starting to think we'll need every hour of it. We're laid out on the rug in front of the fireplace, a dozen files splayed out in front of us. This is harder than I thought it was going to be. First of all, there are a thousand files in my father's office. Most of them aren't even related to the lab. Most of them are numbers and figures, and not at all what we're looking for.

"Can I just say that you're the perfect partner in crime," Rogue says, skimming through another file. "And I mean that in the literal sense, which no one ever uses that term for."

"How do you know what people use that term for?" I say, tossing another file on the stack.

"I live alone, not in a bubble."

"I live in a bubble," I say, opening another file folder.

"Lived," Rogue corrects. Everything about him challenges everything inside me. And I've never loved a challenge so much. "You popped that bubble. You're free now, babe."

I tuck my nose back in the file, knowing if I don't then I'll make a mess of the files stacked between us. He gives me a tempting look and then continues to read, seeming to have sensed my thoughts.

I've been scanning the files, looking for the list that must be buried deep inside the transcriptions of different histories. Zack had said that they'd recently reorganized the labs and there were inventory lists detailing where everything had been sorted. Zack's father, the City Treasurer, had told him about this when he inquired. His father, unlike Rogue's and mine, isn't purely bad. Maybe he's misguided, but John Conerly is more of a lemming who's been following higher officials, believing they know better than he does. He's an honest man, one who tells Zack everything he knows. Zack probed his father for information, and not ever suspicious of his son, for good reason, he told him about the reorganization that happened a few months ago. John must not know about the injections; otherwise, he would never condone them. He's not the type. I want to believe that anyway.

I toss another file on the stack and sigh. Rogue's eyes flick up to me. "No luck?"

"No, that had exactly what we were looking for. That's why I threw it on the discard pile," I say dryly.

"Look who gets sarcastic when she's frustrated," Rogue says, looking amused.

I turn around and size up the area behind me, like someone could be standing there. I turn back to Rogue and give him an ultra-serious expression. "Who?"

Rogue whistles through his teeth. "Oh, and she can act too."

"Are you talking about me in the third person?" I ask.

"I am."

"Is that a result of spending too much time with goats and horses?"

He seems to think about it for a minute. "No, they all refer to themselves in first person."

"Rogue, do you know what I love about you best?"

He bristles at the question. I'm not sure why, and he recovers so quickly I don't have a chance to think on it. "I'm sure the list is long. Give me your top ten."

I shake my head. Smile. "You don't take yourself too seriously. Everyone here does. They run around looking for a reason to be offended. I think half the time they offend themselves by not following some etiquette."

Rogue nods and allows a slight seriousness to creep into his eyes. It's quickly whisked away by a mischievous smile. I'm growing accustomed to those smiles. I'm starting to enjoy them, although I probably shouldn't. "That's what you like best? You need to see me without my shirt on," he says.

I toss the file I've already reviewed at him. He doesn't even complain that my lousy toss sends a dozen papers scattering out around him. Although he scowls at me, he unquestioningly goes to stacking them right and sliding them into their folder.

The next manila folder isn't all the way opened when I quickly spy a half a dozen words that catch my interest. This file doesn't have the inventory list. It tells a different story, not related to the reorganization of the labs. It's dated four and a half years prior. Four lines gain my attention at once.

"The first specimen's spinal fluid was harvested on January 11th shortly after birth. It didn't survive the harvest."

"After the failed harvest the specimen was taken directly to the lab for a full autopsy".

"The council decides to wait to harvest specimen's spinal fluid for injection materials until six weeks after birth."

"Ciphering spinal fluid from Middling infants is believed to create a successful serum for injections for Reverian Defects."

And just like that, a world I didn't know could tumble further, cascades through space until it must be sucked into a black hole or into whatever would completely shred it in two.

I flip my head up from the file. Rogue must sense my anxiety because he looks up at once from the file he's reading and finds my gaze.

"They killed Dean's child," I say, hearing my voice in my head, but disbelieving the words.

Chapter Twenty-Nine

"What?" Rogue says, pushing the stack of files aside and staring at me, not at the file I hold clenched between my fingers. "Do you mean Dean Cooper? The farmer?"

I nod. "His baby died on January eleventh of that year." I hand him the folder. He scans it and then his eyes widen with shocked repulsion.

"They harvest Middling children to get the ingredients they need to create the injections for Defects?"

I nod, my stomach turning over in my physical body, the feeling echoing in my subconscious form. "Rogue, I've got to get out of here. I'm going to be sick."

"But we haven't found the inventory list," he says, staring at the stack of files in front of us.

"We'll find the meds," I say, standing, gathering the files. "I need to get out of here now. Have to."

He nods, revulsion written on his face. He starts sending files back into the cabinet, one at a time. It's not a quick business and although I want to desert him and be as far away from my father's office as possible I stay by his side.

"Em," he says, as he's waiting for a file to disappear. "They didn't kill all the babies."

He's trying to make me feel better, I realize. He has his eyes trained on me, although I know his focus is on moving the files.

I nod. "I know. I read the whole report," I say, holding it up. "Twelve. They killed twelve babies before they figured it out. They devalued those lives, sacrificing them to find a serum. They killed twelve babies before they realized they had to wait for them to be six weeks older to 'harvest' them. Those were the children we heard in the lab. To this day, they must do this to every Middling born," I say and realize at the same time.

"I knew they were experimenting on children, but I didn't realize that they did it to them all. I didn't know they let some of them die," Rogue says, swallowing hard, like it took a great effort.

"Not let them die," I say, anger rising in me. "They killed them. Experimented on them when they were at their most fragile, early

149

state. They harvested their spinal fluid, knowing the implications. Innocent babies. And now they withdraw spinal fluid from every infant at age six weeks. You remember what the injections felt like. Taking their spinal fluid must be excruciating for those Middling babies, but they do it to every single one born. All to create Defects."

I think of the new batch of Middlings they just recruited. I think of the children they bear who will suffer, all for the purpose of creating a serum. What they take from them will stifle the gifts of so many Dream Traveler children who will grow up to be converted. And then those Middlings and Defects will be reunited to serve the Reverians. Again, revulsion makes my stomach turn.

"Rogue, they take this from Middlings, this spinal fluid, in order to synthesize it into something to stop the gifts in Dream Travelers." I hold my head in my hands, completely confused by this turn of events.

The last file disappears and he steps forward, cupping my face in his strong hands. "I know. I'm sorry."

"Dean's child didn't have to die," I say, remembering the pain in my friend's eyes. "She was an experiment. The very first baby they tried to harvest so they could create..." I can't say the words, the ones we both know are true. The ones that stare back at me in Rogue's eyes and then he echoes like I'm locked inside a vault.

"It was probably her spinal fluid that created the injection they gave to me, since I was the first."

I rush into his arms. There's no other place for me on Earth at this point. If I'm not in his arms then I can't remain upright. He cinches me in, holds me in tight to him. I feel the pain he has recently realized with me. Rogue hasn't been whole for a long time, but to know they had broken him using a dead baby's spinal fluid is further insult to injury. Inside my own head I feel an ache erupting from the years and years of Middling babies' spinal fluid used to make me less powerful. To make me never realize who I was.

My words are muffled, almost nonsense as I say them against Rogue's arm. "Come back to the tent with me. I can't be here any longer."

He nods, a new weight in his eyes.

In the tent we awake to each other. Neither of us says a single word. Instead, I turn and pull his arm around me like it's a shelter.

I've lost every single reservation about allowing Rogue to love me. He's my strength in this revolution. He's my encouragement.

Against my cheek I feel his breath and then his words. "Don't worry, babe. I'll get you out of here."

I encourage his arm tighter around me. Bury my body more into his, seeking redemption in his embrace. It doesn't work so I turn over and kiss him. Only once, but it still erases a piece of the pain my father created in me. Before, when I realized what President Vider had done to Rogue, I didn't know how to respond, but now the words rush out of my mouth. "I'm so sorry. I'm sorry it's your father who's behind this. I'm sorry he did it to you first. And if I ever see him again I will do everything in my power to kill him," I whisper, feeling him more acutely than I did moments before.

His breath pauses. He looks at me, but all I can make out is the whites of his eyes. "If anyone can do it then it would be you, but I refuse to allow you to mark your soul with his blood."

"But he has to be stopped," I whisper in the darkness.

"And he will be."

He rubs his nose against mine and whispers against my lips. "No more worrying about this tonight. Rest now, babe."

And in the protection of his arms, I find it easy to close my eyes and drift away.

Chapter Thirty

I awake at dawn and slip out of the tent, not wanting to disturb Rogue, who looks peaceful and happy in his sleep. However, he spills out of the tent two minutes later, a look of worried horror on his face. It quiets into relief when he catches sight of me stacking wood for the fire. His hand claps onto his chest as he releases a breath.

"What, did you think I went off and got myself eaten by a bear?" I say, unable to keep from laughing at his worry.

He doesn't smile back. Doesn't laugh. His face is too serious. The expression doesn't look right on him. "When I awoke and you were gone..." He shakes his head, his sleep-tangled hair falling down in his eyes. "I was just worried, that's all."

I've never seen him rattled like this. When he tore out of the tent he had that look of panic a parent has when their child briefly goes missing, and they fear the worst has happened to them. I stand, move in close to him. Push his hair from his eyes. He's so tall that I have to stand up on my toes to reach him well. "I'm fine," I assure him.

"Good." Rogue nods and then his eyes fall down to the fire I was building. "But you still don't know how to build a fire." He shakes his head at me. "How many times growing up did I show you?"

I shake my head and purse my lips at him, rebellion in my eyes. "Well, I guess you'll just have to give up any hope I'll ever learn." I sling my duffel bag with over my shoulder and set off. "You build a fire. I'm going to freshen up."

"Whoa, whoa, whoa," Rogue says, grabbing my hand and twisting me around. He's fast, his movements sharp, but still gentle. "Where do you think you're going?"

"To. Freshen. Up," I say, rolling my eyes at him.

He seems to consider me for a minute, then nods. "Okay," he says, going back to the tent. "Let me grab my boots first."

"Rogue, you weren't invited," I say, watching him slip on his socks, a look of determination on his still tired face.

"And I don't need an invitation," he says, pulling on his tan leather boots.

"Rogue…"

"It's cute when you say my name like that. Like I'm in trouble," he says.

"If you think you're going to chaperone me down to the stream then you *are* in trouble."

He slaps the side of his boot and stands, brandishing a smile. "I promise to be a gentleman. I could use a little of this freshening up you speak of. Anyway, I'll stay away from you, scout's honor." He holds up his three middle fingers.

"I don't see how you're going to give me any privacy if you won't take your eyes off me for a single second."

"I will, as long as I can hear you and you check in with me regularly." He's smiling, but I sense his seriousness.

"Okay, fine," I say, turning around and trotting off. "But stay on your side of the stream."

***

"Oh, good, you're here, brother," Rogue says to Zack when he arrives late morning. "You can entertain Em while I excuse myself. She's been demanding my constant attention."

"I've done no such thing," I say.

"Yes, you command my attention whether you realize it or not," Rogue says, shaking his head at me like I misunderstand something of great importance.

Zack watches him walk off and then turns to me. "What's that about?"

"Rogue thinks I'm going to disappear or get myself caught in a patch of thorns if I'm not supervised," I say, rolling my eyes.

"He's probably worried that your father will find you. He's not wrong to worry. You're not safe here for too much longer."

"Why do the two of you always have to gang up on me?"

"Did the clothes I brought you not work?" Zack asks, gesturing to my shirt. It's the one Rogue let me borrow when I first arrived.

Absently I hug the shirt into me. "No, the clothes were great. Thanks. I just prefer this one." I roll down the sleeves a little so they meet my wrists; my hair is still wet, making me cold in the morning air.

Zack watches me quietly, his mind working as he does.

"What?" I say when he gets that look on his face, the one where he wants to say something, but doesn't want to. He wears it all the time lately.

Zack sighs, seeming to resign a little of the tension in his shoulders. "Is something going on between you and Rogue?"

"Going on like how?" I ask, feigning ignorance.

"Going on like romantically," he says, and I spy a tinge of red color the tips of his ears.

"Maybe," I say, ignoring Zack's gaze that watches me as I go to work organizing the camp, tidying.

"Oh," he says, like the word contains multiple syllables. The disapproval in his tone is obvious.

"What?" I say, spinning around and facing him. He's wearing a tight expression, his denim blue eyes heavy with concern.

"Nothing, it's just that it's..."

I wait for him to complete his complaint but he doesn't. His tentative gaze just keeps shifting between me and the ground, an uncertainty in it.

"It's what?" I say.

"It's just that it's Rogue."

"So?"

"It's just weird and—"

"Zack, you know I am a girl, right? Or maybe you don't."

He shakes his head at me. Clenches his eyes shut. When he opens them he actually looks angry, a state he's rarely in. "You have this disillusion that I don't see you as a girl. I'm not sure why. Maybe because we're friends, but nothing could be further from the truth."

"What's that supposed to mean?" I say.

Zack stares at me, a meaningful expression in his eyes. I stare back, challenging him with a single look. He shakes his head again, the morning sun reflecting off his shiny, blond hair. "Nothing. That's not what I meant to say." Zack always says what he means. Always thinks before he speaks. He gives me a regretful look. "I just meant that you drive me crazy because you make these insinuations about me."

"Like what?" I say, pinning my hands on my hips.

"Like that I don't know you're a girl. Or that all I care about is my career. Maybe you're the one who doesn't see *me* accurately."

154

I stare at Zack, really stare. Watch him take a steadying breath. Watch the nervousness in his eyes morph into defeat.

"Hey, brother," Rogue says, striding back into camp. "Why do you look like you're planning your own funeral?"

His eyes flick to Rogue and then back to me. "I'm just worried about what happens next."

I peer at him, trying to understand what he's not saying this time. Trying to comprehend how I could misunderstand someone I know so well. Trying to determine how I've hurt him, which is the only thing I do understand from the conversation we just had.

Zack pulls a piece of paper out of his breast pocket and hands it to Rogue, who's taken the position beside me. "Here. That's the code. It will get you into the lab."

My face brightens, releasing some of the tension I've been holding. "You got it! Thank you."

He nods. Doesn't smile. A morose expression in his eyes.

"You've been more successful than us," Rogue says. "We didn't find the inventory list."

"What?" Zack says, his face falling with even more disappointment. "They weren't in your father's office?" he asks me.

I shrug. "They probably were." I'd been able to section off the sadistic facts we learned about our government all day. I'd been successful at not allowing it to contaminate my thoughts, but now it pours through the barrier, bringing with it a sickening feeling. "I had to stop looking," I say, looking at Rogue, seeing the nightmare I feel in me display on his features, bringing a coldness to his eyes. "Zack, we found out that they synthesize the formula in the injections from spinal fluid they steal from Middling babies. That's the testing they're doing. But Middlings don't know. They think they are testing them for a defect, one they told them was responsible for infant deaths a few years ago."

Zack closes his eyes. Shakes his head. When he opens them he looks struck by an epiphany. "They're the ones who killed the infants, aren't they? Our government?"

He's too smart sometimes, figures things out so quickly it makes me feel dumb. "Yes," I say in a hush.

Taking a seat on the large rock, he pins his elbows on his knees, his head hanging low. Zack is doing the opposite of what Rogue and I did last night. He's retreating inside himself with this news. He doesn't want us to see his face as he processes. I was only able to section off the grossness of that history because I retreated into Rogue's arms. And again I'll need to push this all to the corner of my mind, where it can motivate me without blinding me with anger.

"I'll see about getting the inventory list today," Zack finally says, his eyes still on the ground. "If I can get it then I'll bring it to you tomorrow, maybe tonight."

If he was looking at me then he'd see I'm shaking my head. "No," I say. "We have to go tonight. We'll just have to search for them." I can't put off getting the meds. Rogue needs them. I will need them soon.

Zack agrees at once. I'm sure he's glad he doesn't have to sneak into my father's office.

"And then what?" Rogue says.

"Then I've got to figure out how to get Nona," I say.

Zack shakes his head and finally brings his eyes up to meet mine. "She wanted me to pass along a message to you. Nona says she's working on something, but she'll need a few months to get it right."

"What?" I say, half appalled and half curious. "What is it?"

"She wouldn't say, but she said that it's worth her attention. I told her you wanted to get her out, save her from getting converted, and she agreed. However, she says she's not at risk for conversion yet."

"So, what am I supposed to do? Camp in the woods until her secret mission is complete?"

Zack gives me an indignant look. "You need to get out of here. It's not safe."

Rogue nods in agreement. "After we get the meds, I vote you go with me," he says, a small question in his voice.

I nod. Of course I'll go with Rogue. I'd go anywhere with him.

"Nona said she'll let you know when she's ready," Zack says.

"How?" I ask.

"She said she'll leave you notes in the old oak tree?" He says it like it makes no sense.

"Oh, that's perfect," I say. "She's so clever." Nona really thinks of everything. I can dream travel into the Valley at night, to the old oak outside the Japanese garden in the park. As kids we used to leave each other messages there. Nothing of importance. We just loved the opportunity to have a covert way to communicate. In dream travel form I'll be able to read her messages and if I bring a pen with me, I can write back to her, since I can't leave or take anything from the physical realm while dream traveling.

"Okay, that's a good plan," I agree after ruminating on it.

"There's one last thing," Zack says, standing. "When you leave, I want to go with you two. I want out of this valley."

Chapter Thirty-One

"Now you're talking, brother!" Rogue says, holding his hand up for a high-five.

Zack slaps it, a sliver of a smile on the corner of his mouth.

"No," I say with a firmness in my voice.

Both guys whip around to face me, confusion screwing up their expressions.

"What?" It's Rogue who asks the question they both are thinking.

"I need you here, Zack. I want you to watch over Nona," I say.

Disappointment colors every single feature on Zack's face. "She has your tutu, Em. And she will be leaving you messages," Zack says, all his attention on me, Rogue at his back. "She'll tell you if she needs help."

I nod because he's right.

"I can't stay here now," he continues. "I can't intern in a government who weakens those who might be a problem. Labels them Defects. Ostracizes them from their own people. I'm going to be assigned an occupation soon. I can't work in this government or for it. I want to be with you two."

"But from inside the government you could help," I say. "That's where you could make the most change."

Rogue looks at me, a pitiful look that says, "How could you be so mean to him?" I shake off the guilt.

"I want you with us too," I say. "I don't want to leave you, but there's no one I trust more to watch over everything. I know it's not fair to ask that of you. I'm sorry."

"Em, I'm not sure much can be done," Zack says.

"Well, something has to. We can't let them get away with what they're doing to our people and to Middlings. It sounds like Nona is working on something and if I know her it's a revolution. Maybe I was cowardly to think of just getting us out. We need to get everyone out. We need to put a stop to this."

"Em, I admire your beautiful tenacity, but what you're talking about is unrealistic," Rogue says.

"What I'm talking about is exactly what Zack was born for." I round on Zack. "All you've ever wanted was to be a part of a government which supported the people, to help them flourish. I'm sorry that's not the government we have and they fooled us all into believing the opposite. I'm sorry they've heartbroken us all with this treachery, that they've scarred some of us with their manipulation. But Zack, you're the one person I know who can help make the changes which will actually make a difference. If you stay here you can infiltrate them. Find their secrets. Help us figure out how to expose them to Middlings, to the Reverians, to larger forces, ones that can help us bring them down."

Zack looks at me, a strong conviction in his stare. "You really think we have a chance?"

"Yes!" I say, almost stomping.

"She does have an excellent point. Maybe I've stayed away too long. Maybe it is time for a revolution," Rogue says, clapping Zack on the shoulder.

"Yes, Em, you're right," Zack says.

I look between the two of them with a bit of disbelief. Rogue smiles at me, then at Zack. "She didn't expect us to agree with her so easily. Look at that look on her face," he says, elbowing Zack in the ribs.

"Is there a reason you're talking about me like I'm not here?" I ask.

Rogue leans into Zack's ear, his gaze firmly on me as he does. "I think she can hear us talking about her."

I shake my head at Rogue, but smile at Zack. He's looking less hurt and a lot more motivated than he was moments prior.

"So, you'll stay?" I ask him.

Zack nods. "I'll stay. This is where I can make the most change. I'll learn everything I can and I'll leave messages with Nona's. We'll organize something grassroots, but it won't stay that way." Zack really looks angry now, but it's a quiet anger that burns in his eyes. Makes his strategic mind seem to work faster. "We need to do something that will tear the current government out of Austin Valley. And it won't be easy, but I think with planning we can do it."

I throw my arms around Zack's shoulders. Usually I hate his political talk, but right now he's appealing to me on a different level. He's making me see why this interest of his has always mattered. He pats me on the back a little nervously, which gives me the cue to pull back.

"Sorry, you just made me so proud," I say, poking him in the shoulder.

"Well, you're right," Zack says. "We can't escape this problem. We have to find a way to fight it. I'll figure out what Nona is working on and help. And before I leave here we should all strategize while we have the opportunity."

"You know, Zack," Rogue says, "they didn't put you on the Defect list because they didn't see you as rebellious. But they're wrong. You're more rebellious and dangerous than all of us because you know how to hide. If anyone is gonna bring them down, it will be you."

I'm indescribably sad that I'm the one who convinced Zack to stay. It was an incredibly hard position to take. I kept picturing the three of us living off somewhere on Rogue's farm, making a life full of laughter and fun to make up for everything else. But our happiness would always be plagued by the people we left behind, by the injustices we turned our backs on.

***

For the next hour we strategize, the session led by Zack. He makes us set up every detail for our break-in tonight. He's not happy until we've thoroughly planned out how we'll search the labs and make our exit. Then we move on to what we can accomplish over the next few months, how we can start a rebellion. It's more involved than I would have thought, but with Zack leading the initiative I should have expected this.

"Zachariah, can you stick around camp for another hour or so?" Rogue asks, stretching to a standing position with a long yawn. With his hands stretched above his head I'm granted a glimpse of the underside of his long biceps. They intrigue me in so many ways, the most obvious being that the men of our society don't have bulk muscle mass. Their jobs are not labor intensive enough to produce that. And the President maintains that walking and stretching are the most ideal exercises for Reverians. So again and again I find my curious eyes trailing the toned muscles of Rogue, wondering how he built that definition. I'm unaware that my eyes are trained on his movements so acutely until I catch Zack watching me.

160

He darts his eyes down on his silver watch. "I've got a meeting this afternoon, and it will take me an hour to get back, but I can stay maybe a half hour. Why?"

"I've got to check on my horse. Get her ready for the ride. Keep an eye on Em, will you?"

"I don't need a babysitter," I say, knitting my arms across my chest, realizing after the fact that the gesture indeed makes me appear childish.

"Of course you don't. I'm the baby, and it would just make me feel better if Zack was here with you while I stepped out. Humor me," Rogue says, winking at me over his shoulder as he pulls back the flaps to the tent.

"Doesn't it spook your horse when you dream travel around her, since she can't see you?" Zack asks, a curious look on his face.

"Used to," he chirps. "But she knows me well enough now."

"How did you learn how to ride and care for horses?" Zack asks.

"The same way I learned half the stuff I do. I watched experts while dream traveling," Rogue says, staring at the far-off hills. "I stalked this one Middling ranch for months. A cute family-run one in East Oregon. Learned most of what I know from them."

"That's genius," Zack says.

"Oh, no, it's just what people who are free to dream travel do. They maximize their potential. And you, my friend, have more than most, so I look forward to you being set free," he says to Zack with a wink.

Zack smiles to himself. Seems to ruminate on the idea with his eyes pinned on the ground.

"Well, I'll be back in a few," Rogue says and then shuts the flap.

I set back to work, breaking down parts of the camp since we'll be leaving it for good tonight. It doesn't just feel strange to think about leaving the Valley, it's absolutely mystifying. I realize I'm standing, not moving, holding a bag of rope and the first aid supplies. I'm frozen in place because my thoughts are frozen by this idea of leaving the only place I've ever known.

Suddenly I feel Zack by my side. He tugs on the sleeve of my shirt, well, Rogue's shirt. It's an endearing gesture he hasn't done in a long time. It's how he used to try and get my attention when I was

161

giving him the silent treatment. I turn and face him. Looking at his familiar eyes makes my heart ache suddenly. I'm leaving him behind. My best friend. It suddenly feels all wrong, but I have to do it. I need Zack here working, watching over Nona.

"Come sit down with me. We don't have much time left together," he says.

I nod, setting the supplies down. I take a seat on the ground, leaving the rock for him so he doesn't get his khakis dirty. However, he sits down on a patch of pine and crushed leaves beside me.

"I always thought that we'd have all this time," he says, his words slow and robotic. "That you'd always be here in Austin Valley. I never considered a reality where you left."

"Me either."

"I'm sorry for what they did to you. I'm sorry for what they're making you do."

I nod and lean my head on his shoulder. "I know."

"What I was trying to say earlier," he begins and pauses. I sense he's waiting for me to look at him. I pull my head off his shoulder and when I do, he smiles at me. "I was trying to say that there's no two people I want to be happier than you and Rogue," Zack says, his voice firm. "If you're happy together then that's even better. It just surprised me, I guess. That's the reason for my reaction." And because I know him so well, I spy the crack in his voice, and the disingenuous smile he flashes.

"It just kind of happened. Rogue and me. I don't even know how," I say, a little embarrassed.

Zack laughs dryly. "You were born, that's how."

I give him a confused look.

"He's had a crush on you since forever," Zack says, shaking his head at me like I'm clueless. "Why do you think he always threatened to kiss you? He was hoping in your rebellious nature you'd call him out on it."

I smile inside. *That's exactly what happened.*

Zack continues. "We used to arm wrestle and the winner would marry you and the loser would marry Dee." He stares off like he's fallen back into the memory. "I lost every time."

"What?" I say with a giggle. "You did not! Why would *you* arm wrestle over me?"

162

He looks at me askance. Shakes his head. "I guess it's because I like a challenge."

"Wait! That's why you wrestled or why you wanted to marry me?"

He laughs again. "We were just kids fooling around."

I nod. And strangely, I deflate a little. "Yeah, and there's not many girls to wrestle over in Austin Valley."

"You know, Em, you've always been the tie between Rogue and me. The reason we became friends and stayed friends. We bonded watching you make a fool out of yourself trying to get the ball during keep away."

I scowl at him. "I hate that game."

"I bet you do, Shorty."

"I'll have you know, I'm average height."

"Well, you didn't play games with average height people, so you always put yourself at a disadvantage."

"I always preferred you over people my own height," I say.

"You mean gender."

"Girls are…girly," I say like it's a disgusting thought.

An abrupt laugh pops out of Zack's mouth. "And the sun is sunny and air is airy. I think what you mean is some girls are a bit more prissy."

"Don't tell me what I mean." I plant a soft blow on his arm.

It feels like we're saying all this right now, reminiscing, because it's all ending. That makes me want to stop, but I can't. I need to hear Zack talk for as long as I'm afforded. I want to store every memory, in case we never get another one.

I look directly at him and spy the sentimental expression on his face. It makes me want to punch him again. Instead I lay my head on his shoulder so I don't have to see his false smile and regretful eyes.

"Em, I'm glad you preferred us over other friends."

Tears press at the back of my eyes. Burn and creep closer to the surface. I nod into his shoulder, but don't trust my voice to speak. Zack has seen me cry dozens of times, but right now I can't. I want him to see me strong in this moment, or at least not as a sobbing baby.

"As I was saying before," Zack continues, "if it wasn't for your insistence then Rogue and I'd never be friends. You always invited me, and dragged me out of my house when I was resistant. I never

163

had much confidence to be the President's son's friend. The idea intimidated me for years, although my father had encouraged it."

"He's just Rogue," I say. "There's no one more down to Earth."

"That's what you said before when I asked if there was something going on with you two," Zack says, nodding his head. "I think that's why he's always had a crush on you. You never treated him differently because of who his father is. You liked him for who he is. I don't think many people did that. And he isn't just Rogue. He's a guy who left here when he was thirteen and survived. He built a house. Runs a farm. By himself."

"Wait, do you have a crush on him?" I say, grateful for the laughter that breaks up the constriction in my throat.

"No." I feel Zack shake his head. "I admire him. He has everything I want."

"I never took you for the 'farmer' type," I say.

Zack gives an impatient sigh and again I feel him shake his head. I wrap my arm around his, careful not to wrinkle his shirt.

"Make sure that Dee doesn't antagonize Nona," I say.

Zack cinches my arm in closer to him. "I'll tell her it's a real turn-off."

"That's genius. That will work for sure."

"It's difficult to know that after today we'll live in different worlds," Zack says, and for the first time I hear regret in his tone.

"I'm coming back, Zack."

"I know, but you'll be gone for a while and you've always been here. Even when Rogue disappeared you were here. I'm not sure what my world looks like without you in it."

"Probably a lot less chaotic," I say with a fake laugh. "And you'll be so busy that you won't even miss me."

"There's no wa—"

The hum of the zipper pulling back interrupts Zack's words. Rogue pokes his head through the tent, spies us on the ground, and smiles—one so big I squeeze Zack's arm tighter. In a few strides Rogue takes the place on the other side of Zack.

"Ugh," Zack groans. "You're not as light as Em."

I lift up my head to see Rogue with his head on Zack's shoulder, his arm tied around his, the same as mine.

"I wish mean ol' Em would let you go with us, instead of electing you to fix and inherit the society," Rogue says in a whimpering voice.

"Shut up, Rogue," I say, tucking my head back into place.

"How's the horse?" Zack asks.

"Ready to go," Rogue says. "I guess then we should let you go too."

I pull my arm out of Zack's as he stands up. Rogue is already on his feet, a hand extended to me. I take it, but keep my eyes on the ground.

Don't cry. Don't cry. Don't cry.

"I'm sorry, brother, that I never told you goodbye before and that I made you think I was dead," Rogue says, standing in front of Zack.

I bring up my eyes to see Zack's eyes twinkle. "Don't be absurd. I'm just happy you're alive."

Rogue nods. Extends his hand and when Zack takes it he pulls in, hugging him with the other arm. Slaps him on the back, a loud sound that makes Zack sound hollow inside.

From over Rogue's shoulder I catch a look in Zack's face, a determined sturdiness. And it makes my insides break apart.

Rogue holds Zack out at arm's length. "Don't you worry. I know you will, but try and not." And then he leans in and whispers something in Zack's ear, which he nods to before stepping away.

I feel small as I step up beside Rogue and stare at Zack, knowing what I'm expected to do now. I shake my head. "This is dumb. We're all going to be back together in a few months. I don't know why you two are acting so sentimental."

A flat smile forms on Zack's face. "Be careful tonight, Em. Don't get caught."

"Have a little faith in me."

"I do, believe me," he says with conviction.

"Fine then, shut up and give me a hug so you can get out of here. If you're late, they'll get suspicious."

Zack nods and leans down, wrapping both his arms around me. I unabashedly bury my face into his shoulder. "You be careful too. Don't take too many risks."

He pulls back and gives me a shaky smile. "You know me well enough to know I'd never do that."

As I press my lips hard against each other one bandit tear escapes my eyes. It races down my cheek and lands on my collarbone.

Zack takes a long blink. Tries again and fails to give me an encouraging smile and then nods. "Bye, Em." And then he turns and walks away.

Chapter Thirty-Two

After Zack left I retreated to the tent, volunteering to clear it out. Rogue nodded, not questioning the few clipped answers I gave to his questions regarding packing up camp. I did clear the tent while I was in there, but I also cried a flood of quiet tears. Each one a token of the loss that seared my heart. Each tear labeled with a different hurt. My father's betrayal. The lies I'd been fed my whole life. The unnecessary pain of the injections. My mother's indifference. Dee's heartlessness. Leaving Nona behind. Leaving Tutu. And letting Zack walk away. Each of my tears felt full of my pain, so much so that they fell as fat drops on my cheeks and soaked one of Rogue's T-shirts I used to dry them time and time again.

While I cried I listened to Rogue work outside the tent. From the noise he sounded to be tearing the camp into pieces, but maybe he was just working fast. The sun would set in an hour and we'd agreed to have everything done before then. I was half grateful for the noise he made, doing whatever he was doing, hoping it drowned out my sobs. And then suddenly the noise died completely and I wondered if Rogue had gone, maybe to the stream or somewhere else.

When I'm certain that no more tears will leak from my eyes I exit the tent. I find Rogue stationed right outside it, reclining against the rock, his head back, eyes closed. He has my iPod in his hands, the buds in his ears. He smiles at me when I squat down next to him.

"I hope you don't mind me borrowing this," he says, plucking the buds from his ears.

"Not at all."

His hand reaches up, but pauses beside my swollen cheek, and then he strokes his thumb along it. The gesture brings tears I thought had dried up to the corners of my eyes. The look of hostile sadness on his face triggers them to flow again. "Come here," he says, pulling me into his lap. "Gods above, I'd love to kill everyone who's hurt you." Rogue cradles me against his chest and suddenly I don't cry. I breathe him in. I tremble in his arms. I wrap my arms tighter around him, but I don't cry. He rubs his stubbled face along the top of my head and draws me in even closer, so I'm sitting across his lap.

We sit like this for what feels like a long while. I count the time by his heartbeats and can't fathom pulling my ear away from his chest. This closeness seems to fix me somehow and I fear that as soon as our embrace is broken, the pain will storm back. Still, I pull away after maybe a thousand heartbeats, maybe more. We've lost most of the remaining sunlight when I peek my head up from under its hiding spot below his chin and find his eyes. "Hi," I say, my voice sounding frayed.

"You know, your crystal blue eyes are even more intense after you've cried," Rogue says, looking at me intently, studying my eyes.

I don't know what to say so I drop my gaze to the ground.

Rogue's fingers find my chin and angle it up, drawing with it my focus back on him. "Do you want to go with me still? After we get the meds? Have you changed your mind?"

And it hits me so acutely that I feel like my chest has hollowed out. He thinks I don't want to leave. He doubts my commitment. The uncertainty he feels laces around my heart like a vine and begins to constrict it. Before I lose any more breath to this suffocating feeling, I sit up and straddle him, one knee on one side and the other on the other side. His eyes widen slightly. Now he knows I mean business, because I do. "No-no-no-no," I say in a rush. "I'm going with you and I'm not doing it because it's my only option. I'm doing it because I want to be with *you*."

He stares at me, skepticism marking the corners of his green eyes.

"Rogue, I want to go with you for so many reasons. Some are obvious, like I want to see where you live, the place you've made your home. But I also have less practical reasons, ones that are harder to explain."

I hold his gaze as he seems to process me and my words. I wait for him to ask, but he doesn't. He just stares back at me, like we're playing the quiet game. I fear I might lose this round. Finally, after too long, he guides my head down and whispers in my ear. "Will you try and explain?"

I actually smile, feeling victorious somehow. I flip my face up so it's directly in front of his, only a few inches away. Then I hoist myself up so I'm looking down at him slightly. "I can't let you go. If you leave, I'm leaving too. If you stay, I will. Hell, if you march into your father's house I'll be right behind you, because I'm absolutely, terrifyingly in love with you."

He blinks up at me. And I don't need any more reason to hold myself back, but still I do. I lean in close to him, and I wait. I feel his breath, but I wait. Just watch him watching me. He doesn't pull me to him, but instead seems to understand I'm enjoying being at the edge of this moment. The moment before we kiss. When I bring my lips an inch from his a shudder actually escapes my chest. He almost smiles. Right now, under these circumstances, I feel I'm trained on his every movement with incredible intuition. And when I finally close the distance he breathes me in with a rough purr. Kisses me back like in the seconds I feigned a standoff, he starved. Strong calloused hands grip my back and pull me in closer to him. He kisses me with an unmatched intensity, one that unlocks a flood of warmth inside me, erasing any remaining pain. My hands slide around his firm jaw, down his neck, and follow to his chest. He catches them before they complete their path. Holds my hands in his, imprisons them there. He's no longer kissing me, but his lips are only an eyelash distance away. Finally between a series of shallow breaths he says, "I'm going to regret saying this, but we need to pack up camp."

I nod. Slide my head over and rest it on his shoulder and wait for my breaths to steady. "Yeah, you're right," I say.

I roll off him, but as soon as I'm at his side I scoot back closer and tuck my body under the arm he drapes around me. He knows we need to get up as well as I do, but doesn't seem too intent on it either. Maybe like me, he's worried about what lies ahead of us tonight and just wants to enjoy this moment. Maybe he's just indulging me since I announced my undying love for him. I don't really care why he's still holding me when we have other things to do, I'm enjoying the aspects of this moment. The sun setting. The warm, but crisp summer air. The warm hand clapped on my thigh. The guy who holds me like I'm the greatest prize. After spending years being a Defect, it feels amazing to finally win in this way.

And suddenly, something occurs to me. I turn around abruptly and sit back on my knees. Rogue doesn't seem caught off guard by my sudden change in position.

"Zack said you really have always had a crush on me," I say, looking at him with my best determined look.

169

He doesn't blink at my abruptness. He simply shakes his head. "Not a crush. Love. I've always loved you," he says.

I blush and stare at a spot on his chest, suddenly unable to bring my eyes to meet his.

"You didn't believe me before, did you?" Rogue asks.

"I did. I was just surprised that I never knew it. I mean, we were so young," I say.

"Maybe that's why then. But I think it's because of something else. I think because you're so self-sufficient you don't see what you can have until you need it."

I shake my head at him.

"And Em," he says, like he's not paying attention to my head shake, "you need me now and here I am. And you finally see my love."

It's my turn to stop and regard him quietly. A thousand urges are reaching from different places inside me right at this moment. I shake them off and maintain my stoic silence.

"You know," he says, with a slanted smile, "it's a beautiful thing that you finally need me, because I've been dying to be needed by you."

I sit frozen for a long few seconds. Apparently too long because Rogue pushes up. Once he's standing he extends his hand to me. I was already in the process of standing on my own but because I sense he wants to help me, I take his hand.

When we're both standing, he angles his head back down at my iPod sitting by the rock. "So your music, indie folk, it's compelling. A bit slow, but I still enjoyed the poetry."

I forgot he'd been borrowing my music. "You still listen to alternative?" I ask, finding our standing position a little awkward suddenly.

"I don't listen to anything. Living off the grid means no electricity. I've got a well and all but no TV or lights. That gonna be all right with you?"

"I don't care for TV, but that may be because the approved channels are all lame. You wouldn't believe what I had to do to get this music approved," I say, holding up the iPod.

"I'm guessing you were damn persistent."

"Well, if you need electricity then I might be able to help you," I say, holding up a hand and tapping him in the chest.

"Be careful where you point that thing."

I smirk. "Thanks to you I know how to control it."

"Well, now you got me thinking. If I let you leech me then that energy can be converted to power a water heater or furnace."

"Sounds like we get to experiment."

"Oh, I live for home improvement projects. And now I get to use my beloved as an energy source. It just keeps getting better."

Chapter Thirty-Three

It's mostly my fault that it's dark while we try to pack up camp. We both scamper around trying to find lost objects. Rogue stumbles several times over the supplies I've absentmindedly left out or dropped.

"Sorry," I say, when I back into him as he's rolling up the tent. It's like knocking into a brick wall.

In the moonlight I make out a soft smile on his face. "Not your fault."

"That's a lie," I say, kneeling down to help him fold the tent into a neat square.

"I should just throw on the lantern and make our lives easier."

"No, let's not risk it," I say. "We're almost done. I'll stay out of your way with my clumsy feet."

He holds out his empty hand and a second later the bag for the tent appears there. With a wink he says, "I probably can do the clean-up a little easier on my own. Why don't you pack your duffel bag since it's the only thing we're taking with us?"

"What are we doing with the rest of the supplies?"

"Hiding them in that oak tree," he says, nodding to one in the distance. "We'll need them on our return trip."

The idea of returning simultaneously fills me with trepidation and excitement. I long to see Nona, to hear what Zack has learned, and to instigate a change. But there's too much risk connected to each of those desires and I fear that my own thirst for vengeance will hurt people I love if I'm not careful. Just by getting myself caught I'd hurt those who care about me. And if I don't get caught, but fail to strategize properly, then I'll lose the advantage I have over President Vider right now. He doesn't know what I know, what I can do, and that we're organizing something with a potential to pull him out of office. And I know what my shortcoming is. I know what can be my undoing in all of this. My father. The blinding anger I have for him fills my head with erratic thoughts. Makes me impulsive. I fear that my desire for revenge against him will send me into an action that endangers everyone I love. I fear I'll ruin our chances at justice just because I want to see my father suffer so badly. Revenge isn't a healthy emotion. I know that. And right now it's my fuel, but I fear it will burn too hot.

Somehow there are more things I need to stuff into my duffel bag than I have room for. The hike out of the Valley will only take a couple of hours, but still I think we should bring provisions for a day or so, just in case. I look up to catch the silhouette of Rogue carrying the tent on one shoulder and a bag of supplies on the other, managing them easily. Then his form buckles. Falls to the ground. Everything in his grasp tumbling to the ground.

The blankets! I left the stupid blankets out beside the tent and now Rogue has tripped on them. "I'm sorry," I say, rushing to help and then freeze. The moonlight rains down on Rogue, giving me a glimpse that tells a different story than the one I concocted in my head. He's dropped down on one bent knee. His head lies in his hands. The tent and supplies in front of him. The blankets a safe distance away. For a full ten seconds he's quiet, gripping his hair in his fingers, unmoving.

"Rogue?" I take a few cautious steps in his direction.

He shakes his head, discouraging me from approaching, but I ignore him and kneel down a few inches away. Tattered breaths wheeze in and out of his mouth. They're loud in the quiet forest air, but I know Rogue is using everything he has to suppress them. And then a groan escapes his mouth and it rips the caution I'd harbored away. I rush forward and catch his head in my hands just as he tumbles sideways. His form is huddled into a ball, one so large that the force of his head landing in my lap almost knocks me flat. I recover quickly and wrap my body around his head, cradling it.

Rogue's head is against my abdomen and the rest of him lies in front of me. I hug him to me. He doesn't pull away. Doesn't push me away, as I expected. He cringes, but it's from the pain. His face turns white and his hands stay clamped on either side of his head. I push his hair away from his face and hands. I lean down and into his ear I recite the only thing I know to say in this moment. "It's all right, Rogue. I love you." Over and over and over again I say these words to him. And he allows muffled screeches of pain from his mouth, sometimes loudly, but thankfully mostly softly. The pain in him somehow leaks into me and crushes parts of me in torturing ways. Rarely before have I had the misfortune to stand by and watch

173

someone I love convulse with pain. I'm powerless to help him, yet witnessing his pain is compulsory.

After a few minutes his complaints turn to indecipherable mumbles. I allow him to squirm in my lap, holding him as still as I think will keep him calm. I slide down so I'm lying next to him and hold his head into my chest. I think his consciousness has gone, but then he reaches around my waist and wrenches me into him with a desperation that makes me actually smile awkwardly. "Rogue, it's all right. I love you."

And when he nods, I stiffen. He slides his face up until he's looking straight into my eyes. His face is strained, but there's an almost smile on it. "Rogue?" I say, wondering if he's gone completely mad. "Are you all right?"

Too fast he rocks back into a sitting position. I follow suit, although without the same grace. Rogue looks at me like I'm a ghost or something else that's real and also not. He's kind of smiling, but also shaking his head like he's mystified.

"What?" I say, feeling wrong for touching him while he was plagued by that headache, afraid he's about to punish me for it.

"That's the shortest headache I've ever had." He shakes his head, his chaotic hair falling in his face. He slides it back into place, each of his movements careful like he's afraid of his own body. "Somehow, *you*"—he points his gaze at me— "lessened my pain. You made it end prematurely."

I shake my head. "I'm sure it's just a coincidence that I was here."

"I've been getting those headaches for four years. They usually take me out for a full hour, but that one lasted less than ten minutes. That's a first. Explain that, Em," he says, leaning forward, close.

I attempt a smile that feels more like a stretched determined expression. "I-I-I—"

"You make me better," he says, interrupting me. His laughter fills the air and almost rips the mask off my face. Then he pushes forward, encouraging me back until I'm lying flat. Rogue hovers just above me, a hungry look in his eyes. "Thank you, Em." He leans in and kisses me. I expected it to be full of the animalistic emotion he seems to be harboring, but it's soft and thoughtful. When he pulls away I smile at him, but again it doesn't feel genuine.

174

"I'm glad it didn't last long," I say, feeling strange lying in the leaves with him over me in the dark.

"What you're not saying is that it was you," Rogue says, pushing up, and too quickly he's standing and pulling me up with him. "But it was you. Somehow you make me better."

"What? You're saying it's another gift of mine."

He shakes his head. "Sometimes the best thing about us isn't what we're gifted with, but what we can make others feel just by our very nature of existing."

"I'm not sure if I know what that means."

He rubs the side of his head. "Nor I, but right now I'm grateful you exist in my world." He grabs my hand and tugs me into him, wrapping me in his arms.

I smile and into his ear I say, "We're still going to the labs."

"Of course we are," he says with more strength than a man should have who's been through what he has just now. "I was just making a notable remark."

"You're really okay?" I say, stroking the hair off his forehead beaded with sweat.

"I'm better than I've ever been thanks to you." He kisses me once upon the lips. I go in for another but he pushes away. "We've got something we've got to do."

***

"We have to camouflage ourselves?" I ask in surprise.

"You already know what my father's gift is. You should know why we have to do this."

That makes sense now. I nod as Rogue traces a leaf sprayed in skunk juice down my arm. It makes my nose burn. Makes my stomach turn. And still I'm forced to smell it. "So that will cover our scents?"

"It confuses him, which hopefully will be enough."

"Where did you get that?" I ask, directing my attention to the instrument he's using to make me smell repulsive.

He angles his head down at me. "I have my sources."

"Gross."

"If you think this is bad, you get to detail me in skunk grossness next."

"Can't wait," I say.

"Well, no need. I'm all done."

He hands me another leaf, this one fresh with the scent of awfulness. "Seriously, where did you find this and how?"

"Call it a part of my gift," he says with a smile.

"I'm calling bullshit, but it still smells like skunk," I say, rubbing the leaf over his chest. "And it seems like you should be able to wipe yourself down without my help."

He claps a hand over mine, stopping me. "Oh, well if you don't want to do it then I will. I just thought…" He gives me an incredibly perfect pouty face.

"Oh, stop it." I pull my hand from his and run the putrid leaf up around his shoulders. "It's just you finally give me the opportunity to wipe you down and ask me to do it with skunk junk. Thanks."

"Next time will be better," he says, a heated look in his eyes.

"If you make me sponge bathe you with a dead fish then I'm going to call out your sick fetish."

He grips my elbow and pulls me into him. "I only have one obsession and I'm looking at her right now."

And even with the smell of skunk radiating off both our bodies I shiver from his words, have to hold myself back. My eyes shift back and forth between his and I ease my arm from his hand, sliding the leaf down his chest and around to his back. Anything I say won't sound right. It will be too playful or too corny or too serious. Everything I want to say contradicts what we're about to do, so I pretend I don't feel anything and he hasn't said something that makes me want to forget we're facing mortal danger. I slide the leaf around his shoulder blade and down the length of his back.

"To the right," Rogue says. "I've got an awful itch there."

"Get a back scratcher," I say, moving to his lower back. "I've got a job to do."

"Just don't see why you can't kill two birds," he says.

"Here, how does that feel?" I say, indulging him.

"Like you need to put your fingernails into it."

I laugh. "You're insufferable."

"You don't mean that."

"No, I mean the opposite of that, but right now you're making me coat your body in skunk, so that's how I feel."

"I see you're an 'in the moment' kinda girl."

I swipe the leaf down the back of his leg and throw it on the ground. "Done."

He turns and sniffs, grimaces and smiles. "Good job. Oh, and Em, I have something important I need you to do," Rogue says, garnering my attention. "This one is going to be mighty difficult for you, but I need you not to speak when we're at the labs. We need to use hand gestures as much as possible."

"Why would not speaking be difficult for me?" I say.

He presses his mouth together and looks down at the ground as if he hasn't heard me.

"Oh, shush it," I say with a smile. "I know how to be quiet."

"You're not even quiet when you sleep," he says, grabbing my hand and pulling me forward.

Chapter Thirty-Four

I stash my duffel bag beside a tree that we'll have to pass on our journey back from the labs. It's not hidden, but we shouldn't be gone long enough that anyone will stumble across it at this late hour. I want to be able to pick it up and sling it across my chest without stopping so I decide against burying it in brush.

Moving beside Rogue at a steady jog, I'm accosted by something that isn't quite clear to me. It has to do with his pace. We're running on the path, not concerned with passing anyone here since curfew started hours ago. The path will take us to the main plaza and from there the lab is only a half a mile. But moving beside Rogue seems strange. His movements make me doubt my own because he runs differently, like he's not running at all. It almost seems as if he's walking beside me and the faster I move the more he appears to be hardly moving to keep up with me.

Once we're to the plaza I'm sucking in breaths, willing them to steady my racing heart. But Rogue doesn't look as though he's even broken a sweat. He tugs my hand and pulls me into a shadow. Now that we're out of the park, we need to stay in the dark, sprinting when in the light. Knowing he'll catch up with me easily I move off first, and instantly feel him at my back. The way he moves behind me is encouraging, makes me want to move faster just so I keep pace with him. This inspiration somehow delivers us to the lab quicker than I thought we'd be there.

The building, which looks like an ordinary storefront, is dark up front, but its back end is lit with security lights. This is where we'll enter and also where it looks more like a warehouse that contains something huge and not as innocent as its meek front would suggest.

I turn back to Rogue, his features dark in these shadows. "Let's just pop in there real quick," I say.

"In and out," he says, and just as I turn to fill the light with my presence he tugs me back. I freeze, afraid he's stopping me from a danger I haven't spied yet. He pulls my hand up to his shoulder and encourages it around. "Earlier when I had the headache. I had a premonition afterwards."

I blink, trying to clear the dark between us so I can see him clearly. That's right, after a headache he has several abilities at once briefly. Why didn't he tell me about the premonition before now? "What?" I breathe. "What did you see?"

"I can't tell you. I'm afraid if I do I'll change everything," he says.

"Then why are you telling me now?"

"Because I think there's something you need to know," Rogue says. I try to pull my hands away from his neck. He tenses and slaps a hand down on them, keeping me latched on to him. "I haven't told you something about me. When you figure it out, I want you to use it to our advantage."

"Rogue, what does that mean?" I say, pulling my hands off him and this time he allows it.

"Em, if I thought telling you the future would help I would, but I think this advantage comes only if you discover everything on your own."

I shake my head at him. "You're making me want to slap you right now."

He pushes his face in close to mine. Challenges me with a defiant look. "Slap me, baby."

I shake my head and turn. Pause for half a second and sprint into the bright overhead light.

The beeps the keypad sings after I press each number sounds too loud. I picture my father can hear it from our house a mile away. After the six-number code is entered the lock releases with a sharp click. The heavy side door shuts behind us with a gentle clunk. Ahead of us the long corridor is dark, lit by dim floorboard lights. There are more lab rooms than I realized. At least ten doors line this hallway. The meds could be in any of them and even then there are probably a dozen hallways just like this.

"I'll search this room," I mouth without a sound, pointing to the first one. "You take that one." I indicate the one opposite. My hand is on the cold handle when at lightning speed Rogue's arm blocks me and he turns me so I'm facing him. I'm frozen, staring up at his face which is arranged into an angry glare.

"No," he hisses, a flare of fury in his word. Then I realize it's not anger in his face but crazed worry.

"Rogue I'll just be in the next room—"

179

He leans in so close that he's whispering directly into my ear. "Em, I don't care if this takes all night. You're staying with me. That was the plan and we aren't changing it."

I pull to the side and stare back up at him. I want to shake my head, but as if he senses it he catches my chin and brings his mouth close to my ear again. "If anything happens, I want to be by your side."

I nod against his face. "Fine," I mouth.

Rogue turns at once and pushes into the first room, pulling me in behind him. I already knew it was unoccupied by peering through the window in the door, but I didn't realize how unbelievably disorganized it is. It clouds my mind. Overwhelms the mission.

I'm just about to start searching cabinets when Rogue holds up a hand, stopping me. He shakes his head and points back at the door we just came through.

So not this room.

He leads me back out and down the hallway. When we arrive at the next door he pokes his head through and cranes it around. Then he backs out and shakes his head at me. Maybe he's already searched these rooms. Or maybe he's looking for something to match the premonition he saw. I wish he would have explained it to me. I don't like the idea of fulfilling some destiny that I have to blindly walk into. What if I don't make the right decisions? What if I don't understand his cryptic words? What if I get us caught?

After he's poked his head into every room on this hallway, he leads me up to the second floor through the stairwell. His every movement is quick, with a strange precision. Everything, from the way he reaches for a door handle, to the angle of his head as he searches the area around us, has a unique grace. I can't pinpoint what it reminds me of, but it's reminiscent of something.

When we reach the hallway on the second floor, Rogue's back straightens. He's sensed something. I've found that just by watching him, I understand my surroundings better than if I actually took them in properly with my own eyes.

As he has with all the other rooms he pokes his head through a doorway and scans. I half expect him to close the door and lead me down the hallway. Instead he strides into the room, pulling me in behind him. "Here we go," he says, walking directly into the room, confidence in each step.

"They're in here?" I ask. He shakes his head. "No, but they will be."

"What does that mean?" He's hardly even whispering anymore, so I quit as well.

"Trust me," he says. And strangely any complaint stays tucked in my mouth. Those two words send away all my hesitation. Of course I trust him. I step into the room mimicking his confident steps. It looks similar to the other ones I've seen. Lab tables sit in the center, cluttered with various objects. Cabinets line the walls. On the far side of the room is another door leading to another identical room. Rogue leads us in that direction. I almost bump into him when he stops. His hand points to a bottom cabinet which faces the back wall. "Search that one. I'll look up top," he says.

I nod and kneel down, opening the cabinet to reveal a hundred or so medicine bottles. All at once my eyes take in every label and I know the right meds aren't here. I'm about to move to the next cabinet when I'm distracted by Rogue, who's standing just in front and beside me, not moving. He's not searching. Not doing a thing. He stands frozen. Staring. A hostile anticipation in his eyes.

I shuffle my feet underneath me, about to stand, when the door we entered through pushes open, hardly making a sound. I duck down low, my ears prickling from the patter of the soft-soled shoes on the linoleum floor, the sound of fabric rustling against fabric as the person who enters the room moves. His breath is like a steady stream of quick breaths. And I'm quite certain he had summer squash and goat cheese for dinner. All this information floods into my mind as Rogue's words fill the air.

"Hello, Father. I've been expecting you."

181

Chapter Thirty-Five

"Hello, Rogue," President Vider says, that familiar growl in his voice a little more gravelly.

Beside me Rogue's heartbeat speeds up. He swallows a lump in his throat. I hear skin run against skin and look up to see him rubbing his thumb against his fingers. I spy the pores on the back of his hands, the knitting of his shirt, tiny specks of dust on the floor on the other side of him. My eyes are like telescopes, zooming in and out at will. Again I have hyper senses. President Vider's gift.

"Don't you want to give your dear father a hug?" President Vider says, amusement in his voice. "We've been parted for so long. How good it is to finally see my son."

He moves a step and a half into the room. He rustles a hand into his pocket. "I've missed my boy. And here you are, all grown up. And how much you have grown, Rogue. You're as strong as an ox."

"Give them to me," Rogue says, his voice flat, unaffected.

"Oh, no hugs?" President Vider says, taking another step forward, running his hands along the marble countertop. My eyes are trained on the dark corner in front of me; even so, I perceive all of this and know my senses are drawing an accurate picture for me.

"You know why I'm here. Give me what I want," Rogue says.

"How about we talk about what *I* want. There are a few things. For starters, I want to know where you've been." President Vider sniffs the air. "In the woods, no doubt, and obviously without real plumbing. Tell me, son, have you found your years outside the society to be pleasurable? Or have you missed the comforts you took for granted?"

Rogue slams his palm down on the countertop. "Do you have the meds?"

"In fact, I do. I'm hiding them," President Vider says in an almost playful tone.

"Give them to me before I kill you."

President Vider laughs; it's a deep booming sound. "I'll show you what I'm hiding, if you show me what you're hiding. Because in this room I count, one...two...three heartbeats."

182

My eyes flick up, but Rogue's back is still facing away from me. "Show me the meds first. Then I'll show you who I'm hiding."

"Oh, you were always so tiresome. So irritating with your negotiations." Fabric bristles. An object moves against the fabric. A medicinal odor hits me, one full of chemicals which is reminiscent of the injections.

"This is what you were looking for, right?" President Vider says. He shakes the bottle I'm sure he's holding between his fingertips, the capsules in it clanging around the plastic. "This is why you invade my valley with your filth?"

"Yes, and haven't you wondered what my gift is, Father?" Rogue asks.

"No, I don't wonder about you, but to hope you're dying alone in a ditch. Imagine my disappointment at seeing you here now."

I almost stand and charge the President, but somehow force myself to stay crouched as I know Rogue wants me.

"I imagine you're in store for more disappointment, then," Rogue says. "This will not be your night."

And I hear the clang of the capsules as they clink against the plastic bottle followed by silence. A gasp from the President's mouth. And then an object collides with Rogue's hand.

"You really should have cared, Father, what my gift was. Otherwise you wouldn't have showed an apportational the object they most desired," Rogue says.

The President grinds his teeth. "Nice trick, boy. You can keep your meds. It's a fantastic exchange for what you're harboring on the other side of that cabinet."

From the door closest to us, I hear movement. Thunderous footsteps. I want to reach out for Rogue, warn him somehow, but I know I shouldn't break his concentration on his father.

"There will be no exchange," Rogue says, drumming his fingers on the bottle.

A tired breath shoots out of President Vider's nostrils. "Stand up, Em Fuller. I want to see you."

Rogue's eyes finally cast down on me. He gives the slightest nod and I push up at once and turn to face the President, trying to also keep my attention on the approaching presence. However, at the sight of President Vider my focus crumbles. The wicked grin on his face makes a shiver escape my lips. He's wearing a black suit, his hair the same color and perfectly parted on the side and pushed back in a neat arrangement. The smile twitches on his face. He sniffs the air. "Oh yes, I heard your heartbeat, knew you were here, but I smelled you first." Again he takes in another inhalation, like he's smelling a rose. "Even with the camouflage my son so cleverly put on you I still smelled the sweet essence that is Em Fuller. It's delicious." He licks his top lip from one corner to the next. "Rogue, before I tell you about my big plans for Em, let me introduce you to Maurice."

From the doorway behind us a teenager who's almost seven feet tall steps in. He ducks his bald head under the doorway as he enters. He's wearing a gray suit. "Maurice came to me shortly after you abandoned me, Rogue. And he's been ever so useful for dealing with those who stepped out of line. I really wish he would have been here for you as a child, maybe then you wouldn't have been so disobedient."

"Father, what does this have to do with us?" Rogue says, eyeing Maurice, who blocks the doorway on one end of the room and then swinging his head around to President Vider, who blocks the other exit. "Just step aside and let us leave. We don't want trouble."

"Oh, but I believe you do. And you aren't going anywhere with Em. That's why Maurice is here. She belongs to me now and he's going to ensure that she goes home with me." President Vider turns and looks directly at me, his eyes reminding me of a ravenous wolf. "You see, I think before you become a poster child for the Defects, you should be tied to the post of my bed. How does that—"

Rogue rushes forward, so quickly his motions blur. But simultaneously Maurice lunges out and claps a single hand down on his shoulder. Rogue's in the process of deflecting it when he drops in a series of convulsions, pain screaming in his voice. A single touch from Maurice and he appears to be frying from the inside.

"Rogue!" I say and rush forward, but Maurice throws out an outstretched hand. I halt inches from the splayed fingers, eyeing them and then Maurice's threatening stare. He has Rogue pinned on the ground, his hand hovering a few inches from his neck, his other hand extended to me.

"You see, my dear sweet, Em," President Vider says, taking a step in closer to me. "Maurice's touch is lethal. It's quite the unique gift. An embrace from him would stop the heart of his lover. Poor

184

boy hasn't been hugged since he hit puberty, but I've loved him the best I can, given him a job. I do care about my people. Aren't I kind?"

I step away from Rogue and Maurice lowers his hand. Anger boiling my insides, I turn and face the President. "Your manipulation doesn't work on me."

"No, I see it doesn't." He steps forward, reaches out, and almost strokes a single finger down my dirty cheek, but stops himself, holds back. "And I do love a challenge. And more than that I love that you, my pet, are going to encourage an entire population of Defects to rush toward their fate."

"Why would I do that? Even if you convert me, I won't be happy about it. Promote it for your evil agenda," I say, disbelieving the rebellious tone I'm daring to take against the President.

"Oh, my fine young lady, you seem to think I'd leave you with the memories you have now." He shakes his head, his eyes trailing over me, making me want to step behind the counter again to shield myself from his prying gaze. "First you'll be converted to Middling and then your memories will be receded using the modifier. You'll believe what you're told, as you should have from the beginning. I do love the opportunity to create model citizens. And I love that I'm giving you a chance at redemption."

Down on the ground, Rogue lies, flinching from his recent pain. His eyes connect with mine and I want to drop to my knees and shield him from anything Maurice can do to him. But his eyes seem to be communicating a different message to me. "Let him up," I say, my eyes firmly on President Vider.

"You're not in a position to make demands," the President says.

I turn and take in the scene at my back. Maurice hovers over the prone Rogue who is unable to negotiate a single inch without being touched by him. I'm too far from Maurice. Five feet. I take a few steps backward and President Vider holds up a hand. "Stay away from my son."

"You lost the right to call him that," I say and take another step backwards.

"Maurice," President Vider says, and the giant pain-inducer places his fingertips to Rogue's cheek, making him jerk wildly and scream out like he's on fire suddenly.

"No," I yell, but remain frozen.

"Isn't that the way it always is," President Vider says, "you hurt the ones you love by trying to help them. That's my unfortunate plight. I tried to help my poor son, make him a usable member of this society, but he didn't appreciate my efforts. But you, Em, it's not too late for you. You'll have the distinct honor of being the poster child for Defects. I gave you that honor. You will prove to them that they have a salvation. They will worship you. And I assure you that honor is better than anything my son has promised you."

"Freedom! That's better than my freedom?!" I yell.

"Em, don't be goaded by him. Just ignore him," Rogue says from the ground, his voice shaky.

President Vider gives a minute nod to his minion. Maurice pokes Rogue, sending him into a series of screaming howls.

"Stop!" I scream. "I'll go with you. I'll do whatever it is you want." My hands vibrate by my side. "Just let him up. Let me look at him and say goodbye." And President Vider nods at Maurice, who motions to Rogue. And he shuffles to a standing position. I look at Rogue and open my mouth to say something, to apologize, but then I feel his thoughts in my mind. A thought I know is his. *Gods above, Em, you're beautifully impossible.* I smile at him and round on the door just as my father enters.

Chapter Thirty-Six

My father strolls into the room, a coolness in his self-satisfied expression. He takes the place next to President Vider, unbuttons his pin-striped jacket, and slides his hand into his pocket, not even making eye contact with me. He removes a watch on a gold chain and then slips it back.

"As Lyza foretold, they're right on time," my father says to the President, looking at him with a prideful expression. My own mother. She's the one who told them when we'd be here. She must have seen it with her clairvoyance. *Damn bitch.*

"Father?" I say, waiting for him to look at me with his crisp blue eyes. Finally he brings his gaze to mine, an indignant look on his face. He always seems too young, with his polished look and head full of blond hair. He ages, but not enough. Not enough to feel like he's that much older than me. It's wrong and I hate that about him. I hate how he makes everything feel wrong.

"Em, did you really think you were going to get away from being converted?" He looks at me with a sneer, his nostrils flaring. *Oh gods, she stinks,* I hear him think.

"And you're wearing entirely too much cologne," I say, pulling my chin down low to my chest. I sniff the air once. "Oh, and a bit of perfume too, but that's not the kind mother wears."

My father's eyes widen with horror. "Why did you say that? Where did that come from?"

"Wouldn't you like to know?" I say.

How does she know I smell like a perfume? I changed my jacket, it should have been enough.

"It wasn't," I say, with a guilty smile.

"Why did you say that?" my father says.

What kind of game is she playing? he thinks in his head.

"The kind you've played on me my entire life," I say.

He raises a knowing eyebrow, a wicked grin on his face. *So you're telepathic? Well, congratulations, but very soon it won't matter,* he thinks.

Oh, yes, I'm telepathic, as well as other things, I say in my mind.

187

He tapers his eyes at me. *What else?*

You'll find out, I think.

"Em," he says out loud, a strange edge to his voice, a bit of nervousness escaping. "Tell me what other gifts you have."

"Damien," President Vider says, snapping my father's attention on him, "what's going on?"

"It appears my daughter has inherited my main gift."

"Oh," President Vider says, sounding pleased. "So you'll know exactly what I want, when I want it, won't you, Em? This keeps getting better."

No! Behind me I hear Rogue's heart pound faster, louder. I turn and give him an encouraging look.

"Don't worry, Rogue," President Vider says, sensing the rise in tension in his son, the same as me. "We have plans for you too. You'll be converted and your memories receded. The people of Austin Valley will be so touched when my son returns to me, after being lost for so long. And after I'm done with Em, you two can live in some awful Middling dwelling, where you can be complacent and serve us as you were intended."

I flash a look at Rogue again, but it's Maurice's round face that catches my attention. There's a confused expression on it. *But I thought I was supposed to kill him tonight,* the ogre thinks.

I turn with a slow stealth and face my father.

He shrugs, a relaxed grin on his face. *Oops. Now you know.*

"Em," he says out loud, "I want you to come here. This time you won't be escaping conversion."

The little girl in me cowers. The old subservience overtakes me, the one I've been plagued by since childhood. My feet move forward, like I don't control them, but he does.

Down the hallway, far off, a door clinks. I stop, focus my attention on it and the tiny noises that follow. Someone shuffles into a room. Moves multiple metal objects, placing them on a metal tray. Their breath smells of barley and plantains. They haven't showered since this morning. And they walk with a slight limp.

I raise my eyes to my father's just as President Vider says, in a delighted growl, "Dr. Sanders is ready for her?" he says, looking confused, having heard the same noises I did. "But I thought we were going to wait to do her conversion tomorrow."

My father shakes his head at me, his face slack. "I want it done now. You can do what you like afterwards. Kill her for all I care."

"Oh, no, she's way too valuable to our campaign," the President says.

Instinctively I back up. My eyes flick in the direction of where I hear this doctor preparing to convert me. I'm scanning for options. My eyes take in thousands of objects all at once, a dozen possibilities occurring to me. "Maurice plans to kill Rogue, but how do you plan to take me?" I say.

President Vider shakes his head, clicks his tongue. "I'd never kill my dearest son," he says. Lies. "But if you don't consent to follow us then I will have him tortured." He flicks his eyes at Maurice and nods, such a subtle movement, but instantly Rogue wails behind me and I almost lose the ability to hold myself up. His pain is so distinct in his cries, more so than when he's been plagued by the headaches.

I'm growing more into my gift, and suddenly surrounded by Dream Travelers I feel all the distinct powers around me. With the need to survive and protect leading my motivation, I feel everyone's abilities at my fingertips. President Vider's enhanced senses and my father's telepathy are strongest right now because they use their gifts automatically, like breathing. But I believe the other gifts, Rogue's apportation and Maurice's killing touch, are at my disposal too. And still I sense other powers around me, and I don't know what they all are, although I sense someone has the gift to shield, because I know I'm easily keeping my father out of my head right now, only feeding him the thoughts I want him to hear. It's easier to shield him than ever before. Behind me Rogue groans again, this one a guttural sound.

I spin and face Maurice. "Stop! Don't touch him again or *I'll* kill you."

In front of me my father laughs, one full of ridicule. President Vider joins in with him. "Em, do you really think that you can pull something out of this young man's thoughts that will help your cause, let alone give you the opportunity to kill him? You're out of options. So admit defeat and come with me now."

"As you wish," I say and step forward, my hands loose by my side, my head giddy with the opportunity to have close proximity to

189

my father. I'll take him hostage, leeching Maurice's powers. I'll get Rogue out of this.

Behind me I hear an object slip out of Rogue's pocket. The air swishes by the sides of the container as it falls. I twist around and seize it with my eyes before it's even touched the ground. The bottle of meds clatters to the tile floor and rolls off under a cabinet, but I spy it easily. My reflexes when I turned around had been strange, too fast. Like how I'd spied Rogue moving when we first entered the lab.

Rogue doesn't look remorseful, but rather has a cunning look on his pained face, held hostage by Maurice standing too close beside him. "Oops," he says, "I'm such a damn klutz. Maurice, you mind picking up those pills for me? I've got a migraine coming on."

I have no idea what he's up to or why he doesn't look perturbed by the fact that he's lost the meds we came here for. Maurice shakes his head at him. I turn back around to my father, but his eyes are not on Rogue, they're studying me. He pushes his heel into the ground, a tiny movement, but I notice it before it even happens, having telegraphed his move. President Vider's eyes flick down to his heel too. My father rubs the heel against the linoleum, making the slightest of movements, creating the slightest of irritating noises. Instantly it soaks up my attention. Soaks up the President's.

"Why are you doing that?" the President asks.

Because, my father thinks.

And then he rubs his fingers together. My eyes flick to them. So do President Vider's. He stops, rubs his fingers together on the other hand. Instantly my eyes are there.

Too late I realize what's he's doing. I rush forward.

My father holds up his hand. "Stay away from me, Em."

"You told me to come with you," I say, continuing forward.

My father looks at Maurice. Nods. Instantly Rogue screams out in pain.

"Stop!" I say, freezing in place. "Stop!"

"Don't come a step farther, Em," my father says. "Actually I'd feel more comfortable if you backed up a few steps."

"Like the President said to me earlier," I say, gritting my teeth together, "I don't think you're in a position to make requests."

He raises a single eyebrow at me, nods his head again, and Rogue's scream makes me crumble. Why do I think I can win at their game? I've already lost. Obviously. *Okay, fine, you win,* I think and hold up my hands in surrender.

"Well, well, well. How extremely interesting. It appears that my daughter is a leech," my father says with almost a hint of pride in his voice.

Alarm registers on President Vider's face. "Oh gods!" he says, taking three steps back.

Chapter Thirty-Seven

"That's right," I say, taking a step forward. "I'm a leech." I leech the energy out of Maurice, feel it tingle on my fingertips. Hold it in my hand with a new confidence. I reach out both my hands to the President. "Still want me?"

"Stay away," the President says, a sneer in his voice.

"I read your thoughts. I hear your heartbeat. And I can make you feel a lot of pain," I say, angling my head over my shoulder at Maurice.

"You forget," President Vider says, with a growl, "that we still have control here." A tiny nod and behind me I know what I'll hear next.

I whip around and face Maurice, again my movements like that of a cat's or more appropriately a cheetah's. Quick. Efficient. "Stop!" I yell. After a delay he does. "You don't have to do this. You don't have to do what they say."

The boy—I call him that because he's younger than me—looks at me with strange, sad eyes. After a quick perusal of his thoughts I realize that he does. He absolutely has to do everything that President Vider says. Where does my advantage lie if they can torture and kill Rogue and I'm unable to stop it, even having all of their abilities? I need to have something they want, to hold it over their head, but I don't know what that is. From below the cabinet I spy the white bottle peek back at me. I'm not sure why, and I know that it robs him of energy, but I still leech Rogue, apportioning the bottle of meds into my hands and then slipping it into my pocket. *If we get out of this, then we'll need these.*

My eyes flick to Rogue's, which are rimmed in pain, but still looking relieved for some reason. *Thank you. Now take my other gift,* he thinks.

Other? I think to myself. I don't know what he means so I turn and face our fathers, who look like they've backed up a few paces.

"I want you to let Rogue go," I say. "If you do then I won't race forward and put you both in debilitating pain."

"If you take a single step forward, then Rogue will die," President Vider says too matter-of-factly.

My father shakes his head at me, a dismissive look. He slips a phone out of his inside jacket pocket and holds it to his face. "Send in unit eleven to the second floor of the labs." Without another word he drops the phone into his pocket. It simultaneously terrifies and frustrates me that I can't find the upper hand. I have the skill of every person in this room and still I can't overpower my father.

He smiles, having sensed my thoughts. "That's right, Em. Read our thoughts, sense everything around us, use Rogue's apportational ability, but know that we still control you, because we have what you want. You can have it all, but you're still powerless against us. And soon, you'll be even more powerless." He nods again and Rogue screams. Fury wraps around my head, constricting my rationality. *If you hurt him again I'm going to sprint forward and kill you.*

"He'll die too," my father says in response to the words in my head. "Will it be worth it then?"

President Vider eyes my father and then me, realizing he's missing parts of conversations between us. "Enough of this. It's time you're relieved of this gift and all the pressures it puts on you. So sad you ended up being so powerful because I was really looking forward to your company tonight."

And my father, who should have looked sickened by such a thing, doesn't make a single grimace. *You're a sicko,* I think at him.

And you're a slow learner. He glances at Maurice and again Rogue howls with pain. My legs weaken, my body weight falling forward, and I almost tumble to my knees. But right before my knees hit the ground I hear Rogue's voice in my head.

NO! DON'T!

My reflexes catch me with a strength I don't own and pull me back up to a standing position. I turn to the person who I hear in my head. Rogue stares at me, looking half drunk but also determined. He rights himself to a full standing position.

Watch, Rogue thinks at me. And I do, taking in every ounce of him like I'm about to never see him again. I see his form as it is to me, perfect and strong and full of a grace which seems like it belongs to the gods. And then it hits me like a bullet in the chest. I watch him again swipe his hand across his hair, so fast that without President Vider's gift of sight I would have missed it. Would have never seen his hand move away from his side. I watch the way his feet shift and realize what I missed before. I realize he's giving me a display. To be able to see Rogue in that light is a gift in itself.

Now I know what Rogue's other ability is. I know why he can't use it to his favor, with Maurice too close to him. But I also recognize how I could employ it if given the right opportunity.

My father, who I realize only sees a fraction of his world because he's trained on thoughts, watches me with a quiet annoyance. President Vider watches the hallway behind them as well as my every movement, afraid I'm about to turn Maurice's gift on them.

"Soon," my father says, "this ugly mess will be over with."

"Because I'll have killed you all and you'll be hanging out in hell," I say.

He shakes his head at me. "Em, if you want to leave then do it. We all know you have that power, but we also know that if you do Rogue will die, and if you try and attack us using Maurice's skill then Rogue will die. So will you please stop with the threats, because they're quite tiresome?"

"Oh, and after the long day you've had screwing your secretary, I'm sure this is too much," I say.

Don't say that!

"Come and stop me, Father."

"And this is exactly why you were put on the Defect list, Em," my father says, looking at me with a tired expression.

"Yeah, kudos for trying to exterminate the Defects," I say.

"It's not an attempt. It will happen," the President says with a conceited knowing.

"What about these new Dream Travelers you're recruiting into the Valley? Aren't you afraid they may be Defects?"

"We screen them," the President says.

"And what about all these ideas they have of the outside world?" I ask, stalling.

The President gives me a delighted look. "We recede most of their memories using the modifier. An especially useful technology. They have no memory of any outside influences." His smile resembles a wolf with its hackles pulled up high. He also looks pleased, like he's halfway to a feast.

I deflate, realizing how much further ahead they are than I realized.

Yes, that's right, Em. There's no stopping us, my father thinks.

"You know, I realize you have reinforcements coming, which I think is cute, since the three of you can't handle me on your own," I say. "But you do understand that I could just drain you all to death?" President Vider laughs. "That would take all night."

"You're wrong," I say, "I've drained—"

"Those who aren't pregnant or sick aren't as easily affected," my father says in a tired voice, having read my thoughts.

Tammy's pregnant? Rogue is sick? What? I shake my head at him.

Oh, didn't you know? my father says in his mind.

I hate his answers. They make me feel like I'm constantly on the losing end of this battle, when I have every advantage. I keep listening for these reinforcements. So does President Vider. They aren't in the building yet.

I should make my move now, but the problem is that using a skill of this sort before practicing it in a setting like this isn't just dangerous, it is a lunatic move. And still so perfectly do I know what Rogue intends me to do. I know the skill he intends me to leech. I keep buying time. Delaying.

"You know, Dad," I say and watch him cringe. He always made us call him Father.

"You're downright evil. That's not a judgment of you as my father, but rather a judgment of your thoughts. You make me sick." I turn to President Vider. "And your thoughts are wicked and could easily put you behind bars. One day, I'll make sure the Reverians know the truth about what you did." And finally I turn and angle myself so I'm looking half at Maurice, but still have my father and the President in my eyesight. "And you, well, you're just a minion who's been brainwashed and are under mind control."

I turn back to the President and take a step forward, which sends both men in front of me stumbling backwards. "I realize now why you really created the Defect list. It's not just because we threaten your authority, it's because we have a gene inside us that prevents us from being put under your mind control. And how can you rule people who don't do everything you make them? It's nice to sense everything, but even better to control people. Too bad you can't control everyone."

"You will suffer for this," the President says.

"You have to catch me first," I say, and using the gift I just realized Rogue owns I race to Maurice in less than a quarter of a second. My feet hardly touch the ground. I feel myself blur across the space. Both my hands seize one of Maurice's, which is easily the size of my head. Instantly I'm incapacitated by a shock so jarring it makes my teeth hurt. His face registers the same pain. But not the same pain. More. Between our skin to skin touch we suffer a double burn. His eyes widen as I push more of his power at him, having leeched a great deal of it while I stalled. Stored it for this moment. And still only a couple of seconds have passed. And then Maurice drops to the ground like a great ship sinking. His eyes wide open. Unmoving. He's dead.

I almost pass out from the pain still surging through my limbs. Rogue reaches out for me, but then halts. Knowing I have to, I leech his power to move at rapid speed and dash out the door behind us, just catching the look of horror on my father's face as his slow eyes take in what just happened. Behind me Rogue moves at the same pace. A super human one. The space around me blurs as I shoot through room after room and finally to a back hallway. I'm moving like I do during dream travel. Like I'm a roller coaster. Moving like this, beside Rogue, feels incredible. Like we're two lions in a jungle, each movement so precise it makes my heart pause.

I don't leech any more from Rogue after I leave the lab room. And soon I know this speed which is granting us a serious advantage will dissipate. We sprint down the stairwell, through a different hallway, to a set of double doors. The whole time I'm aware of the energies around me, the people. But none are dangerous. None are leechable. We break into a giant warehouse full of stacked boxes. It's only halfway through that that Rogue's energy leaks out of me and I slow until I'm moving at my usual pace. He passes me and then circles back when he realizes I'm no longer at his side.

"Take more," he says, walking by me as I jog.

"No. You'll need it," I say.

"We just need to get out of here," he implores.

"No. We have a long journey back. You need your energy."
And I worry about what my father said. About Rogue being more affected by my leeching.

"Fine."

"Why didn't you tell me about your other gift?" I say.

"It just came out recently. Like really came out," Rogue says. "I've always been strong and had good stamina but it came out on my way into the Valley this trip and I hadn't had a real chance to practice and hone it yet, well, not until now."

"But you knew it was there," I say as we round a corner. "And you didn't tell me."

He gives me a sideways smile. "If I would have then you would have overthought that moment. You wouldn't have done it so perfectly. Escaped so wonderfully."

"How can you know?"

"Because I saw the future," Rogue says with a devilish smile. "We have a lot to discuss. Let's go."

I chance touching his arm, hoping the gift I leeched from Maurice is completely gone. He smiles. Grabs my hand and we run. Taking off even faster, him pulling, almost dragging me. We swing around corners, trying to find our way out of this too big warehouse. Several times we backtrack, finding dead end after dead end.

Finally a door. I push through it and into a two-story room. Cold stings my skin. The temperature in this space is at least ten degrees colder than the warehouse, which was already frigid with its metal walls and concrete floors. Server cases stand in rows upon rows in front of us. Blue radiance shines from them, providing the only light in the room. Above the terminals a metal catwalk crisscrosses around the room, wires snaking along its belly.

What is this place? What in the world are they trying to control with this all? I turn once. Twice. Three times, trying to determine which way to run. It's a maze of rows which stretch for as far as I can see.

"Do you sense a way out of this?" Rogue asks, staring around.

"Why me?"

"Because you're Ms. Badass," he says.

"No." I shake my head. "Maybe you should scout ahead? Do your cheetah move and find the exit."

He gives me a punishing look. "You know damn well I'm not leaving you."

I nod, having expected that answer. The good news is that I think I'll sense my father or the reinforcements if they close in on us. I take cautious steps and angle my head around the first row of cases, which stand taller than Maurice.

Maurice. Guilt prickles my throat. Threatens to close it up. I shake off the feeling, but not entirely.

The rows stretch for twenty feet, with short breaks between them and the next. In the dim light it's hard to see the wall on the far side of the room, but I think I almost do. I grab Rogue's hand. "Come on. We have to get out of here."

Disappointment unravels in my stomach when we reach the darkened wall to find no exit. And ahead of us stretches the same row of servers, one after another. Too many rows to count. My eyes strain in the blue light.

On my next step I'm assaulted by an intense burning in my chest. It doubles me over. Steals my breath.

"Em." Rogue races back, pulling me upright. "What is it?"

Both my hands press against my chest. Press against the burning. My heart feels ready to explode. And I try to say something, but I can't speak past the pain. He grips my neck and tips my head back, looking deep into my eyes. Searching my face. "Gods, you're burning up, Em. What's happened to you?"

I blow out a hot breath. Feel it so acutely against the cold of the room. I shake my head at Rogue, as the corners of my vision start to darken.

Again he's studying me, his face blanketed with confusion. Finally a determined look takes over his features and he sweeps me into his arms. "I'm getting you out of here."

"You're not going anywhere," my father says, his voice coming from up high, his pale face swimming into my vision.

Chapter Thirty-Eight

Rogue halts. We both turn our faces up to where my father and President Vider stand on the catwalk above us. Seeing the sniveling grins on their faces sends my adrenaline into overdrive. It takes over the intensity building in my chest. Clears my vision. I squirm until Rogue releases me from his arms, standing me upright. His hands stay clasped on my shoulders. My father leans on the railing of the catwalk, his knuckles white. President Vider stands, feet shoulder width apart, hands casually clasped behind his back.

"You killed someone, Em," my father says, shaking his head with slight disappointment like I've done something trivial.

"You made me!" I scream up to him. And although I'm still roasting, my anger is giving me strength over the ailment that's recently zapped by chest with pain.

President Vider sighs. "Don't you see what a danger you are to other people? Don't you see why we gave you the injections all along? You thought we were trying to control you, but we're just trying to protect innocent people. People would suffer if Defects like you and Rogue were free to have your gifts."

"Father, I do believe you've brainwashed yourself into believing that," Rogue says, his voice filling up the large room. "But you can't warp us."

I focus on my father. Try to reach into his thoughts and come up short. I scan the room, trying to use President Vider's gift to find an exit. Nothing comes. All I feel is Rogue's power inside him at my access.

"We're too far away," my father says with a satisfied grin.

"What?"

"You can't leech us from this far back," my father says. "And if you continue to leech Rogue after his ordeal and with his condition you'll kill him. It's time to stop acting irrationally and surrender to the conversion we all know is inevitable."

I hate the confidence in his voice. I hate that I'm half nodding in agreement to my father's words. I hate that he still has a leash on me somehow.

"Why don't you come down here and get us?" Rogue says, sounding slightly amused. "We'll wait for you. Promise."

"Mr. Vider, do you take me for an idiot?" my father says.

"Quite frankly, yes," Rogue says, a sideways smile on his lips. "Which is why my father chose you as his Chief of Staff. Idiots are easy to control. They think the way he tells them to."

"Well, while you've satisfied your ego berating me, we've trapped you," my father says, threading his arms across his chest, looking victorious. The whites of eyes all around us pop out of the darkness as men approach from the shadows. Dozens of men. All wearing jeans and T-shirts. Middlings. Their slack faces take on a sinister look in the blue light. "Who's the idiot now?" my father says, his chin down, eyes treacherous.

I step in closer to Rogue. His arm tightens around my waist. Twenty men, maybe more, inch in closer to us, forming a tight circle. The men appear cautious, and also driven, taking calculated short steps.

"They've come to take you back to where you belong," President Vider says, leaning over the rails.

Rogue holds up his hands. "Look, guys," he says, swinging his head around, speaking to the men crowding us, "we don't want trouble."

"These exceptionally loyal Middlings know you *are* trouble," the President says, his voice laced with that persuasion he uses to brainwash. "They know you are their downfall and if allowed free you'll destroy the Valley they've grown to love. My fine citizens will not allow terrorists to endanger their lives. Isn't that right, men?"

A collective and low "Yes" hums from the men's lips.

"And the best part is, Em, you can't leech a Middling. You're powerless against them," President Vider says, drawing his chest up high. "And Rogue, you can fight them, but even you can't defeat twenty-five men. You two are done and soon you'll both be converted. Soon you'll be like these Middlings, who succumb to my rule."

"And that's what you've always wanted from us, isn't it!" I yell, my anger making me shake all over. The burning returns to my core, but not like before. It's a pulsing supremacy, and it's uncontrollable, as though it's about to overpower me. "You want to control us. You want to think for us. But I will die before I allow that."

"I don't really see what the problem is," my father says rather coolly. "You've always been more Middling than Dream Traveler. I would think you'd be grateful that we're putting you with your people."

"Why don't you read my mind if you want to know what *I* think about it," I say.

"You're so uncivilized, Em. This is the grave you have dug. Get over it," my father says.

The men approach faster; they're only ten feet away. Nine feet. Eight. Close enough that I recognize faces from the fields. Men I've worked alongside. "Dean!" I say, grateful to see his kind eyes staring back at me. But there's something different in them. An uncertainty maybe. "I'm not a bad person, Dean. You have to help us. It's the President who can't be trusted."

His face contorts with confusion. He pauses. The men around him halt too.

"It was the President who killed your—"

"Don't listen to her," President Vider says. "She's a liar who's trying to confuse you. Don't let this rebel manipulate you with her deceptions."

"That's funny, coming from you," I say, scowling at President Vider.

"Get them!" the President commands.

The men lunge forward. And I know that it's futile to fight them. We're outnumbered. I hold up my hands. Feel Rogue behind me, pull me into him tighter. "Wait," I say. "I'll go, willingly. We both will."

"Em, what are you doing?" Rogue whispers at my shoulder.

"Shhh…" I keep my hands up as I speak. "But before I surrender I have one last thing to say to my father. Will you please give me that?"

The men freeze in a perfect circle around us. Dean nods, a real battle seeming to go on within him. I flip my head up.

"Father," I say, glaring at his smug face.

"Yes, Em," he says, sounding bored.

"You've always known I was uncooperative, right?"

"Yes."

201

"And you knew you were stripping me of my gift by giving me the injections, right?"

He blinks a few times. "Yes," he says, his patience waning.

"You've seemed to know so much about me," I say, my hands still in the air. Palms facing toward him.

He leans over the rail, looking down at me with a narcissistic smile. "That's right."

"Well, one thing I don't think you know is that even from a distance, I'm dangerous." From my raised hands bolts of electricity fire. They're bright, so much so that I can't look at them directly without my eyes squinting from the bluish light. The bolts shoot through the air faster than anyone can react. They gallop for a target and finally connect with the metal railing both my father and President Vider are gripping with white knuckles. The two men don't have a second to react and there's nowhere for them to go. The electricity assaults the railing and instantly spreads out, shooting through everything connected to the rails. The beams linked to the catwalk. The catwalk. My father. The President.

The electricity that had been lying across my heart, building with intensity, burdening me, burning me from the inside out, is now a weapon I've thrown at the two most powerful men in Austin Valley. Now with the electricity released I'm suddenly light. I feel like I can sprint for a hundred miles. And above us, my father and President Vider grip the metal bars like they're welded to them as they fry under the electricity. Both men's eyes bulge. Their bodies vibrate with a violent intensity. Smoke from somewhere begins snaking its way through the blue light. I watch them fry for what begins to feel like too long. Their suffering is a strange one that leaves an ambivalent weight over my conscience. Redemption and guilt somehow live simultaneously in my thoughts as I watch the electrocution of the two vilest men I've ever known.

And then as if synchronized, they both shoot off the bars and land in crumpled messes a few feet back. Each man convulses, like trying to move but unable to control their limbs properly. My father sits up, but electricity continues to snake through him, pinning him to the ground. Blood, dark, almost appearing black, snakes down from the President's nostrils. And although I know I shot a great deal of electricity at them, they both still stare at me with blinking, vengeful eyes before slumping back on the metal grate below them. My father's attempts to breathe echo with a strange rattling sound. And yet, I find a slight bit of consolation that he breathes. For the moment he is powerless, but not dead.

Around us the crowd of men steps back. The faces of men who have trusted me, worked beside me, stare back with disbelief and distrust. "No!" I yell. "I won't hurt you! I'll protect you. I'll save you from them. Don't be afraid."

And still they revolve their gaze on each other and seem to come to the same conclusion as they back away. Away from me, like I'm going to hurt them with the same power I just unleashed against my father. Dean looks at me, terror in his eyes. "I want to help you," I say, taking a step forward, but he shakes his head and backs up and then the group disperses, running away from me like I'm a monster.

I touch Rogue's hand only slightly, afraid I might hurt him with my touch. When nothing happens I clench his hand. He grips it tight.

"Let's get out of here," I say, and we run forward, toward where the Middlings are going. Hopefully to an exit.

Chapter Thirty-Nine

We race out of the building, through empty lots, past the plaza. And then Rogue scoops me into his arms and sprints at lightning speed. It's the most beautiful thing I've ever witnessed. To feel safe and secure and also move like I'm dream traveling. That's what Rogue can do. He moves like my consciousness does, with a graceful agility. His body has that instinct and I instantly worship it.

He sets me down when we arrive at my duffel bag. He's sprinted, carrying me, for four miles, and isn't even winded. I'm certain now I don't spy half of his movements, which are like tiny sparks, quick and powerful.

"Rogue," I say, touching his face, marveling at his greatness. "Are you all right?"

He nods. "I'm fine. Let me carry you farther."

"No," I say, pulling away from him. "I've got this. Let's go." I tug his hand behind me as I hike up the hill in front of us. Then I remember something and turn around to catch a deliriously happy smile on his face. "What are you smiling about?"

"I've got a long list," he says.

I nod, smile back. Then I pull the bottle of pills out of my pocket. "Sorry, I forgot about these." I open the bottle and pop one small oblong pill into my palm and offer it to Rogue. He swallows it dry.

"You were incredible back there. You electrocuted my father and yours," he says, his eyes sparkling with life.

"I don't think I killed them."

"No, I'm afraid you probably didn't, but still you knocked them out and that's a good start to a fight."

"I did kill Maurice," I say, guilt crowding my throat again.

"No, you put him out of his misery."

He kisses me and then tugs me forward, holding my hand as we rush through the forest. We hike two more miles to the top of the ridge and then our journey becomes more treacherous for the next two miles down, sliding on screes and almost falling off steep blunts. But Rogue navigates our route, every time making sure we finagle ourselves out of danger.

The canopy of the forest is so dense, I didn't even know the moon was hanging overhead until we come to a clearing. Its silver light kisses the grass and wildflowers in the field. And then on the far side of the clearing I spy movement. I startle at first but then realize whatever it is isn't human. The motion is a sweeping one. Hidden just on the other side of the field under the trees is an animal. And then my eyes adjust to the moonlight and I catch the movement of the swish of a magnificent horse's tail.

I turn to Rogue. "That's...?"

He nods. "Indeed."

I almost cry realizing we're so close. So close to freedom. Each step away from Austin Valley now feels coated with a potential doom, like my father will fly in and steal me away. Convert me. Being this close to escaping his and the President's oppression is terrifying. And still I move forward, taking each step with a deliberate focus.

When I'm ten feet from the horse I really see her. See how extraordinary she is.

"Wow," I say in a hush, coming to a halt.

"She's a beauty, isn't she?" Rogue says.

I've never seen such a large animal. She's the length of a car and taller than Rogue. Her coat is golden and her mane and tail are white. She exudes a mystic strength I've never witnessed before. I wonder if all animals have this beautiful power inside them. Something tells me I will soon find out. I have so much to discover now.

"She's stunning," I finally say in response to Rogue's question.

Rogue tugs on my hand, encouraging me toward her. He pats the horse's neck. She whinnies at him, shakes her head. "Say hi to Em."

"Hi," I say, putting my hand up to her nose so she can smell me. I assume that's what you do with a horse, so they know you're all right. "What's your name?" I say, rubbing her nose, which is soft and wet.

"I just told you. Her name is Em," Rogue says, with a guilty laugh.

My eyes go wide. Mouth drops opens. Somehow a smile forms on my face. "You named your horse after me?!"

He nods, a clever smile on his face. Shrugs. "She's not just any horse. She's the best one out there." He stands back and looks at her, checking her over. "And she's the most beautiful."

"Do you have a horse named after Zack too?" I laugh at the ridiculousness of the perfect man in front of me.

"Yeah, he's my second best horse. Not as pretty, but he's still a looker."

The laugh that bursts out of my mouth echoes around us. As though he was born on a ranch and not confined to a suit most of his life, Rogue steps into the saddle and slings his leg over the side. Again the way he moves chills me. His gift of agility is unbelievably mesmerizing. His movements blur with grace. He extends a hand to me and I realize I'm holding my breath. Somehow by just watching him I've forgotten to breathe. "My lady?"

Sitting up tall on his horse, the moon casting him in a flawless light, I see Rogue for the first time for who he has truly become. A man. But not just any man, he's become one who can steal anything he wants, pull it to him with just his sheer desire. And he's stolen my heart. I've always loved Rogue, but not like I do in this moment. I don't love him like a friend anymore. He doesn't remind me of the boy who used to knock on my door at the same hour after dinner every night. I love him like my life depends on it. And in this moment I know it does. Our love has freed me.

I grab his hand, and with a strength that tightens my heart he pulls me up and onto the horse, whom I refuse to call by my name. My hands seize onto Rogue's waist to steady me. "I've never ridden a horse before," I say, looking down at the ground which feels too far away. The horse feels warm under me, and strangely like I'm straddling a tractor.

Rogue turns around and gives me a sideways smile. "It's just like riding a bike."

"How's that?" I ask, looking down at my feet that hang loosely on either side of the horse.

"If you fall off, it hurts like hell."

I laugh and snuggle my face in his neck, before lifting my chin and planting a single kiss on his cheek.

He turns back around and straightens up. "Hold on tight, babe."

I snake my arms more snugly around him and press my chest to his back.

"Come on, Em, take us home."

Rogue digs his heels into the horse, flicks the reins, and we take off in a steady trot down the hill, away from the land where I was born and to a place where I hope to be reborn.

Don't miss book two in the *Reverians* series, *Rebels*. Available starting September 15, 2015.

Flip to the end of this book to continue your journey with the Reverians and read the first chapter of the next installment: *Rebels*.

And if you have a moment then please leave a review for *Defects* on Amazon. Sarah loves to hear what readers think.

Acknowledgements:

I can't believe I actually get to say this, but my first thank you goes out to my readers. I have readers?!?! You all reached out and supported me so much after my first series was published. I'm not going to lie. I was mortified by the experience. Would the world hate it? Love it? Line dog crates with it? But you all told me how much you enjoyed the Dream Travelers' world. You asked for more. You encouraged me. Every single comment and review and email has given me confidence to step back in the author ring and put my heart on the line. Thank you for giving me that encouragement. Thank you for your insights and thoughts and sharing with me.

Thank you to my beta readers. Seriously, this would be a way different story without your help. I'm more than grateful for the time you give making my stories better. Without you I would be lost. Thank you to first chair, Colleen. Thank you to some of my biggest supporters Heidi and Mike. Thank you to Kelly for tightening the storyline. And thank you to Dane and Meghan who are eagle eyes. Thank you to Katy and Mathew for their incredible insights.

Thank you to my editor, Christine LePorte. Your work really polishes my story and your encouraging words have been a huge support to me.

Thank you to Andrei Bat. Can you believe I roped you in to do another cover for me? Bhahahaha! You can't get away from me.

Thank you to my Facebook, Goodreads, Twitter and Instagram family. I have so much fun with you all and you have no idea how much the interaction encourages me. Thank you to the fantastic bloggers out there who have supported the first series and this one. I feel so fortunate to be able to work with you all.

Thank you to my family who is constantly building me up. Specifically a huge thanks to Randy and Edie. Your unconditional love just blows me away. Thank you to my dad, Kathy, Bea and Anne. Love you all.

Thank you to my friends. Seriously, you all amaze me with your support. I love you all so much and just want to make you proud. Thank you to Marie, Susie, Nicole, Nicole, Anna, Melinda, and Heidi for all your help with the books.

Thank you to spirit for granting me so many blessings. I have said before, and firmly believe, I have written very little of my own. I'm a recorder of sorts, writing down the inspiration you give me through some strange cosmic source. To me, there's no other real explanation.

A colossal thanks to my husband, Luke, for putting up with me. When I write I turn in to a crazy, multiple personality kind of person. I reason that I'm channeling my characters, but to the outsider it would seem that I'm a little bipolar. At least I'm honest about it. Anyway, Luke doesn't just allow this, he actually admires this to an extent. Luke, you are my first reader and my best critic. And I love you dearly. Thank for putting up with me.

And the last thanks goes to my beautiful daughter, Lydia. I'm always trying to make you proud because you, sweetheart, make me so very proud. I never wrote like I did once you entered my life. You are my inspiration.

About the Author:

Sarah is the author of the Lucidites and the Reverians series. She's been everything from a corporate manager to a hippie. Her taste for adventure has taken her all over the world. If you can't find her at the gym, then she's probably at the frozen yogurt shop. If you can't find her there then she probably doesn't want to be found. She is a self-proclaimed hermit, with spontaneous urges to socialize during full moons and when Mercury is in retrograde. Sarah lives in Central California with her family. To learn more about Sarah please visit: http://www.sarahnoffke.com

Check out other works by this author:

The Lucidites Series:

Awoken, #1

Around the world humans are hallucinating after sleepless nights.
In a sterile, underground institute the forecasters keep reporting the same events.
And in the backwoods of Texas, a sixteen-year-old girl is about to be caught up in a fierce, ethereal battle.
Meet Roya Stark. She drowns every night in her dreams, spends her hours reading classic literature to avoid her family's ridicule, and is prone to premonitions—which are becoming more frequent. And now her dreams are filled with strangers offering to reveal what she has always wanted to know: Who is she? That's the question that haunts her, and she's about to find out. But will Roya live to regret learning the truth?

Stunned, #2
Revived, #3

REBELS – Book II

Chapter One

Hard to believe three months ago I'd never even seen a horse, and now I'm crouched down low on one who shares my name. I tried to rename her, but Rogue said it would confuse the horse. Wind races through my hair as we canter across a rare stretch of flat ground. Most of the trek between Rogue's farm and Austin Valley is dense brush and steep hills. However, Em easily manages the trails, which have been carved into the side of the hills by Rogue's many commutes to and from the Valley over the years.

"Only a little farther now," I say to Em, the golden palomino I'm riding.

A stiff ache has formed in my neck from checking my back, hoping he's not following. The sun is just now coming up over the eastern mountains and hopefully Rogue is still sleeping. He'll wake up soon and discover I'm gone. Discover I've left. And he's probably going to kill me for what I'm doing, but if I can accomplish what I returned to Austin Valley for, then I'll endure his anger.

I've only been gone for a night from his house and already I miss it. Miss the way it has its own personality, one which is comforting and also intriguing with its many oddities. Rogue's house was built following the strictest of construction protocols, but he snuck in many of his own ideas, adding secret compartments in walls and drawers in the stairs where we keep our shoes. I know I'll be returning to him and that house soon, but to be away after these long three months feels wrong, like I've left a vital organ behind.

When Rogue told me about his house he said he had a garden. He lied. He had a patch of weeds. *Now* he has a garden. Good thing he didn't tell the same lie about his house. Otherwise I would have been living in a shack. It was obvious he'd spent all his time on the house, sustaining himself on cans of beans and freeze-dried fruit during its construction.

As the terrain in front of us grows denser with brush, I slow Em into a trot, intent on keeping a quick pace. Rogue was right about

Em; she's an incredible horse and her competent navigating allows my mind to wander back to when I first entered this new world full of Rogue, his farm, and his animals.

After our escape from Austin Valley, Rogue and I rode continuously, me holding on to him, trying to absorb the steady bounces of the horse. Rogue made me close my eyes when we finally neared his house. I listened with shut eyes as he dismounted and then pulled me off the horse and set me on my unsteady feet. My back ached from the ride and I never thought my head would stop vibrating from the constant rattling of the hooves on uneven terrain. I heard something approaching but with Rogue's giddy breath by my ear I didn't worry.

"Keep them closed, Em," he said to me.

And then a wet soft sensation nipped at my fingertips.

I gasped, pulled my hand to my chest. "What was that?" I said, jumping back into his arms.

He laughed, one so pure I immediately relaxed. "That's Athena. Specifically her tongue."

"What? Gross! Dogs lick you? What did I do wrong?" I said, my eyes still dutifully closed, but the idea of an animal wiping its tongue against me made my mind cramp with strangeness.

"Nothing," he said with a chuckle. "It means she's likes you."

If these strange animals did that if they liked me, I was worried to find out what they did if they didn't.

With Rogue's hand guiding me at my back I stepped roughly twenty feet. Then he spun me around to face him.

"Open your eyes," he said, an eagerness in his voice.

I peeled open my eyes to find the sun setting over Rogue's broad shoulder. We'd ridden most of the night and day to arrive there before dark. Clear rolling hills the color of spring moss stood in the distance at his back. Forest punctuated the areas to the sides. And to the north I could just spy a small stream snaking between two hills. My eyes finally found Rogue's, which were overflowing with excitement. His smile widened, a perfectly crooked one. His almost black hair was wilder than usual, having been swept every which way by the wind as we rode.

At his knee I caught movement. I dared to look down. Only in books had I seen dogs. This one had a long black snout, perky ears, and a coat of black and brown fur. I jumped at the sight of her.

Which made her ears perk up more and she struck a protective stance.

"Heel, girl," Rogue commanded, and she sat her hindquarters back on the sandy dirt ground. "She's never seen one of you."

"A girl?" I asked, taking another step backward, as the dog tweaked her head to the side at the sound of my voice.

"I was talking to Athena," Rogue said, with an amused smile. "You've never been in the presence of a dog, right?"

I nodded. "Do you always talk to them like they're people?"

"No," he said with offense. "I treat animals with way more respect."

He had his hand down at his side and Athena looked between it and me with a tentative expression in her brown eyes. "She senses your fear, Em. It makes her worried you mean her harm."

"I know what she's capable of," I said, tension laden in my tone. "She has teeth, and aren't dogs like her police animals outside the borders of Austin Valley?"

"Yes, she's a German shepherd. And need I remind you, you're outside those borders now."

All my life it had been about what happened inside versus outside Austin Valley's borders. Black and white. Safe and unsafe. Happy and unhappy. I figured the world outside the Valley was full of savages. An unforgiving world where nothing went the way you wanted and no one did as you pleased. A world that was unkind and imperfect. Of course, I'd seen the world outside Austin Valley during brief dream travels but that had always been to an approved location, like a college auditorium or a closed down amphitheater. Before Rogue showed me Amsterdam I'd never seen a place in color. The irony was my life in Austin Valley had been in black and white and now I was seeing everything in high definition.

Athena regarded me with doubt when I reached out a hand to her. "I'm all right," I said, willing my hand not to shake and my voice to remain steady.

Rogue waved his hand at her and she stood, taking two steps in my direction. Her nose touched my fingertips, a cold slippery feeling. Her long snout grazed my pant leg. And then, as though she'd confirmed I wasn't a threat, she suddenly made a circle and took the spot next to Rogue's leg again, his jeans caked in dirt from the long ride.

He looked way too entertained by that exchange. "See, that was easy."

"I have my hand, so I'd say it wasn't a complete failure."

He stepped forward and pointed over my shoulder. "Well then, if you're ready I have more to show you."

I turned, and there nestled between an assortment of trees was a house as clean and perfectly built as the ones we have in Austin Valley. Well, not exactly like them. Better. It was a Craftsman style house with a front porch. An A-frame roof. Four columns and four steps leading up to a mostly windowed door. It was small. Four rooms. And it was painted in the ideal shade of mossy green, blending in flawlessly with its surroundings.

What astonished me wasn't the precision of the lines, or the big windows on the front of the house. It was another dog—this one yellow—bounding in my direction. It was wet and smelled like fish and dirt. I found that out firsthand when Poseidon rammed both his paws on my shoulders, knocking me to the ground and licking my face like I was dinner. As opposed to Athena, there wasn't a hint of threat in his approach. All unabashed affection. I found my hands were in his hair and my mouth laughing.

"What am I, Poseidon? Chopped liver?" Rogue said with a laugh. The excited dog bounded off me and gave Rogue a similar welcoming but without knocking him over. I stood with Rogue's assistance, dusting off my pants and immediately realizing I smelled like dog.

"Sorry, even after all my strict training that Lab won't mind. Makes sense you two became fast friends," Rogue said, pulling a twig out of my tangled long hair.

"Shush it, Rogue," I said, grabbing his hand and pulling him toward his house. *His house.* Four steps led me to the front door. Everything was perfect. Not a flaw anywhere I could find. And my eyes were busy searching, not for flaws, but rather hungry to absorb every detail. My palm was on the handle to the front door before I caught myself. I turned, giving him a questioning look.

"Go ahead," he okayed. "It's not locked."

I twisted the stainless steel handle and stepped into a room unlike any I'd ever seen. The walls were paneled in polished wood. A soft rug greeted my feet as I moved forward. My neck craned to see the exposed beams overhead on the ceiling, which was at least twenty feet high.

It was dark, but my eyes studied everything I could see around me: the stone fireplace on the far wall, the entryway which spilled into a kitchen and then the arched hallway.

"You did all this?" I asked.

He nodded, a cute coyness on his stubbled face.

"When?" I asked in astonishment.

"Every night while dream traveling. You like it?"

I turned around a full circle, my eyes sweeping over every detail it could capture within that minute. "I absolutely love it. I've never seen anything that feels and looks so much like…well, it's like you captured the true idea of home in this place."

Rogue laughed. "I knew you'd say something complex."

"Is that all right? Was that an okay reaction?"

"Anything you said would be fine. It would be perfect."

In that moment I wasn't merely in love with the guy who had built that house, I was in awe of him. In awe that he was someone I knew and could reach out and touch and hold against me. I snaked my arms around Rogue's neck, urging him down closer. He kept a smile on his face and a distance of a few inches between us. His hands pinned against my hips and his eyes held mine. Finally he pulled me in close and kissed me, one so pleasing I didn't even care that we both smelled like dog. Each time our lips met my chest tightened and my legs grew wobbly. And then as my mouth continued to move against his he said, "Hey, Em?"

"What?" I said, not particularly liking the idea of words at that moment.

"You wanna meet the goats?"

Not especially. Not right now. I sighed, utterly deflated. Rogue would let me close, but not close enough. Always interrupting our intimacy with a distraction. But inside this small house built with his hands, I knew he wasn't going to be able to avoid me. Which was what I thought he was doing. I was wrong. Rogue wasn't afraid of being close to me. He was hiding something.

To continue reading, please purchase your copy of *Rebels*

54443561R00134

Made in the USA
Charleston, SC
01 April 2016